SAVING
MOSSY
POINT
IN THE FIFTY-FIRST STATE
OF SUPERIOR

Donna Winters

Bigwater Publishing LLC

GreatLakesRomances.com

Garden, Michigan

This story is dedicated to those who love the State Parks of Upper and Lower Michigan

Note

Yooper (sounds like "you-per") is a nickname derived from U.P.-er, an Upper Peninsula (of Michigan) resident.

"The bridge" refers to the Mackinac Bridge, spanning the Mackinac Straits between Lower and Upper Michigan.

CONTENTS

CHAPTER 1 1

CHAPTER 2 13

CHAPTER 3 31

CHAPTER 4 43

CHAPTER 5 55

CHAPTER 6 69

CHAPTER 7 81

CHAPTER 8 93

CHAPTER 9 107

CHAPTER 10 119

CHAPTER 11 131

CHAPTER 12 141

CHAPTER 13 153

CHAPTER 14 165

CHAPTER 15 181

CHAPTER 16 195

CHAPTER 17 207

CHAPTER 18 219

CHAPTER 19 225

CHAPTER 20 235

CHAPTER 21 249

CHAPTER 22 261

CHAPTER 23 275

CHAPTER 24 289
CHAPTER 25 299
ABOUT DONNA WINTERS 305
GREAT LAKES ROMANCES® 306
MORE DONNA WINTERS TITLES 313

CHAPTER 1

"Mr. Engstrom, you *can't* sell Mossy Point State Park!" Betty Hanson slid to the edge of her chair and stared straight into the pale blue eyes of the head of the General Land Office in the recently formed State of Superior. She'd sought this meeting with him at his office in Superior Bay, the new state capital, to warn him of the devastating effect a park closing would have on the Village of Mossy Point. But convincing him wouldn't be easy. His gaze never seemed to meet hers for more than a nanosecond.

"Is that what you came here to tell me? You said you had some urgent information on a serious threat to state land. I assumed it concerned illegal activity, but selling a park? Come, now."

"Selling the park *is* a serious threat."

"Why *not* sell it? That park's a real money pit." As Mr. Engstrom leaned his bulky torso back in his creaky leather chair, Betty envisioned a button popping off his too-tight shirt and splashing in the coffee mug on the edge of his desk. Her lips twitched into a smile that she instantly suppressed. Now was no time for humor. She narrowed her brows and followed his wandering gaze like a guided missile locked on a target.

"Think of the consequences, Mr. Engstrom! Without the park, the village where I have lived for the last forty of my sixty-five years, will fold up! We've already got half-a-dozen ghost towns in this county. I understand you were originally from Mossy Point. You don't want to add your own hometown to the list, do you?"

He took a deep breath, exhaling the stench of stale cigar smoke. "Now I doubt Mossy Point will turn into a ghost town anytime soon." His dismissive attitude fueled her sense of urgency.

"Seventy-thousand people come through there every year for one reason, and one reason only—to get to the park. Without it, every business in the village will close, and then the Post Office and the school."

Mr. Engstrom put his palm out. "That park loses money. When we were the Upper Peninsula of Michigan, Lansing funneled off income from the parks farther south to keep Mossy Point open."

"And now that we've become the State of Superior?"

"If parks don't support themselves, they're done." He propped his feet on his desk as if the case were closed.

A yellow sticky note had taken up residence on the bottom of his shoe. She casually leaned forward and pointed to a figurine on a bookcase a few feet to his left. "Mr. Engstrom, what's that thing next to the ream of paper on your bookcase?"

When he craned his neck to look, she snatched the note and tucked it into her pocket.

"A snapping turtle. If anyone gets in the way, snap 'em where it hurts the most."

"Sounds like the campaign you ran in Lansing to pass the resolution for us to separate from Michigan."

He grinned.

"By the way, I never quite understood why you moved back up here after that. I assumed you'd stay below the bridge and take advantage of the economic improvements."

He cocked his brow. "Opportunity."

"You were promised this job if the resolution passed?"

"Your words, not mine."

"But if you snap at Mossy Point by selling off the park, this state will lose even *more* revenue. Once businesses close, folks will move to Michigan or Wisconsin. Tax dollars will disappear right across the state line!"

"The legislature doesn't see it that way." He checked his watch, swung his feet to the floor, and pressed against the arms of his chair with a grunt, eventually reaching a vertical position. "Now, you've had your say, Mrs. Hanson, and I have another meeting to attend."

Betty slung her bag over her shoulder, took one step toward the door, and turned to face him. "Just promise me one thing, Mr. Engstrom. Promise me you'll keep the park open if it's self-supporting this year."

He shrugged. "I'm only one voice among many when it comes to these things."

"Don't be so modest. Everybody who knows the first thing about politics in the State of Superior knows you have influence over the legislature and the governor when it comes to land."

He shook his head. "You flatter me, Mrs. Hanson. As for promises, I usually avoid them, but I suppose there's no harm this time. You know why?"

She drew a breath to say, "Because it's the right thing to do," but he went on before she could get the words out.

"Because Mossy Point State Park has never paid its own way, not since it opened back in 1959. That park has the same chance of running in the black as a turtle has of flying." He winked.

Betty thrust her hand out. "It's a deal, Mr. Engstrom. The park's going to make money, stay open, and a turtle will fly."

He pumped her hand once and ushered her through the office door, past his secretary, and into the historic oak-paneled hallway that led to the lobby of the former Superior Bay Hotel. "So how are you going to do it, Mrs. Hanson? How are you going to get that park to make money?"

She shrugged. "I'll think of something. Then I'll be back here at the end of the season to show you a flying turtle."

"Looking forward to it, Mrs. Hanson, but not holding my breath. Good luck!" When they reached the lobby, he passed the security guard with a nod, burst out the front door of the state office building, and disappeared down the street quicker than any three-hundred-pounder had a right to.

Betty returned her visitor I.D. to the security guard and stepped outside. She slipped her hand into her pocket and retrieved the yellow sticky note she'd pulled off Mr. Engstrom's shoe. "ExlandGroup, 11:30 Monday." Evidently that was the meeting he was headed for. But what or who was ExlandGroup? She'd look them up later.

Tucking the note back into her pocket, she drew in a deep breath of the late April breeze blowing in off semi-frozen Lake Superior, a block away. Azure ripples between ice floes sparkled with sunlit diamonds, beckoning her. She headed down Hill Street and across Lakeshore Drive to Superior Bay City Park on the shoreline. A pang of nostalgia pricked her heart. She'd met Harry here in April forty-seven years ago when she was a freshman and he was a sophomore at Superior Bay Community College. How she missed him. Would she ever get used to widowhood? After five years, probably not.

She sat on a bench facing the water. Icy reality washed over her. How was she going to save Mossy Point? She lifted her gaze heavenward. "Well, Lord, what have I gotten myself into this time? In sixty-five years of living, you'd think I'd have learned by now that I can't fix everything that's wrong with the world, or *my* world, anyway." She paused, her mind in a spin. "I haven't the slightest idea how Mossy Point State Park can make enough money to stay open. If it's going to happen, you'll have to show me the way."

She slumped down until she could rest her neck against the top of the park bench. The sun warmed her cheeks, tempered by gentle gusts off Lake Superior. She closed her eyes. The cry of gulls made melody against the dull roar of Lakeshore Drive traffic. Just as she started to drift to sleep, a thought bolted her awake.

Start a folk school.

Her eyes sprang open and she sat upright, her mind racing. Could it work? She and Harry and Angie had loved their classes at North Country Folk School. Probably the best family vacation ever. Of course, Petite Baie, Minnesota, with its artsy, upscale atmosphere, had a lot more going for it than Mossy Point. But it could work. The up-north location on one of the most picturesque stretches of the Lake Superior shoreline ought to be a draw.

But what building could she use for classes . . . ? There was the old Lahti cabin at the park, a board-and-batten place about twenty feet by sixty feet, probably full of junk. It needed work. Paint for the wood siding, a new coat of paint on the metal roof, and who-knows-what on the inside. Big job.

Who could she get to help? Lee Nylund for sure, maybe Wayne and Doris Reed. Some others came to mind.

She'd need teachers. Steve Taylor. He was an ace with that photography club at school. If he could get two-dozen high school kids to shoot artistic photos with digital pocket cameras, he could get adults to do it, too. Lee could teach fly-tying. Maybe Wayne Reed would teach decoy carving. He'd created some really amazing ducks since retiring from his plumbing job.

Her stomach grumbled. She checked her watch. Time for lunch; then she had to get back to Mossy Point and talk to Thad. She recalled her phone conversation with the park supervisor that morning before she had headed to Superior Bay. She'd speed-dialed his landline and caught him before he'd left his office for the morning rounds.

"Thad, did you see the article in yesterday's paper about the possibility of selling the park? I just got around to reading it a minute ago."

"I saw it. Not much I can do if the State decides to close us up and sell."

"I'm going to see Mr. Engstrom. Tell him he can't sell our park."

"Good luck. And Betty? You'd better pray for me that I can get a transfer. It'll be tough finding another job in the State of Superior that will support a wife and two kids."

"This park won't close, not if I can help it. But you can count on the prayers, buddy. Talk to you later."

That promise had been made three hours ago; now she had to make good on it. Rising from the bench, she set a brisk pace for her truck. A roast beef sandwich at the Beef Palace would quiet her stomach, then off to meet with Thad.

o0o

Half an hour later, Betty hit the road to Mossy Point. There was hardly a car to be seen in either direction, and nothing but woods and an occasional cabin on either side for twenty-five miles. The hardwoods hadn't quite leafed out yet, but soon their canopy would dapple the sun, turning the road into a storybook lane.

She eased down on the accelerator, eager to get to the park, talk to Thad. While trees sped past, she organized her thoughts. Half-an-hour later, she pulled into the parking lot marked "Employees Only" behind the administration building.

Thad's truck was there. Good. She wouldn't have to hunt him down. Moments later, she headed through the workshop and down the hall. Thad's office door was open and he was sitting behind his computer, staring at the monitor and running a hand through his wavy chestnut hair.

"Hey, Thad!"

He looked up with an unconvincing smile. "Betty, how'd it go?"

"Great!" She helped herself to the chair beside his desk.

"You convinced Ray Engstrom not to sell this park?"

"Not exactly. But he *did* promise to keep it if the park runs in the black this year."

His shoulders slumped. "Fat chance. I'd better update my resume."

"Not so fast! I've got an idea. You know the old Lahti cabin?"

Thad's brow wrinkled. "What about it?"

"A folk school, that's what!"

"A folk school?"

"A place where folks of all ages come to learn arts, crafts, recreational skills, all kinds of things. Harry and Angie and I went to a folk school over in Minnesota on our vacation one year and it was fabulous! Angie learned jewelry making, Harry learned birch bark canoe construction, and I sewed a pair of Chippewa-style moccasins. I figure we can start small here at Mossy Point with the old Lahti cabin, fix it up for classes, put the word out, and cha-ching! Money will flow in faster than you can count it!"

"D'ya think?"

"Absolutely! Folks coming for classes will stay at the campground, fill up those empty sites you're always complaining about, buy your firewood for campfires at night, and tell all their friends to get up here and join the fun."

"You make it sound easy."

"Hard work, more like. Come on. Let's go take a look at that cabin, see what has to be done."

He put his palm out. "Not so fast. I'll have to clear it with the higher-ups."

"I'm sure you can convince them, or let me. What's your boss's number? I'll talk to him." She reached for his portable phone.

He grabbed it first. "*Her*. Eva Underwood. And I'll do the talking."

"Maybe we should call her later, after we've inspected the building and know how much work has to be done."

"Good idea. You can ride with me. First, I have to find the key to that building." He searched his desk drawer, pulled out two keys on a tag, dropped them into his shirt pocket, and escorted her to his truck.

They proceeded down the gravel road into the campground where a familiar young woman was cleaning a fire ring at one of the campsites.

"I see you've got Janna Jarvis on the job again this year. Seems awfully early for her to be out of school."

"Her term at Superior Bay Community College ended last week."

"I'd forgotten how early they go on summer break." One more person who would lose a job if the park closed. Betty couldn't let that happen to a nice kid like Janna who needed the money to stay in school.

As they approached the far northwest end of the park, Thad turned to her. "Have you got any idea where the start-up money is going to come from for your folk school? We've got a moratorium on spending in Parks and Recreation right now."

"I've got some ideas. I'll hit up the home improvement place in Superior Bay for a few gallons of paint."

"Stain, Betty. Board-and-batten needs stain, not paint."

"Stain, then. Maybe they'll throw in a few sticks of wood for any broken boards or battens that need replacing."

As Thad drove along the road through the deserted campground and out the other side, his questions continued. "Who's going to do all this work? My staff is already cut to the bone. It's all we can do to get the campground ready to open in the next two weeks."

"I can get volunteers."

He rounded a curve and pulled to a stop in front of the building. Betty's heart sank at her first glimpse of the place in—she couldn't remember when. The last time she'd seen it, years ago, she'd thought of it as quaint. Now that she needed to make it usable, it looked more like a neglected shack surrounded by juniper and weeds. Boards covered the windows; streaks, stains, and moss obscured the old metal roof; a metal bar and padlock secured the double front door.

She turned to Thad. "A good pressure washing and new paint on the roof ought to freshen the place up for starters, don't you think?"

"Roof coating, you mean. Metal roofs need a special coating, and it's not cheap. You'll have to hire a contractor that's licensed and insured to apply it. Volunteers aren't allowed to use ladders or stepstools."

"You're kidding! Not even if we have our own insurance?"

"Not even. You'll have to get each volunteer to sign a waiver, too, to hold the state harmless in case of an accident or injury."

"Not a problem. You give me the forms and I'll get them signed." She pushed through the juniper and stepped around a wooden box-like protrusion to reach the other side of the building, the side that faced Lake Superior. The view gave her pause. Nothing but cool blue waves lapping a rocky, sandstone shoreline as far as the eye could see in either direction. Beautiful. Remote. Inspiring. The perfect place for a folk school.

Then she turned to look at the building. Not so perfect. Wind off the lake had torn at the siding. Some pieces of batten were missing. Others had buckled. She'd need a good carpenter to make it right. The door, barred and padlocked like the double door on the road side, appeared ready to rust off its hinges. At least the foundation seemed solid. They continued around the building, making a path through the brambles back to the roadside door.

Thad pointed to an overgrown juniper bush. "You can have your volunteers trim back the foliage near the building. It should have been done years ago."

"Check." Betty added the chore to her mental list of jobs.

After some wrangling with the rusty padlock, Thad managed to force it open. The wooden door, evidently swollen from spring rains, didn't want to budge. Thad yanked on it once, twice. The third time, the door popped open so fast he nearly fell to the floor.

Betty covered her mouth to stifle a laugh and stepped inside. A strong, musty odor emanated from the dark interior, so black because of the boarded-up windows that she could make out nothing of the contents. She heard Thad click a light switch, but the building remained dark.

CHAPTER 2

"Power's probably off at the electrical box," said Thad. "I'll get a flashlight from the truck and see if I can turn it on."

While he was gone, Betty closed her eyes. "Lord, what have I gotten myself into? I don't know much about fixing up a place like this, but I can see it all refurbished and buzzing with students. I'm counting on You to lead me. And Thad is counting on You to keep his job. Be with us, both. Amen."

Thad returned, flashlight in hand. A minute later, the overhead light came on.

A tangle of old junk cluttered the room—broken cots, an old wood-burning sheet metal stove with its pipe extending up through the center of the roof, a couple of trunks, a wooden ladder, a fifty-five gallon trash barrel, and an oak lectern with a cross carved on the front. Betty pointed to a piece of equipment that looked as if it belonged behind a small tractor.

"What on earth is that? A lawn mower on steroids?"

"It's an old brush hog for making a trail through the woods. Might even be the one they used to make the first trail back in the day. It's nothing but a piece of scrap metal now."

She stepped past it to the trash barrel. The musty odor grew stronger. A ratty old blanket lay in a heap on top. She grasped it gingerly between her thumb and forefinger and lifted it. Beneath lay old rags, empty tin cans, and a couple of empty glass milk bottles from decades ago. She pulled out a quart milk bottle and held it up. "Looks like a collector's item. Are you going to have your staff clear out all this stuff?"

Thad shook his head. "I don't see anything here worth saving. It can all go to the landfill, far as I'm concerned."

"What about your boss? Think she'll give the okay?"

"I don't see why not."

Betty pointed to the brush hog. "Scrap metal is up in price. You might be able to get a few bucks for that at the scrapyard in Superior Bay."

"If you can get something for it, use the money for fixing the place up. I haven't got time for hauling junk. Like I said, we've got our hands full just getting the campground ready for campers."

Along the east wall stood a sink, and beside it a toilet. Betty wandered over to take a closer look. Bathroom partitions had long ago been torn out. Rust stains colored the white porcelain of the basin, along with a layer of grunge. The same with the toilet bowl. She turned the single brass handle on the sink. It moved easily but nothing came out of the spout. "This place must have a well. Does it work?"

"Let's take a look. The pump house is outdoors—that wooden extension you went past to get to the lake side of the building."

She followed him to the little wooden extension. He stamped down a juniper bush to give clear access to the pump house door, held secure by another rusty padlock that held the lid and one side together. With some effort, he managed to open the lock, flip up the lid, and lower the door. Shining his flashlight on the pump, he punched a button. A motor groaned.

"Amazing!" He punched another button and the motor went silent. "This is an old-fashioned motor with oiling cups. See them?" He shined the light on two tiny cups. "You'll need to put a few drops of oil in each cup before using the well pump, then add a few drops every so often. And you'll have to prime the pump before you'll get any water out of the ground."

"How good is the water from this well?"

Thad shook his head. "Rich with iron I'd say, from the looks of the sink and toilet. I wouldn't use it for drinking water unless you get it tested and know for certain there's no bacteria. It ought to work for cleaning purposes, but I didn't see any water heater."

"That explains the single handle on the sink. Let's go back inside. There are a few more things I need to look at." She headed indoors to take a closer look at the ceiling, walls, and floor, while Thad locked the pump house.

When he joined her a few minutes later, she turned to him. "Is it my imagination, or do I see wood paneling on the walls and ceiling, and pine boards for a floor?"

"You're absolutely right. A new coat of paint on all that wood will make a world of difference for the least amount of money. Of course, you'll have a little patching and cleaning to do first." He pointed his flashlight to the ceiling where the stove pipe exited. "You're going to have to remove this old stove. It's a fire hazard—too much of a liability. On the positive side, you'll have more metal for recycling."

"But how will we heat the place on those chilly days before summer, and again in the fall?"

Thad ran his hand over his chin as he studied the pipe running up through the ceiling, and then a smile lit his face. "Back when we were part of Michigan, Lansing sent us a new propane stove for the snack shack. There was nothing wrong with the old one, so we saved it. You can install it here, and get the propane company to lease you a tank."

"Good idea. I think I've got the picture here. What do you say we go back to your office and get your boss on the phone for approval?"

Thad turned off the light and closed and locked the door.

oOo

Back in Thad's office, Betty sat beside his desk while he speed-dialed his boss. After a brief explanation of plans for the Lahti cabin, Thad pulled the receiver away from his ear by about an inch. Eva's voice came through as if she were on speaker phone.

"Make sure you get a holds-harmless waiver signed by everyone before they start working. And don't let anybody climb a ladder or a stepstool. Got it?"

"Check." Thad doodled on his scratch pad. "What about money from scrap metal? Can I put that into fixing up the building?"

"Absolutely. The few bucks you'll get will only create a problem if you send them to accounting. Good luck, Thad. Let me know how it goes. I'll come take a look when it's finished."

"Talk to you later, Eva. Bye." He rolled his chair to the file cabinet near his desk, pulled out a form, rolled back, and handed it to Betty. "Get each volunteer to sign a copy of this waiver and bring them to me before you start."

Betty glanced at the fine print covering the form, then up at Thad. "Could you give me about ten more copies of this?"

Thad shook his head. "That's the last one in my drawer. I'm fresh out of copy paper and there's a freeze on spending until next month. You can make your own, can't you?"

"I can, but . . . " Her jaw tensed. "I can't believe this state is so cheap they don't even supply enough paper to print the forms they require of volunteers!"

Thad leaned back, a wry smile curving his lips. "If you think that's bad, go take a look in the lavatory."

"Why?"

"No paper there, either. No towels or toilet paper."

"Holy wow!"

Thad laughed. "We've adopted a new motto here. BYOP. Bring your own paper."

"That's disgusting! What are you going to do when the campers show up? They're going to expect toilet paper, at least."

"We'll have it by then."

A thought struck Betty. "I'll tell you who's got copy paper. Mr. Engstrom. I saw a ream of it on his bookcase when I was in his office. Figures he'd have plenty."

"I should have had you beg some from him while you were there."

Betty chuckled. "I suppose it's a waste of breath to ask if you have any extra supplies tucked away that could be put to use in the Lahti place."

"I'll look around, but I doubt it." He checked his watch.

Betty took the hint and rose quickly. "I know you've got work to do, and I need to go and round up some volunteers. See you later, Thad."

"Good luck." Thad's voice trailed her as she set a brisk pace for the parking lot.

No toilet paper. No paper towels. No copy paper. The State of Superior was far worse off than she'd imagined. Mr. Engstrom probably had plenty of toilet paper. Of course, he probably needed more than most with his prodigiously plump posterior.

"Betty Hanson, shame on you! Your mind has gone right down the toilet!" She scolded herself as she got into her car.

On the short drive home, she mentally reviewed the names of potential volunteers—friends from church, neighbors, and former colleagues from her teaching days. She'd invite them over for coffee tomorrow morning and pitch her idea for the folk school.

Once inside her three-bedroom ranch house, she wasted no time making phone calls, purposely avoiding Frank Schram. No point inviting trouble. An hour later, only five had said they'd come. Three had said, "Maybe."

At her computer, she checked email and deleted spam. She was about to put her computer on "Sleep" when she remembered the sticky note she'd picked up in Mr. Engstrom's office and fished it out of her pocket. ExlandGroup was the name she needed to look up. A search brought little in the way of results. She clicked on the first listing and learned that the company was privately held and specialized in land development. Maybe Mr. Engstrom was an investor.

Leaving the computer on "Sleep," she headed to the great room to dust and vacuum. Web-catcher in hand, she ran it up the corner to the ceiling, pausing to admire the drywall. The new roof and ceiling repair had emptied her emergency cash account a few months ago, but the work had to be done. Maybe someday, little by little, she'd be able to replenish the emergency fund. She set aside the web-catcher, plugged in the vacuum, and continued her cleaning chores.

At six, she fixed herself a salad for supper. Afterward, she made photocopies of the holds-harmless waiver, gathered several pens, and headed to the table near the fireplace. The framed photo of Angie, Manuel, and Carlos stared at her. As she gazed at them, a dull pain throbbed in her chest. Why had her daughter frozen her out of their lives for the last two years? Only God—and Angie—knew the reason. There was nothing more she could do to mend their relationship but pray.

She set the forms and pens beside the photo, settled into her recliner, and sent off a prayer for the thousandth time that somehow God would mend the rift. Following her "Amen," she turned the satellite radio on to the Sinatra channel, picked up her Kindle, and immersed herself in the romance she'd acquired on a free download. The evening passed quietly except for a couple of phone calls expressing regrets from folks who couldn't come tomorrow. Heaviness descended on her. She'd been so sure more would accept her invitation.

At half-past ten, she checked email messages. More regrets and a couple of maybes. She turned off the computer and headed off to bed, thoughts of tomorrow's meeting running through her mind as she dropped off to sleep.

o0o

Her eyes popped open early the next morning. After a shower, a cup of instant coffee, and half a breakfast bar, she headed to the Quick Shop for supplies. By nine forty-five, the inviting aroma of fresh-brewed coffee filled the open kitchen and great room. Mugs, French vanilla coffee creamer, spoons, plates, napkins, and a platter of sweet rolls and donuts lined her granite countertop next to the coffeemaker. At the last minute, she filled her electric kettle with water, turned it on, and set out a variety of teabags—herbal, black, white, red, and green.

She checked the sitting area of her great room, a few feet away, where chairs and end tables formed a U-shape in front of the fireplace. Morning sun streamed in the windows on either side, offering the promise of a pleasant spring day and a glimpse of budding trillium and wild leeks in the woods that rimmed the backyard. Above the mantle, Zeb, Harry's trophy ten-point buck, appeared ready to preside over the meeting.

Her gaze shifted to Harry's old leather recliner facing the fireplace from the bottom of the U, and for an instant she imagined him sitting there. "Wish you were here to help, Harry. You'd know just how to do all this stuff."

"You can do it, Betty."

The sound of a truck pulling up jogged her from the imaginary conversation. She headed for the front door. Lee Nylund's pickup was parked in front. Figured that he'd be the first to arrive. Since Harry's passing, he'd been quick to come anytime she'd needed a man's help. If ever she were to remarry, it would be to someone like Lee.

She opened the door and watched him coming up the driveway. His silver hair was neatly combed back, and his paunch overlapped his belt, as usual. Even at his weight, he walked with a brisk pace, until he tripped on his untied shoelace. Scrambling to catch his balance, he somehow managed to avoid falling face down in the gravel. He knelt to tie his shoe.

She opened the storm door. "Watch out for those rogue shoelaces, Lee. They'll get you every time."

He rose with an impish smile. "Good morning to you, too, Betty." He took the two steps to her stoop with one stride, kissed her cheek, and stepped inside. "Smells great in here."

"Help yourself to the coffee and sweet rolls. I see Steve Taylor pulling up, and Karen Baker right behind him. I'll be there soon as I let them in."

Steve floated up the driveway, every hair in place, golf shirt and pants making the most of his trim physique. He looked ready to take on Pebble Beach, not the restoration of a park building.

"Good morning, Steve. Thanks for coming."

"Hey, Betty, what's this about teaching photography at the park?" He pulled a comb from his shirt pocket, ran it through his receding hair, and tucked it away.

"I'll explain later. Help yourself to some coffee." She pointed to the kitchen counter and then turned to welcome Karen.

Now there was a woman who looked ready to work— un-styled hair brushed back from her face, T-shirt and jeans spotted with paint stains. She greeted Betty with a mild punch to her upper arm.

"Mornin', Betty. So ya got some work needs doin' over at the park, eh?"

"That's right. You know the old Lahti cabin at the northwest end?"

Karen nodded, her gaze shifting to the kitchen counter and back again.

"I'll explain it all when the others get here. Meanwhile, why don't you have some coffee and something to eat?"

She nodded and moved on, nudging her way past Lee and Steve, who were holding a conversation in front of the sweet rolls.

Within minutes, Doris and Wayne Reed joined the get-together. Doris's henna hair and ample waistline had survived a winter in Florida, as had Wayne's Green Bay Packers cap. Shortly after their arrival, Patsy Webb, a relative newcomer to the area, a kind of a recluse, and one of the "maybes" on Betty's list, quietly joined the gathering.

Betty poured herself some coffee, put a donut on a plate along with a generous dose of guilt, and caught up on her friends' latest news.

"Sorry to say I didn't lose a pound down in Florida." Doris patted her waistline. "But I found out about a great new diet. Grapefruit and toast broiled with sugar!"

Steve made a sour face. "You don't need a diet, Doris. Just come golfing with me. You'll walk off the extra pounds."

"Thanks for the offer, Steve, but no thanks. Right now I couldn't see past my belly to hit the ball, even if I knew how to swing a club, which I don't."

"Patsy, do you golf?" Betty asked.

"Never been golfing." Patsy spoke quickly, her focus on her mug of coffee. Curtains of long, straight, blue-black hair fell on either side of her cheeks, concealing much of her olive-skinned face. Someone had said she had ties to the Ojibway community in Baraga.

Wayne adjusted the cap on his balding head. "I've never been golfing, either. Who wants to follow a silly ball, anyway?"

Steve smirked. "At least I don't waste my time following a has-been football team, Cheesehead!"

"All right, you two." Betty sent them a warning look as if she were back in the classroom with a couple of recalcitrant teens. "I guess I'd better get this meeting started before I hear any more name-calling. Why don't you refill your cups and plates and find a seat near the fireplace?"

When everyone was settled, Betty stood beneath Zeb, her gaze taking in each of her guests.

"First, I want to thank you all for coming. As I mentioned, I have some news for you about Mossy Point State Park. How many of you saw the article in Sunday's paper about the possibility of the park closing at the end of this season?"

Three hands went up, one of them Wayne's. "I saw the article. The park's been there for more than half a century. I can't see the state closing it down."

Steve's brow rose as he focused on Wayne. "You couldn't see the Upper Peninsula becoming a separate state, either, but it happened."

"Yeah, thanks to those separatists below who voted us right out of the State of Michigan. I still can't believe they barricaded the governor on the bridge during his Labor Day walk two years ago, and threatened to blow it up if he didn't speed up the schedule for cutting us loose."

"It's all about the money," said Lee. "They wanted to stop the migration of their tax dollars across the bridge ASAP."

"Now look at us," said Doris, "dead broke and selling park land, *our* park land, to balance the state budget. Governor Pleven warned us when she was inaugurated that things are tight and we should expect changes, but I sure didn't think it would come to this during our first year of statehood."

Steve sighed. "Everything would have been fine if Yogi Vanderveen had become governor."

"I'm not so sure," said Karen. "He shoulda known better than to bop a moose on the nose with a tire iron, even if she *was* in the middle of the road when Yogi was tryin' to get to his inauguration."

"Before Vanderveen lost his battle with that PMS moose and earned himself a resting place six feet under, he had businesses all ready to move up here," said Steve. "Our economy would be recovering right now, if he were in the governor's mansion. Instead, his skinflint lieutenant governor, Pleven, took office and vetoed the tax concessions. Now she's threatening to close our park. It makes no sense." He set his mug on his plate with a clank.

"It does when you realize our park has never run in the black since the day it opened," said Betty.

"Who told you that?" Wayne asked.

"Ray Engstrom. I had a meeting with him yesterday. I told him closing the park would kill business in the Village of Mossy Point, maybe even turn it into a ghost town. I made him promise that if the park makes money this year, it will stay open. But in order to make money, we need a plan."

Steve raised his hand. "I've got one. Hire some pole dancers and put the word out over in Superior Bay."

Patsy gasped.

Lee rolled his eyes.

Doris shook her head and laughed. "If it were that easy, they'd already have done it."

Betty nodded. "Besides, parks are about families and outdoor recreation and good old-fashioned fun. So I have an idea. Do you all know the old Lahti cabin out at the northwest end of the park?"

"Sure do," said Karen. "Lahti used it as his home base for trapping. After that, a preacher bought it—forgot his name—and it was a church, sorta. Then the park bought those forty acres. It expanded their hunting grounds, but they didn't do anything with the cabin—except to use it for storage. How ya gonna make money there, anyway?"

Betty smiled. "So glad you asked. With your help," Betty's hand swept the room, "I'd like to turn it into a folk school."

"Folk school?"

"What's that?"

"Never heard of a folk school. How does that work?"

The questions from Doris, Wayne, and Steve flew at Betty. She put her palms out, ready to answer when Patsy spoke up.

"A folk school is a wonderful place where people of all ages come to learn a new skill." Color flooded her face and she lowered her gaze.

"Thank you, Patsy. That's exactly right. Students at a folk school could learn photography, like Steve teaches in his after-school club, or fly-tying like Lee does, or the decoy carving that Wayne is so good at."

"A folk school sounds great," said Lee, "but how will it make money for the park?"

"I'm so glad you asked. The classes will have tuition and the materials needed will be paid for by the students. The tuition can go directly to making the park profitable. In addition to that, most, if not all of the students will camp at the park while they attend class. Could be one night, two nights, even a week, so the camping fees will help, too."

"What are us teachers getting paid?" Wayne asked.

Betty smiled broadly. "The satisfaction of knowing you helped save Mossy Point State Park."

Steve grumbled. "Another volunteer gig. I'm already doing that with the photography club. I'm not liking the sound of this, Betty. First, we have to rehab a building. Then, when we teach, we can't even earn a greens fee. And to top it all off, there's no guarantee it will be enough to keep the park open. I'm outta here. Superior Bay Golf Course is calling." He started to rise.

Lee clamped a hand on Steve's shoulder and forced him back down. "Not so fast, Fancy Pants. You can't afford to let the park fail. None of us can."

"Won't hurt none to get a little dirt under them manicured fingernails of yours," said Karen.

Eager to get back to business, Betty continued. "Lee's right when he says none of us can afford to let the park close. Losing traffic to the park will mean losing customers for Wayne and Doris's daughter at Mossy Point Pizza and Steve's son at the Quick Shop. Businesses will close, families will move away, and the Post Office and school could both shut down. Then we're a ghost town."

"Sounds alarmist," said Steve.

"Want to take that chance?" Lee asked.

Steve sighed and slumped down on the couch.

Betty continued. "Now, about making the old Lahti cabin usable as a classroom."

"Sounds expensive," said Doris.

"Yeah. Nothing's been done to that place in years, decades even," said Wayne.

"Except for the mess Frank Schram probably left there, using it as his personal deer blind." Doris rolled her eyes.

"It's been years since that old coot used it as a deer blind," said Karen.

"Deer blind or not," said Betty, "Thad and I took a look at the place yesterday, inside and out, and most of what it needs is cosmetic. I'll get the building supply store over in Superior Bay to donate what we need in the way of materials. The rest is elbow grease. First, we need to clean out the junk inside and trim back the bushes around the foundation. I'd like to start this afternoon. I'll drive my truck over for hauling scrap metal when I go to Superior Bay tomorrow morning. We need another truck for the underbrush, and one for junk to go to the land-fill."

Wayne's hand went up. "We can use mine for the brush. I'll bring my trimmers."

"I'll make the haul to the landfill," said Lee.

"Great! We'll start after lunch, then, okay?"

All but Steve voiced approval.

"Is there anyone here who thinks we can't do this?"
Betty asked.

Steve's hand shot up.

Betty scowled. "Anyone but you, Steve."

No one else raised a hand.

"Let's meet at one o'clock at the Lahti cabin," said
Betty. "Bring your work gloves. See you then."

Betty's guests had started for the kitchen when she
caught sight of the waivers and pens she'd left on the
table near the fireplace.

"Hold it!" She picked up the pens and forms and
headed for the kitchen. "One thing I forgot. Everyone
has to sign a holds-harmless waiver for the state before
we start work. Please sign one before you leave so I can
turn them in to Thad. And another thing. No one is to
climb a ladder or stepstool at the park, so don't bother
bringing anything like that to the work session."

She began to pass out the waivers. When she offered
a form to Steve, he jammed his hands into his pockets.
As Betty stepped away, he grabbed it from her, almost
tearing it in two. She handed him a pen and he scribbled
his name on the bottom in an illegible scrawl.

When everyone had left, she picked up the phone,
called Thad, and arranged to have him meet her at twelve
forty-five to unlock the building. Then she loaded dishes
into the dishwasher, wondering how many from the
meeting would show up at one o'clock. With an attitude
like Steve's, she might be better off if he spent his afternoon on the Superior Bay Golf Course.

CHAPTER 3

At exactly quarter to one, Thad pulled up beside Betty at the Lahti cabin. She hopped out of her truck, waivers in hand, and stepped up to the driver's side of the DNR truck. "Here you go, all signed and dated."

"Thanks!" He set them on the empty passenger seat and got out, keys in hand.

The padlock opened more easily than it had a day ago, but it still remained difficult. She'd have to ask one of the fellows to work on it, and also the padlocks on the lakeside door and pump house.

Thad opened the door and switched on the light. "I'll try to swing by later, but we're pretty busy in the campground." He headed for his truck.

"Thad, wait!"

He turned to face her.

"Before you go, could you please unlock the lakeside door and the pump house, and leave me the keys? I'll have someone clean up the three padlocks and lubricate them tonight, and we'll put them back on tomorrow morning, if that's okay. The building will be empty overnight."

He hesitated a moment, then gave a nod and headed for the pump house.

Betty followed.

He worked the lock loose and handed it to her, then did the same with the lakeside door. "Good luck with your work session. I've got to run." He gave her all three keys and took off at a jog.

Betty collected the lock from the roadside door, put the three locks on her dashboard, and reached for the brown jersey work gloves she'd stashed in her pocket. Tires crunched on gravel as Lee pulled up, followed by Karen and the Reeds. They joined her for a look inside the building.

Karen peered into the fifty-five gallon drum and wrinkled her nose.

"Do you think we can clear this place out today?" Betty asked.

Karen nodded. "Don't see why not."

Lee took a look inside the electrical box and shook his head. "This system needs updating."

"Sounds expensive," said Doris.

Wayne headed for the door. "I'll get started clearing brush."

Two SUVs pulled up. To Betty's surprise, Steve came dressed in worn jeans and a sweatshirt. Patsy wore overalls stained with paint, a kerchief on her head, and a dust mask around her neck.

"Let's get started hauling things out of here," said Betty. "Scrap metal, like that old brush hog, goes on my truck. Trash goes on Lee's."

"What about this barrel?" Karen asked. Do we hafta sort through this junk?"

"Why don't we dump it out on Lee's truck. Then we can see if there's anything worth saving."

Betty helped Karen walk the barrel to the tailgate of Lee's truck. He followed them carrying a broken wood box. He tossed it onto his truck and then helped Betty and Karen lift the metal trash barrel to the tailgate and turn it on its side.

Lee climbed into the bed of his truck, poured out the contents of the barrel, and sorted through it with his foot—old rags, glass milk bottles from the '50s, empty food tins. A moldy odor wafted up, making Betty sneeze.

"Well, look at this!" Lee pushed an old blanket aside with the toe of his shoe to reveal a rusty metal box.

"An old tackle box," said Karen. "Wonder if there's anything inside."

Lee knelt down, worked the latch loose, and lifted the lid. "A few old lures. Betty, is it okay if I take this home? With a little work, I can get rid of the rust, make her look like new."

"Sure, on one condition. Take the rusty padlocks from the doors and pump house and clean them up too."

"Done."

Steve and Patsy came out of the building, hauling the brush hog toward Betty's truck. Lee closed the tackle box and hopped down from his truck to help Steve lift the old piece of equipment onto Betty's tailgate.

Patsy headed back inside, but Steve relaxed against Betty's truck, pulled a comb from his back pocket, and ran it through his hair. "Time for a break."

Karen glared at him. "Break, my Aunt Petunia. We've gotta keep working if we're gonna get this building emptied today."

Lee started to roll the empty barrel toward Betty's truck, and then paused. "What do you say we take this back inside and fill it with more junk. It will save us a lot of trips back and forth."

"Great idea," said Betty.

On her way to the door, she paused a few feet from where Wayne was clearing brush. He'd removed everything to the left of the roadside door. "Looks much better already. Thanks for your help, Wayne."

"No problem." He tossed another armload of prickly branches onto a pile.

"Say, Wayne, I was wondering if you'd take a look at the old well pump after we get things cleaned up. We'll need to get water running again, and you being a former plumber, I figure you're the man for the job."

"I'll take a look after I get the brush cleared out."

Betty smiled. "Thanks, Wayne."

She joined the others inside, filling the barrel with broken dishes, rusty cans, rags, and even a couple of moldy hunting magazines. Lying on its side against a wall was the old wooden ladder she'd seen yesterday. The bottom rung was broken, others were cracked. She dragged it outside and leaned it against the tailgate of Lee's truck. Keeping her back straight, she bent from the knees, lifted the ladder from the bottom, shoved it onto the bed atop the other junk, and returned inside.

A few minutes later, voices outside drifted in through the open door. Someone was talking to Wayne, but who? She paused to listen.

Frank Schram. Nosey old coot. He'd want to know what they were doing. No doubt he'd disapprove. She didn't need to hear it from someone who never even bought a park entrance permit for his vehicle, but instead left his car on the shoulder of the county road and walked in to hunt and fish. She put Frank from her mind and focused again on the work at hand, tossing rags into the barrel.

"What about this?" Karen ran her hand over the oak lectern with a carved cross on the front. "It's in decent shape. Be a shame to haul it to the landfill. Suppose some teacher might use it? A little furniture polish would fix it up real nice."

Betty took a closer look. "You're right. Keep it for now. We can always haul it out of here later if it's in the way." She returned to the pile of rags she'd been tossing out.

A few minutes later, something hit the ground with a thud. Someone groaned. Betty rushed outside. The others followed her. On the ground a few feet from the door lay Frank Schram, his unshaven face wrinkled in a wince, his shirt and pants soiled and torn as if he'd worn them for a month. Next to him, against the building, stood the decrepit ladder with a newly broken rung three up from the bottom.

Frank tried to get up, moaned, and lay back down. "I . . . my hip."

"Stay still," said Betty. "You need an ambulance."

Steve flipped open his cell phone.

Lee shook his head. "There's no signal out here."

"Broken hip, most likely," said Doris.

Patsy's gaze rested momentarily on Frank; then she headed back inside.

Karen looked at the ladder and then at Frank. "Tried climbing that old ladder, didn't ya? Fool! Anyone can see it's a piece of trash."

"I'll drive to the phone at the campground." Betty headed for her truck.

Lee followed. "Let me go instead."

Betty shook her head. "I'll have to let Thad know."

Lee gave a nod and closed her tailgate.

Betty had to remind herself not to drive too fast on the gravel road. Thad was in the campground working with Janna when she pulled up to the phone. By the time she had dialed the emergency number and told the operator where to send the ambulance, Thad had joined her.

"What's up, Betty?"

"I think you mean, what's down. Frank Schram. Fell and can't get up."

"Sorry to hear that."

"I've called for an ambulance. Probably take half an hour to get here from Superior Bay."

"Good thing you got those waivers signed."

Betty gasped and covered her mouth with her hand.

Thad's gaze narrowed on her. "You *did* get a waiver signed by Frank, didn't you?"

She shook her head. "He wasn't one of my volunteers, wasn't even at the meeting. He just showed up."

Thad pulled off his cap and ran his hand through his wavy chestnut hair. "Lawsuit, guaranteed."

Betty's heart raced. "How can he sue? He took an old ladder I'd put on Lee's truck to go to the landfill, set it up against the building, and—"

Thad's cheeks flushed. "No one saw him? Tried to stop him?"

"We were all inside, except for Wayne, and he was on the other side of the building clearing brush. No way he could've known what Frank was up to."

Thad pulled his cap on and walked away.

"Sorry, Thad! Really, I am!"

He raised his hand in acknowledgment, and without a backward glance, kept walking.

Betty's stomach churned. She got in her truck and headed back to the Lahti cabin. Nothing to do now but wait.

When she arrived, Lee was sitting on the ground next to Frank.

Her gaze met Frank's. "The ambulance will be here in about half an hour. Is there anyone I can call for you? Your son?"

Frank shook his head. "Little Frank's working in North Carolina this month. Ain't nothin' he can do."

"What about your daughter?"

Again Frank shook his head. "In Wisconsin, tied up at her store."

Betty sat down beside Lee to wait. She tried to think of something to say. From an accident years ago, she'd been told by her insurance adjuster that expressions of sympathy would imply guilt, even when the other party was totally at fault. Silence reigned until she worked up the nerve to ask the one question that burned in her mind.

"Frank, why did you climb up on that ladder?" She'd managed to keep her tone free of blame. No point angering the man.

"Wanted to take a look at the roof. Wayne said yous guys was fixin' up the place. Makin' a school. Gotta have a good roof for that."

"Yes," was all Betty could think to say except to add a royal scolding. She bit her tongue.

Steve and Karen emerged from the building, horsing the barrel toward Lee's truck.

Lee rose. "I'd better get back to work."

Betty nodded. What would she do when the ambulance arrived? Ride with them? Follow in her truck? Or let Frank go to the hospital alone? Her insurance company would tell her to keep her distance. But that seemed callous, even if it did imply blame according to the legal beagles.

She'd have to follow him to Superior Bay General Hospital. This was going to be a long day. She went to her truck to get the three rusty locks from the dashboard, and then she stepped inside to give them to Lee and tell him her plan.

"I'll follow the ambulance to the hospital and make sure Frank gets admitted. Here are the locks. We won't be able to lock up tonight, but there won't be anything in the building anyway, except maybe some scrap metal. I'll come back for it tomorrow."

"Do you want me to go to the hospital with you?" Lee's sympathetic gaze searched hers.

His offer was tempting, but Betty shook her head. "You can do more good here."

"You're sure?"

After a moment's thought, she nodded.

The ambulance pulled up and she went to speak with the EMTs. In no time, they had Frank loaded onto a gurney and into the ambulance.

o0o

Several hours later, Betty switched on her headlights, pulled out of the hospital parking lot, and started for home, praying she wouldn't fall asleep behind the wheel or hit a deer along the way. She punched on the satellite radio, selected the '60s channel, and sang along with "Louie, Louie," tapping the steering wheel to the beat. Several songs later, she entered the Mossy Point Village Limits and cruised past the business district. The Quick Shop and Mossy Point Pizza were already closed up for the night.

A half-mile down the road, she made the turn into her driveway. The fringe of her headlights revealed a young fellow sitting on her front porch next to a backpack.

He waved and came toward her through the beam of her headlights. Carlos. Her grandson was supposed to be in California finishing his senior year of high school. What was he doing here?

When she rolled down her window, he leaned against the frame. Even in the dim light, dark circles showed under his eyes and a shadow of whiskers darkened his face. A trace of body odor drifted in on the breeze.

"Hi, Gram. Been waiting for you." He sounded like she felt, all done-in.

"Hi, Carlos! I'm surprised to see you here! Shocked, in fact! I thought you were in California."

He shook his head. "Left there in January."

"But how did you get *here*? Did your mother drive you?" She glanced down the road. Maybe she hadn't noticed Angie's car in the dark.

"Mom didn't come. I hitchhiked."

Betty's gaze snapped back to Carlos. "Hitchhiked? Holy wow!"

"Do you think you could fix me something to eat? I haven't had anything since this morning."

"You poor boy! Let's go inside."

"I'll get my backpack."

She hit the garage door opener and parked the truck, still grappling with Carlos's situation. He followed her inside. He was taller than she was now. He'd probably grown four inches in the two years since she'd last seen him. She wrapped her arms around him, hugging a very bony frame.

They parted and she stood back and gave him a good looking over. His baggy T-shirt was frayed at the neck, his jeans were grease-stained with holes at the knees, and his walking shoes looked like they wouldn't last another mile. A million questions flooded her mind, but they'd have to wait. She turned toward the kitchen.

"Come on. I'll get you some dinner."

He followed her into the kitchen, parked his backpack on a stool by the counter, and sat down next to it. The backpack, badly worn and stained, looked ready for the trash can.

She washed her hands and opened the freezer. "Do you want Salisbury Steak, mashed potatoes, and peas, or would you rather have turkey, dressing, green beans, and yams?"

"Do you have any fajitas or enchiladas?"

"Sorry, no Mexican food in here. We can get some tomorrow." She moved a frozen turkey roast aside. "Oh, here's a beef pasty, if you'd like?"

"No thanks. I'll have the steak, please."

She pulled the frozen dinner from its box, punctured the clear covering, and popped it into the microwave.

"While your dinner is cooking, maybe you'd like to wash up."

"Sure."

"Grab your backpack. You can put it in your room." She led him to the smallest of the three bedrooms where he'd stayed years ago on visits with his folks.

He set his backpack on the floor and paused to gaze at a photo of Harry on the dresser. "I miss Gramps."

"Me, too. Wish he were here to see you all grown up." Harry would know just how to talk to his wandering grandson. She'd have to do her best to figure out what was going on. After dinner.

She opened a dresser drawer. "I don't know what you've got in your backpack, but if you need a clean set of jammies or some fresh underwear, your Grampa's are right here. And his bathrobe, shirts, and pants are hanging in the closet. Help yourself to whatever you want."

Carlos nodded.

"Tell you what. Why don't you put your dirty laundry in a pile outside your bedroom door before you get in bed tonight, and I'll stick it in the wash."

"Thanks, Gram."

"Now, let me get a set of towels. Your dinner is about ready to come out of the microwave." She headed to the bathroom, hung his towels, and returned to the kitchen.

While she waited for him, her mind raced. Why was he traveling alone? Did Angela know he'd come to see her? Where was he headed from here?

CHAPTER 4

Betty's questions would have to wait until Carlos finished eating. She made herself a cup of herbal tea and sipped it while he ate.

He took a bite of steak and looked up at her. "Do you have any salsa?"

She shook her head.

"Tabasco sauce?"

"No tobacco sauce."

"*Tobacco* sauce? I said *tabasco* sauce."

"I know. I was just teasing about how you used to say it when you were small."

He grinned. "Okay. No tabasco sauce. What about ketchup?"

"That, I have." She got it from the refrigerator and sat down again.

He poured a liberal amount of ketchup onto the steak, cleaned his plate in no time, and polished off a second glass of water and a sweet roll for dessert. She put his dirty silverware, plate, and glass in the dishwasher and turned to him with a smile.

"Would you like to come and sit in the great room? I'd love to hear about your trip across the country."

He shook his head. "If you don't mind, I'll take a shower and get some sleep."

"Sure. We'll talk in the morning. But Carlos, there's one thing I'd like to ask. How's your mother?"

"Don't know. Haven't talked with her in a while." He got up from his stool and kissed her on the cheek. "Good night, Gram. And thanks for the dinner." He started down the hallway.

"You're welcome. Don't forget to put your laundry out. Good night, Carlos. Sleep tight."

He flashed a smile over his shoulder. "And don't let the bed bugs bite."

"You remembered!"

He nodded and disappeared into his bedroom.

They'd traded those phrases starting when he was a little tyke. When he turned thirteen, he decided he was too old. Hearing the saying again warmed her heart. She grabbed her Kindle, turned off the kitchen light, and headed for her bedroom. By the time she'd read another chapter in the romance, Carlos had finished in the bathroom and piled his dirty laundry in the hall.

She picked up the armload of clothes and carried it to the laundry room where she sorted it into darks and lights. His jeans, shirts, and underwear were worn out rags not worth washing. But she put them in the washer as promised. Maybe tomorrow he'd go shopping with her for some new duds.

While the washer ran, she took a shower, trying to let all her questions about Carlos and concerns for Frank wash down the drain. It was well past midnight by the time she took the second load out of the dryer. She left all of Carlos's clothes neatly folded and stacked in the laundry basket.

When she finally got into bed and pulled up the covers, a vision of Frank lying on a gurney flashed through her mind. "Lord, be with Frank and help him to heal. And with Carlos, too. And let me get a good night's sleep so I can serve you tomorrow. In Jesus's name, Amen."

oOo

The phone woke her the following morning. Who would call so early? Eager to stop the ringing before it woke Carlos, she picked up the receiver without checking caller I.D.

"Hello?" It came out a sleepy half-whisper.

"I didn't wake you up, did I?" It was Lee's cheerful voice.

"Lee, what time is it?"

"Nine."

"I can't believe it. I never sleep past eight. I did get to bed awfully late, though." She pushed back the covers and swung her legs over the side of the bed.

"Sorry I woke you. I wondered how things went at the hospital."

"Fractured hip. They're going to operate this morning, insert a couple of pins. I probably ought to go in and check on him. What happened after I left the park?"

"Got the building all cleaned out except the scrap metal. I'm hauling trash to the landfill in a few minutes. Thought maybe you'd like to ride along. After that, we can load up the scrap metal and make a run to the salvage yard. Oh, and I've got the locks all cleaned up."

"Thanks for doing the locks, Lee. I really appreciate it. As for the other—good idea, but I've got a wrinkle on my end. When I got home last night, Carlos was on the front porch waiting for me."

"So you and Angela have patched things up?"

"No, no. Carlos came alone. Says he's been traveling across the country since January. Looked like he hadn't eaten a square meal since he left home. When I asked how his mother was, he told me he couldn't say. He hadn't talked with her for a while."

"I see. Tell you what. Bring him along. I'll treat you both to lunch in Superior Bay."

"Thanks for the offer, but I really need some time with Carlos, once he gets up. I've got to find out why he left home, how long he plans to stay here, and where he's headed next. Maybe he'll fill me in on Angela, at least what he knows from the last time they spoke."

"I've got an idea. I'll run to the landfill, and at eleven, I'll give you a call. Maybe by then, you'll have had some time to sort things out, and you and Carlos can come with me to load up the scrap metal. We'll haul it to the salvage yard and then go to lunch. We can stop by the hospital afterward, if you want."

"I hope you like Mexican food. I have a feeling that's what Carlos will ask for. I promised him last night we'd get some. And we'll need to stop by the thrift store and get him something to wear. His clothes are shot, and Harry's are way too big for him."

"No problem. Before we come back, we'll stop by the thrift store and the supermarket."

"It's a deal! Oh, and one more thing. When we stop by the Lahti cabin to pick up the scrap metal, I need your help making a list of the supplies we'll need to make that place usable. Then, while we're in Superior Bay, I'll stop by the building supply store and see if I can talk them into contributing the items on the list."

"We can do that. I'll talk to you at eleven. Bye."

"Bye."

Betty dressed, prepared two scrambled eggs, toast, and a cup of decaffeinated tea, and carried her breakfast to the dining table at the south side of the great room. While she ate, she consciously pushed aside thoughts of Carlos and Frank and contemplated the beauty of God's creation through the huge picture window.

The trillium blossoms were starting to pop out. Soon, nearly all of her little five-acre plot of woods would have a new carpet of white blossoms beneath the bare trees. A paraphrase from the Bible came to mind. Even Solomon in all of his glory was not arrayed like these woods.

In the park, it would be the same. Visitors came annually to see the show. She couldn't let the park close.

After breakfast, she settled into her recliner for devotions and Bible reading. Her head bowed and her eyes closed, she prayed quietly, thanking God for her many blessings. Then she petitioned Him with her needs. "Be with Frank, Lord, and heal him. And help me to do Your will with Carlos, at the park, and in all this day brings, in Jesus's name. Amen."

"Amen."

At the sound of Carlos's voice, her eyes flew open. "You're up! I didn't hear you come into the room."

He was sitting in Harry's old leather recliner, wearing his grandfather's white T-shirt and black pants, all cinched in with one of his belts. The pant cuffs were turned up, revealing bare feet. No wonder she hadn't heard him.

He smiled. "I love you, Gram. You say the most awesome prayers."

"Thank you, Carlos. I love you, too, and so does God. Would you like to pray?"

He shook his head. "Who's Frank? And why were you praying about the park?"

She retracted the footstool on her recliner. "I'll tell you over breakfast. What would you like to eat?"

"Got any more sweet rolls?"

"Sure do. But I'm thinking you could go for something more substantial with it. How about some eggs?"

"Two fried eggs with ketchup, and a sweet roll on the side."

"Coming right up!" She headed for the kitchen.

Carlos rose to follow.

She paused to wrap her arm about his waist. "It's so nice to have you here, Carlos."

He hugged her shoulders. "Nice to be here, Gram."

"Have a seat, and I'll get those eggs cooking."

He slid onto a stool. "Got any café con leche?"

She shook her head. "Not only do I not have any, but I don't even know what it is."

"Espresso coffee with steamed milk, a lot like a latte."

"I've got vanilla creamer and plain old black coffee, if you like."

"Awesome!"

She chuckled. "You young people have made an art of overstating the ordinary." She poured bottled water into the tea kettle and turned on the burner.

"Don't go all grammar-perfect on me, now, Gram."

"Can't help it after twenty-five years of teaching high school English. I'll try to cut you some slack, though."

"Awesome!"

"Hush with that 'awesome' talk. That word is so overused it's lost its meaning."

He grinned up at her. "Just testing. You said you were going to cut me some slack."

"Sorry. I'll try to do better."

"Cool!"

"Case in point. 'Cool' is another overused word." She set out a cup, saucer, and silverware.

"I'll try to watch my Ps and Qs. Pints and quarts, that is, from the colonial tavern days."

"You remembered!" She reflected for a moment on their trip to Concord, Massachusetts five years ago, where an interpreter had taught them the origin of the phrase. "Wasn't that an awesome trip?"

Carlos grinned. "More than awesome. Now, Gram, would you please tell me about your prayer for Frank and the park?"

"I'll explain, but I need to know one thing first. Why are you traveling across the country alone?" She sprayed a frying pan with non-stick spray, slid aside the tea kettle that had boiled, and set the frying pan onto the hot burner. When she poured hot water into Carlos's cup, he gazed up at her.

"Long story. School was tough. I didn't fit in. At home, I messed with tech stuff—cell phones, tablets, computer games—instead of doing my homework. Seemed like Mom was always on my case. There were other problems, too, so I left home the day I turned eighteen. A buddy of mine was traveling with me, but he got a job at a ski resort in Colorado and decided to stay the winter. So I went on alone, working here and there for food and a place to sleep, thumbing rides." He stirred instant coffee into his cup and added vanilla creamer.

"What were the other problems going on at home that you didn't like?" She returned to the stove to crack the eggs into the frying pan.

"Lots of things. But it's your turn. Frank and the park." He sipped his coffee.

"Like you said, long story. I've got a project going at the park. Some friends and I started work on it yesterday. Frank Schram, the neighbor down the road—"

"I remember Mr. Schram. Disagreeable old coot. Tried to tell me and Gramps we couldn't fish in the river."

"Gramps and me."

"He told you and Gramps that, too?"

"No, Carlos. You said 'me and Gramps'. It's 'Gramps and me'."

"Yeah, whatever. Now back to Mr. Schram and your prayer. Spill."

"We were fixing up an old building at the park and Frank showed up. Without anybody knowing it, he climbed an old ladder. A rung broke, he fell, and now he's in the hospital with a broken hip." She turned the eggs.

"Bummer."

"Carlos, change of subject, I washed your clothes. They look pretty well shot. I thought we could get you something better today. How about it?"

"Sure, if you say so. I'm dead broke, though."

"I'll float you a loan, and I know just how you can pay me back."

He raised his eyebrows and took another sip of coffee.

"This building we're fixing up at the park needs a lot of work, painting, and the like. I could really use your help."

"Sure. Got nothing better to do. Say, do you think those eggs are done?"

"Coming right up!" She slid them from the frying pan onto a plate, added a sweet roll, and set the plate in front of Carlos.

"Awesome! Ketchup?"

"Sorry. I forgot." She brought the bottle from the refrigerator.

He doused his eggs with ketchup and took a healthy bite. "Mmm. Thanks, Gram."

"You're welcome." She pulled a stool up beside him. "Carlos, do you remember your Grampa's best friend, Mr. Nylund?"

Carlos nodded and tucked another forkful into his mouth.

"He's helping with that park project, and we need to run some errands over in Superior Bay. We'd like to take you with us, treat you to lunch, and afterward, we'll get you some new duds, and stock up on your favorite Mexican food at the supermarket."

"Sounds like a plan." He picked up the sweet roll and took a man-sized bite.

She wanted to ask more about his reasons for leaving home, but she wouldn't bring it up until the meal was finished. Instead, she spoke of pleasantries—the trillium coming into bloom, the perch running, the birthing season for fawns just around the corner. When he'd finished eating and his dishes were rinsed and in the dishwasher, her gaze met his.

"Carlos, let's sit in the great room and talk for a few minutes. I still don't know much about what's happened since the last time we were together."

"Sure, Gram." He settled into Harry's old recliner, popped up the footstool, and grabbed a magazine from the table beside him.

Betty sat nearby on the end of the couch. "So you left on your eighteenth birthday. Did you get the card I sent?"

"Sure did. Thanks for the gift card. It came in real handy on my trip."

At least he'd made use of the one-hundred-dollar cash card. "You're welcome. Now, tell me, did you finish high school early then? I was thinking you'd graduate this June."

He shook his head, his gaze steady on the cover of the latest issue of *National Geographic*.

"Oh, Carlos. You need that diploma."

He flipped open the magazine. "I can always go back and get it."

"The sooner, the better, or you'll forget what you've already learned in high school and have to work a lot harder. You could study online and then take the test for a GED."

He made no reply, his focus remaining on the magazine. No point pressing that topic.

"Carlos, you said it was a long story, why you left home. There's plenty of time now. I'd like to hear it."

CHAPTER 5

Carlos shut the magazine, tossed it on the table, and twisted his whole body toward her. "Mom and Dad had a fight. He left. Then she was on my case all the time. I just couldn't take it anymore."

"I'm sorry to hear that. Do you know what their disagreement was about?"

"Money, mostly. Dad had been out of work for eons."

"Eons? Is that weeks, months, a year?"

"Months. Half a year at least. The recession killed construction jobs. Dad was really bummed. Then one day, Mom came home with some new jewelry. Not new exactly, but—you know what I mean."

"Collectible jewelry?" Angela had been collecting jewelry made in the mid-1900s since she was fifteen. Had enough to choke a horse.

"Yeah, collectible. Dad said we couldn't afford it. She said the necklace she bought was worth way more than she paid for it, and besides, she was earning the money so she'd spend it the way she wanted. If he didn't like it, he should get out. So he did."

"You said it was mostly about money. Was there something else?"

"Cheating. Dad thought she was cheating on him. She wasn't. She was trying to get back with Dad. A chef came to the house to cook a romantic dinner for their anniversary. Dad thought the chef and Mom were having an affair, so out the door he went."

"And then when you turned eighteen, you left, too."

"Yeah, well, as long as Dad was there, he kinda kept Mom off my case about grades and stuff."

"I'm surprised you didn't go to live with your father."

"Don't know where he is. Mom heard from one of Dad's friends that he's gone back to Mexico to build mission churches with his father. They move around a lot. I wish I'd left with him. Least I wouldn't 've had to put up with all those friends Mom dragged home."

"Oh?"

"First, there was the fruitcake guy. Made his living baking fruitcake. *He* was a fruitcake, far as I'm concerned. Then there was an artist. He was missing part of his ear. Claimed he was the next Van . . . somebody."

"Van Gogh?"

"Right! Seemed to me he was missing part of his brain. And after him was a musician." Carlos turned thumbs down. "And after him, an actor—he was the worst. You know what part he played?"

Betty shook her head.

"Donald Duck! Went around the house quacking all the time. He was a quack, all right."

The phone rang. Betty checked her watch. Eleven o'clock. "That'll be Lee—Mr. Nylund. You're on for lunch over in Superior Bay, right?"

"Awesome!"

She headed for the kitchen phone.

Betty checked caller I.D. and answered on the third ring. "Hi, Lee."

"How's it going with Carlos? Are you two taking me up on the lunch offer?"

"Sure are."

"I'll come by to pick you up."

"See you in a few." Betty hung up and turned to Carlos. "Better put on some socks and shoes. Lee will be here in a few minutes."

Carlos hustled off to his bedroom. Too bad she hadn't had a chance to find out how long he planned to stay and where he was headed next. Maybe it would come out over lunch. And what was she to make of Angela and that parade of men? The girl had always had a "stray cat" syndrome. Sounded like she really indulged it once Manuel left her.

Betty combed her hair, pulled her lime green hoodie out of the closet, and headed down the hall. Carlos was waiting for her by the door. On his feet were Harry's wingtips.

"Those shoes look about three sizes too big. Won't you trip?"

"Nah." He did a spin as if street dancing, caught the toe of his shoe in his pant leg, and started to fall. Then he caught himself by throwing his arms out in wild gyrations.

She laughed and applauded, wiping imaginary sweat from her brow. "Thought for sure you'd land in a heap on the floor, but you recovered beautifully." Her gaze caught Carlos's clean laundry sitting in the basket. "I washed and folded your clothes last night. Since we're replacing them with something different, what do you say we donate the old things to the thrift store?"

"Great idea, Gram! They can have my old shoes, too. I'll go get them."

She and Carlos had just finished stuffing his old things into two plastic bags when Lee pulled into the driveway.

Carlos carried the bags to Lee's truck, set them behind the seat while Betty climbed in beside Lee, and then squeezed in beside her.

"Lee, you remember my grandson, Carlos, don't you?"

He leaned forward and flashed Carlos a smile. "Sure do. Went fishing with Carlos and Harry a few times. Good to see you, son. You sure have shot up since the last time you were here."

Carlos beamed. "Nice to see you again, Mr. Nylund."

"Say, Carlos, how about we do some fishing while you're here?"

"Awesome!"

Betty jabbed Carlos with her elbow.

"I mean, that is a wonderfully fine idea you have suggested, Mr. Nylund, and I look forward to the outing with great anticipation." He smirked.

Betty stifled a laugh.

Lee's brow wrinkled.

Carlos explained. "Mr. Nylund, I am currently being held hostage by the grammar police, subject to severe punishment for overusing words such as 'awesome' and 'cool'."

"I feel for you, son."

Betty nudged Lee.

He smiled, put the truck in reverse, and backed out of the driveway.

When he made the turn into the park, Betty focused on Carlos. "One thing I didn't get a chance to tell you is that we have to load up some scrap metal before we head into Superior Bay. We're going to drop it off at the salvage yard and use the money for fixing up the old park building."

"Cool!"

Betty cringed and bit back a scolding.

Lee drove into the campground where Thad and Janna were offloading a picnic table from the back end of Thad's truck. Thad waved them over. Lee pulled to a stop beside him and rolled down his window.

"Any word on Frank Schram?"

Betty leaned toward the open window to answer, pressing against Lee and catching a pleasant whiff of his spicy aftershave. "Broken hip. He was scheduled for surgery this morning. We're on our way to the Lahti cabin to pick up the scrap metal and take it to the salvage yard. I'm going to stop by the hospital and see how he is. I'll let you know."

Thad slowly shook his head. "Lawsuit for sure."

"Do you really think he'd do that?" Lee asked.

"Some lawyer will get on the case. They can smell money when these things happen." His focus shifted to Betty. "I checked on the Lahti cabin. You made a lot of progress, getting trash cleaned out. Do you have the locks?"

"Lee took them home to clean them up, and he's got them ready to go back on the doors soon as we finish loading the metal. We'll bring the keys back to you."

Thad shook his head. "You keep them so you won't have to hunt me down every time you come in to do work. I have duplicates in my office."

"Thanks, Thad." Betty tucked them into her shoulder bag.

While they had been talking, Janna had come around to Carlos's side of the truck, and he had gotten out to talk with her. They were standing by the picnic table a few yards away. Betty called to him.

Carlos hopped into the truck, a smile on his face. Janna waved to him, and he waved back as Lee pulled out.

"How's Janna doing?" Betty asked.

"Great!" His dark eyes sparkled. "She just finished her freshman year at Superior Bay Community College. Says it was awesome."

"You could go there in the fall, if you get your GED."

"D'ya think?" His brows met.

"What's to stop you?"

He lowered his gaze. "Even if I got the GED, they'd probably turn me down. My grades weren't so hot."

"They take almost all who apply, if they have a high school diploma or GED, that is. I think they'd give you a chance."

Lee backed his truck up to the door of the Lahti cabin and turned off the engine, then got out and held the truck door open for Betty while Carlos got out the other side.

She stood for a moment taking in the changes since she'd left there yesterday afternoon. "The place looks so different with the brush cut back all the way around and the boards taken off the windows. It almost looks cute."

"Some shutters on the windows ought to add the 'cute' factor, don't you think?" Lee's gaze shifted from the building to Betty.

"Are you offering to supply the shutters?"

Carlos turned to her, a sparkle lighting his dark eyes. "I can make shutters, Gram. Dad taught me how. I just need some wood, nails, hinges, and paint."

"And a few tools," said Lee.

"Grampa's got all the tools I'll need in his workshop; at least, he used to have them, unless you got rid of them, Gram."

"I haven't parted with a single one of your grandfather's tools, not yet, anyway. If you're willing to make the shutters, we'll pick up the supplies today." Had Carlos decided to stay around a while?

"Awesome!"

"Give me a shout if you need any help," said Lee. "Now we'd better get that scrap metal loaded up. I'm starting to get hungry for lunch." He lowered the tailgate on his truck.

Betty opened the double doors to the Lahti cabin and walked inside. How different it seemed, emptied of all but the scrap metal and the oak lectern.

When Lee and Carlos joined her, she turned to Lee. "With the trash removed, this place looks a lot larger than I imagined."

"It will look even bigger when we get that old stove and the brush hog out of here." Lee studied the brush hog. "Carlos, do you think the two of us can move that old rascal onto my truck?"

"No sweat, Mr. Nylund." He helped Lee drag it out the door, lift it onto the tailgate, and drag it forward. Within a few minutes, the stove was also loaded and tied down.

"Thanks, fellas." Betty gave a thumbs up.

Lee nodded and turned to Carlos. "We'll need to measure those windows if you're going to build shutters. I'll get a measuring tape from my toolbox."

"No need, Mr. Nylund. I can tell those windows are about forty-eight by forty, and there are four of them. That's all I need to know."

Betty pulled a note pad and pen from her shoulder bag. "Okay, fellas, it's time to make a list of all the things we need from Superior Building Supply. Carlos, why don't you write down what you need for shutters; then we'll add everything else."

"Sure, Gram. I used to write lists for Dad when he'd go out to estimate a project." He set pen to paper, printing neatly. When he finished, he handed the pen and list to Betty.

She put her palm out. "You keep them and help me make a list of the rest of the things we'll need." She headed inside, followed by Carlos and Lee.

"We need a new pine board for the floor here." Lee tapped with the toe of his shoe, which was about to come untied.

Betty stepped up to the door facing the lake. "The hinges on this door are shot."

Carlos made notes and wandered over to the sink and stool. "Are we replacing these with newer models?"

Betty joined him. "Can they be cleaned up?"

Carlos studied the sink, and then handed pen and pad to Betty while he lifted the lid off the toilet tank, looked inside, and carefully set it back in place. "There's not a crack or chip in the porcelain of either one, and the brass handle on the sink just needs polish. I can make the sink and stool look like new with the right cleanser."

Lee joined them. "We probably ought to replace the washers, though, and buy a new toilet kit. I'll get a wrench from my toolbox so we can take the old washers along and match them." He headed for his truck.

Betty ran the toe of her shoe along the floor where old partitions had stood. "We need new paneling to close off the toilet."

Carlos wrote it down, wandered to the oak lectern, and ran his hand over the carving of a cross on the front. "This is really something. Solid oak. All this needs is a cleaning with lemon oil to make it glow."

"I've got lemon oil at home. Are you volunteering?" Betty cocked her brow.

"Sure thing."

Lee returned with a wrench and a tape measure. He handed the tape measure to Carlos. "Just in case you want the true measurements of the windows."

He grinned and began measuring, calling out the dimensions for Betty to write down while Lee worked to remove washers.

She made notes and then pointed her pen to the toilet. "When we build a lavatory around the stool, we could tuck a broom closet next to it in the corner. What do you fellows think?"

Lee gazed up. "Excellent idea."

Carlos extended the tape measure and rattled off numbers while Betty made notes. Fifteen minutes later, the list had grown to three pages in her small notebook.

"Anything we've forgotten, Carlos? Lee?"

Lee's stomach grumbled. "I'm sure there is, but I'm too hungry to think of it right now. I'll lock up and we'll be on our way."

oOo

At the scrapyard, Lee drove onto the scales to get weighed, then drove over to a tall pile of scrap metal. Old cars, metal beams, dented trash barrels, wheel rims, and all manner of smaller items formed a mountain. Lee and Carlos offloaded the stove and brush hog, then got back into the truck. At the scales, the attendant made note of the offloaded weight and then Lee parked the truck in front of the office and went inside to get paid.

A minute later, he came out with money in hand, humming "We're in the Money." Suddenly, he tripped on an untied shoelace and fell forward.

Betty gasped.

Lee caught his balance just in time to avoid falling on his face. He slid onto the seat beside her, his cheeks sporting red blotches.

"Honestly, Lee, I can't understand why you don't keep your shoelaces tied. That's twice in two days you've tripped on them. Nearly gave me a heart attack. Tie them right now. Please."

When his color deepened, she instantly regretted sounding so bossy and irritated.

Shoving the money at her, he got out, propped his foot on the running board, and tied his shoe.

"Thank you, Lee. I'm sorry I was so cross. It's just that I don't want you to end up in the hospital with a broken hip like Frank." She tucked the money into her wallet.

Lee finished tying his shoes, slid onto the seat, and offered a half-smile. "They might even make us roommates. How bad is that?"

"Bad enough to make you keep your shoes tied, I would think."

Carlos leaned forward, his focus on Lee. "You oughta get yourself some elastic shoelaces, Mr. Nylund; then you'll never have to worry about shoelaces coming untied."

"Elastic?"

"Yeah. They turn your shoes into slip-ons."

"You can take a look for elastic laces when we shop for Carlos," said Betty. "He needs new shoes."

"After lunch." Lee started the truck and backed out of the parking place. "Where am I taking you two for lunch, anyway?"

"Wherever Carlos wants to go." Betty turned to him.

"What was the name of that Mexican place you and Gramps took me to last time I was here?"

"Jose's Grill."

"Jose's it is." Lee shifted into forward and gunned the accelerator, squealing his tires.

A scolding nearly escaped Betty's tongue, but she caught it between her gritted teeth. Why did grown men act so childish sometimes?

A half-hour later, in the dim light at Jose's Grill, a waiter served their lunch orders. Betty tasted her taco salad sans cheese and dressing. Not bad, but she'd have preferred the chicken quesadilla that Lee ordered, or even the Mexican steak fajita Carlos had chosen. Why did losing weight always require a choice between what she *should* eat and what she *wanted* to eat?

Lee sampled his quesadilla and then focused on Carlos. "I was thinking I'd go fishing tonight. Want to come along? Perch are just waiting for us."

Carlos's eyes lit up. "That'd be great, Mr. Nylund, if Gram doesn't mind."

"I don't mind," said Betty. "We'll have to get you a license first. I'll loan you the money for it if you promise to work it off."

"Thanks, Gram!"

Betty chewed on her salad, her thoughts drifting ahead. "Lee, are you up for a work session at the park tomorrow?"

He nodded.

"Do you suppose we could get some of the others to come?"

He washed down a mouthful of quesadilla with some coffee. "Probably. Give them a call. Even if none of them shows up, you and Carlos and I could get some work done."

"I'll phone them while you fellas are out fishing."

Carlos finished his steak fajita and a Mexican sundae in the time it took Betty to eat her salad. Was there no bottom to the pit of that kid's stomach?

Lee picked up the tab while she pulled a few bills from her wallet for a tip. When they stepped outside, the bright sunshine blinded her. She stopped to search her bag for her sunglasses and then remembered leaving them in her car. "Doggone!"

"Lose something?" Lee asked.

"What's the matter, Gram?"

"Left my sunglasses home."

Carlos took off his ratty L.A. Dodgers baseball cap and planted it on her head. "Does that help?"

She fought the urge to whip the cap off and hand it back. "Yes. Thanks, Carlos. We'll find you a new one when we get to the thrift store."

"Is that it across the street?" Carlos pointed to Pilgrim Provisions.

"Yes, but before we go there, I want to stop in at the hospital."

A few minutes later, while Carlos stayed in the truck and listened to the radio, Lee accompanied Betty to the hospital's reception desk.

An older woman who could have passed for a prison warden gazed up from her computer screen. "May I help you?"

Lee offered an engaging smile. "We're here to see Frank Schram."

"Are you family?"

Betty shook her head. "We're his neighbors. He doesn't have any family living in the area."

"Perhaps not, but his daughter is with him right now. As for the two of you, only family is allowed today." She returned her gaze to her computer.

Had Betty heard right? Vicky Schram was here? She'd moved to Wisconsin a couple of decades ago and hadn't been back in the area since.

Betty cleared her throat. "Excuse me, ma'am. Could you at least tell us how Frank's surgery went?"

The woman looked up, brow knotted, and exhaled with a huff. "Not unless you have papers permitting you to receive information on his condition."

A door leading to a hallway flew open and a shapely, middle-aged woman with flaming red hair piled atop her head breezed through, the heels of her stilettos clacking as she headed for the exit.

The receptionist nodded in the redhead's direction. "There's his daughter now. Go ask *her*."

The slim, high-heeled woman didn't look anything like the overweight, brown-haired, insolent Vicky from English classes. Betty hurried after her.

"Vicky? How is your father?"

She whirled around, the curious look in her green eyes quickly souring. "Mrs. Hanson from Mossy Point Public School, right?"

CHAPTER 6

Betty's stomach clenched. "How are you, Vicky? It's been—"

"Twenty years since I blew that miserable place."

Eager to avoid a rehash of past problems, Betty swiftly changed topics. "How's your father? Did the surgery go well?"

"Yes, so they tell me. It appears Father will need some long-term care now that they've pinned his hip back together." Her ruby lips suddenly quirked into a smile that appeared ingenuous. "Say, would you mind visiting him from time to time? He doesn't seem to have many friends, and I won't be back here for a while. Got a business in Wisconsin to run." She pulled a card from her designer bag and handed it to Betty.

The card read: *Victoria Schram-Quinn, Victoria's Boutique, Like-New Designer Apparel, Appleton, Wisconsin.* A street address, website, and phone number followed.

Vicky backed away. "You visit him in a few days and give me a call. I want to know exactly how he's doing.

When *I* talk to him, he tends to make things either a lot worse, or a lot better than they really are, depending on his agenda."

"I'll call."

With a nod, Vicky headed out the door at a pace just short of a run.

Lee approached Betty. "Ready for Pilgrim Provisions?"

She nodded. "I guess we're done here. For today, at least."

o0o

At the thrift store, Betty browsed a rack of men's T-shirts while Carlos and Lee carried the bags of old clothes to the donation counter. She pulled out a white shirt with Superior Bay Community College splashed across the front in bright blue letters. Beneath the words, a ferocious, open-mouthed wolf stared at her.

Carlos joined her. "Cool, Gram!" He took the shirt and held it against his chest.

"Good choice, young man." Vicky's voice floated over a rack of dresses in the next aisle. She approached them with half a dozen dresses draped over her arm.

Betty offered a smile. "We meet again."

Vicky nodded, her focus on Carlos. "And who is this handsome young gentleman?"

"My grandson, Carlos. Carlos, Vicky Quinn. Her father is the one we went to visit in the hospital."

"Pleased to meet you, Vicky."

"Looking for some new duds, eh? Here, let me help." Vicky handed the dresses to Betty and began sorting through the rack of shirts. Hangers clacked as she quickly viewed and rejected one after another. Then she pulled out a black shirt screen printed with a motorcycle, and a solid red one with a tiny alligator embroidered on the left shoulder.

She handed them to Carlos. "I bet you need jeans to go with those. What size?"

"Thirty, thirty-two."

"Over here."

Carlos and Betty followed Vicky to the appropriate rack. Again, hangers clacked.

While Vicky sorted through the jeans, Betty looked at the dresses she'd picked out. Too large for the slender Vicky. How odd.

In no time, Vicky pulled three pair of jeans from the rack—one a washed-out blue with knee-sized holes and frayed cuffs, one in black with a designer label on the back pocket, and the third in indigo, boot-cut with traditional gold stitching down the seams.

Vicky smiled brightly and handed them to Carlos. "Give those a try."

"Gee, thanks!"

Vicky checked her watch. "Goodness, it's later than I thought. I've got to hit the road." She took the dresses from Betty and headed for the checkout counter. Could it be that Vicky was going to resell those dresses in her Appleton store?

"I'm going to try these on." Carlos's words shifted Betty's attention.

"The men's fitting rooms are over there." She pointed. "I'll see if I can find you a jacket for cool nights."

Half an hour later, after shopping for a few more things and not finding any shoes for Carlos, Betty stood with him and Lee at the checkout. After the clerk scanned the price tags on the shirts, pants, underwear, socks, a baseball cap, and a denim jacket and began bagging the items, Betty swiped her credit card, punched buttons on the payment terminal, and signed the screen.

The clerk handed the receipt to Betty and the bag to Carlos. "Thanks for shopping at Pilgrim Provisions. Yous have a great day, now."

Carlos took the bag with a smile. "Thanks. You too."

When they had exited the checkout lane, Betty turned to Carlos. "You can pay me back by building the shutters for the folk school."

"No problem, Gram." He hugged her shoulders.

Lee held the door for Betty and Carlos. "Next stop, shoe store?"

Carlos poked him in the chest. "Got to find you some elastic laces, Mr. Nylund."

oOo

At Scott's Shoes, Lee headed for the shoelace rack while Betty followed Carlos to a display of brand name athletic runners.

"Look, Gram! High Flyers!" He pulled out a box in his size and sat down to try them on.

Betty sat beside him, picked up the box to read the price, and gasped. "Carlos, these shoes cost four times as much as all the clothes we just bought."

"But they're half-price, a real steal!" He cinched in the elastic laces and walked in front of the floor-level mirror.

"Take them off. We'll find something more reasonable."

"But I want *these*! After I make the shutters, I'll work every day for two weeks to repay you."

Warmth flooded her cheeks. "I don't care if you're willing to work a month, I'm not buying those shoes! Who are you trying to impress, anyway? Janna?"

He lowered his gaze. "She really got on my case about wearing Gramps's things. Made me feel like a giant dork."

"She's a big tease, always has been. You know that. But she's levelheaded and practical, too. You won't impress her by going out and spending a fortune on shoes. Now take those off and find something else. End of discussion."

He shot her a dirty look, plopped onto a chair, and began removing them.

She ignored him and rose to search for alternatives.

Lee approached, wearing a pair of elastic laces in his shoes and dancing a jig as he hummed "Steppin' Out." He stopped in front of Carlos and extended one foot toward him. "Thanks for suggesting elastic shoelaces. They're just the thing!"

Carlos grinned and gazed up at Lee. "Nice! Now, maybe you can help me convince Gram to buy me these High Flyers."

"Shoes don't make the man, Carlos."

"Thank you, Lee!" Betty shot him a smile and continued her search for economical running shoes.

Fifteen minutes later, wearing a pair of red and black runners, Carlos tucked Harry's old shoes into the box that had held the runners and headed for the checkout counter.

When the cashier had scanned the box, processed the credit card payment, and issued a receipt, Betty turned to Carlos. "After the shutters are done, you owe me a day of work at the park."

"No problem, Gram."

Lee held the door open for Betty. "Are we going to the building supply store next?"

"I guess so." Betty prayed she'd be able to solicit a donation for the shutter materials, paint, roof coating, and hardware they'd need.

o0o

At Superior Building Supply, Carlos pulled out a four-foot by eight-foot panel of birch floor underlayment. "This will make a lot of shutters."

"Floor underlayment?" Betty inspected the panel. "I'd think you'd want pine boards or exterior grade plywood."

"Nope. Birch floor underlayment is put together with waterproof glue and it's a lot more economical." Carlos carefully set the panel on the cart and chose a second one to go with it. "If you want, we can get one-by-ones to trim the edges. Otherwise, I'll sand the edges real smooth before I paint."

"Sanding sounds good to me. What's next?"

"Hardware and paint."

"And don't forget roof coating," said Lee. "I think you ought to buy half black and half white and put it on in stripes. It will make that Lahti cabin look distinctive."

"Or just plain odd," said Betty. "Lead the way, fellows."

Half an hour later, Betty pushed a loaded shopping basket to the front of the store. Carlos and Lee followed with a lumber cart filled with supplies.

"Wait here while I find the manager." Betty walked through an empty checkout lane to the service desk where a pleasant young woman phoned the manager and asked him to come downstairs. Within moments, a dark-haired fellow of about forty approached her with a pleasant smile.

"What can I do for you today, ma'am?"

"I'm working with Mossy Point State Park to restore one of their buildings, and I'm hoping for a donation of supplies."

He scratched his chin. "I see. What type of supplies do you need?"

"Come. I'll show you." She led him toward the shopping basket and lumber cart, explaining along the way. "I don't know if you saw the article in Sunday's paper about the possibility of the park closing?"

"I saw something about it. Didn't read it."

"The park isn't profitable, and since the state doesn't have much money, they're going to close it unless it makes money this year. A group of us is turning an old building there into a folk school to generate funds, but the building needs a lot of work. We've gathered all the supplies together right here." She pointed to the shopping basket and lumber cart. "It would sure help out if you'd donate them to the park for a good cause."

He studied the supplies. "Does your group have a tax-exempt letter from the IRS?" His gaze met Betty's.

"No. Do we need one?"

"I'm afraid so."

"What about the park? Can't you donate the supplies to them?"

"Sorry. We only donate to private organizations that have a nonprofit status with the Federal Government."

"What about a discount? Can we at least get a reduced price?"

"Yes, but that would take a letter from the park and one from your group explaining the reason for requesting a reduced price, and a complete listing of each item by UPC number. Then the discount would be ten percent off the regular price."

Betty glanced at Lee.

He shook his head.

"That would take quite a bit of time. We need these things today. I guess we'll just have to pay the regular price. Thanks anyway."

The manager smiled. "Good luck with that project. And when you get your tax-exempt status, come see me. I'll put you in touch with the donations committee.

Thank you for shopping at Superior Bay Building Supply. Have a nice day!" He strode away at a fast clip.

"'Thank you for shopping at Superior Bay Building Supply.'" Lee smirked. "As if there was another option within a hundred miles. They've figured that into their prices, too, from what I can see."

Betty sighed. "My sentiments exactly. Let's get these things into the checkout lane. We still have groceries to buy before we leave town." She'd have to dig into savings to pay off the balance next month. Her stomach soured. What choice did she have? The park had to be saved. She was the one willing to organize the effort to do it—and evidently she was the one who would have to pay for it, too.

A young woman efficiently scanned each item, sending smaller ones down the moving belt to the exit end where Carlos and Lee bagged them while Betty monitored the checkout display. She nearly choked when the total appeared. Reluctantly, she swiped her card, signed the screen, and pressed the green "accept" button.

On the way out the door, Lee checked his watch. "Betty, would it be all right to stop by the sporting goods store for Carlos's fishing license now? It's getting late. They might close up before we're done grocery shopping. Besides, we need bait."

"Sure. Let's do that."

Carlos grinned. "Awesome! Oops. Sorry, Gram. I meant to say that's a really smart idea, Mr. Nylund."

Betty smiled. "You're catching on, Carlos. In another day or so, you'll be grammar-perfect."

At the sporting goods store, Betty covered the cost of Carlos's license and her own while Lee sprang for the bait. In the supermarket, Carlos picked his favorite foods: dulce de leche Cheerios, dulce de leche ice cream, potato chips flavored with Tapatio hot sauce, salsa, and a couple of bags of tortillas to make wraps with the sliced deli meats she chose.

On the drive home, Betty pushed concern for the oversized grocery bill aside to focus on the folk school challenge. "I was thinking about that lavatory and broom closet. We probably ought to build them before we do any painting inside the old cabin."

Lee's gaze shifted briefly to her, and then back to the road. "Maybe Carlos and I could do that tomorrow, if he's willing?"

"Sure thing, Mr. Nylund. We ought to be able to get it done in a day."

"Great!" said Betty. "I'll set up the next work session for the day after tomorrow."

oOo

At home, Betty sat at the kitchen desk with her stack of credit card receipts and punched each total into the calculator, then hit the "equal" button. The total, high as it was, could have been worse. Thanks to Lee, she didn't spend a cent on lunch out, or dinner either, if you could call it that. His offer to treat everyone to take-out from Mossy Point Pizza had meant she didn't have to cook after a tiring day away, and he and Carlos could get out on the lake to fish before daylight disappeared.

She stuffed the receipts into the envelope in the desk drawer where she saved each month's charges until the credit card statement arrived. How would she pay off the bill when it came? Her savings account was still mighty thin after the roof and plaster repair a while back.

Now, she needed to find willing hands for the day after tomorrow. She reached for the phone and the phone book and began punching in numbers.

CHAPTER 7

On the morning of the work session, as Betty arrived at the old Lahti cabin with Carlos a few minutes before nine o'clock, she was thankful the overnight rain had moved off, leaving only gray skies. She backed her truck up to the door to make it easier to carry in the mops, rags, brushes, towels, buckets of water, and tools Carlos had helped her load earlier.

Lee backed in beside her with the building supplies, hopped out of his truck, and came around to open Betty's door. "Good morning, Betty, Carlos."

"Good morning, Lee." Betty stepped down from the truck, catching a whiff of his spicy aftershave.

Carlos bounded out of the passenger door. "Hi, Mr. Nylund! I'll help you with that stuff on your truck."

Betty put her palm out. "Not yet, Carlos. We need to clean up inside. Let's unload my truck first."

"Sure, Gram."

He lowered the tailgate while she removed the padlock and bar and swung the double doors open. A musty odor wafted out.

Betty glanced up at Lee. "I hope some pine cleaner will kill that foul smell."

"It ought to. Fresh paint will help, too."

Carlos carried in two buckets of water. "Where do you want these, Gram?"

"Against the far wall for now."

Karen, Doris, Wayne, and Patsy arrived and brought in cleaning supplies, including a squeegee for windows.

As Betty returned to her truck for the paper towels and cleaning rags, Steve pulled up, his SUV stuttering and knocking. He got out and sauntered toward the building, his comb in his back pocket and a camera around his neck. If it ever came down to a choice between the two, would he keep the comb and give up the camera? Why couldn't he be more like Wayne, who was unloading wire brushes and a toolbox from the back of his truck?

"Good morning, Steve. Sounds like that SUV of yours needs a tune-up."

"Yeah, someday. Got to pay off my new golf clubs and camera first." He paused by the door, pulled the comb from his pocket, ran it through his thinning hair, and stepped inside.

Betty grabbed the bags of paper towels and rags and followed him into the building.

Conversation filled the room, everyone talking at once, except for Patsy. With her dark hair tied up in a kerchief and a dust mask hanging around her neck, she picked up the squeegee, dipped it into a bucket of water, and started washing windows.

Betty set down the bags and clapped her hands. "Listen up, everyone!"

All but Lee ignored her. He put his fingers to his lips and let out a painfully loud whistle that made Betty cringe. Utter silence followed. Had she gone deaf?

"Betty has something to say." Lee's words reassured her she was still among the hearing.

"Thanks, Lee. And thank you all for coming. Here's the work plan. Karen, Doris, Patsy, and I will clean up inside to prepare for painting. Steve, Lee, and Carlos— did you all meet Carlos, my grandson?"

"We met him." Karen offered a gap-tooth smile.

"Great. Carlos will work with Lee and Steve to wire brush the exterior so they can apply stain. Wayne is going to see if he can get the old pump and well working. Until then, we have only the water we brought, or what we can haul from the administration building. Let's get started!"

The fellows headed outside, all but Steve who aimed his camera at Patsy.

"Patsy?"

At the sound of Steve's voice, she turned to look at him.

He snapped her picture, his flash brightening the room momentarily.

She shook her squeegee at him. "You've got no right! Delete that picture!" Cheeks reddening, she started toward him.

Steve raised his hand in surrender. "Sorry! I apologize. I'll trash the picture right now. See?" He showed her the image in the view panel while he punched buttons to delete it.

"Don't you dare take my picture ever again, you hear?" Patsy's dark eyes sparked.

"Loud and clear." He backed away, turned, and swiftly made an exit.

Betty's gaze followed him as he headed straight for his SUV and stowed his camera.

Karen approached Patsy. "Don't let that hot dog bother ya. He's just got an itchy shutter finger."

Lips pressed to a thin line, Patsy pivoted toward the dirty window, placed the squeegee against it, and pressed so hard a loud squeak cut the air.

Betty winced and turned to Doris. "Guess we'd better do the ceiling first, then the walls, then the floor."

"How are we going to do the ceiling with no ladder?"

"I'll show ya." Karen picked up a sponge floor mop, dipped it into a bucket of pine-scented soapy water, wrung it out, raised it to the ceiling, and swabbed it across the panels.

Betty and Doris followed suit with two other mops. If only Betty could freshen the sour atmosphere as easily as she could clean the ceiling.

The men's laughter drifted inside. Was Steve making fun of Patsy to the others? The turkey. Photos were a good idea, but not the way he was going about it. Betty set her mop in a bucket and headed outdoors to where the men were working on the lake side of the building.

"Uh, oh. Here comes the boss," Lee teased.

"Gram, it's going to be hard to wire brush all the way to the eaves if we can't put up a ladder." Carlos stretched his wire brush as high as he could, coming several inches short of the eave.

"We'll think of something. Any possibility of putting extension handles on the wire brushes?"

"I've got an idea." Steve placed his wire brush against the siding a little below waist height. "The bed of a pickup truck would come about here. What's to stop us from backing a truck up against the siding and standing on the bed to get up under the eaves?"

"Brilliant idea, Steve!" Betty gave a thumbs up. "Now, could I talk to you a minute, please?" She beckoned him away from the others.

"Uh, oh. I'm in trouble now." He winked.

Betty stopped by the edge of the woods a few yards west of the others and spoke quietly. "We're going to have to be careful not to ruffle Patsy's feathers. She's a hard worker, and I need all the help I can get."

"Sorry about that. I'll be careful." He lowered his gaze and dug at the root of a pine seedling with the toe of his sneaker.

"Here's what I can't understand. The first rule you give your photo club kids is to ask permission before taking someone's picture, yet—"

His gaze rose and locked with hers. "I know. Is that all?"

"Not quite. I need your help with something."

He sighed. "What?"

"Photos—of the progress we're making on the building. Wish I'd thought of it sooner."

He smiled wryly. "If that isn't just like a woman! You come out here to scold me for taking a picture, and now you're asking me to take more?"

"I'd like to upload photos and a press release to *SuperiorBayJournal dot com*, see if we can get some online coverage for the folk school. I can mention in the release that you took the pictures and that you're going to teach a folk school class on photography. I could even put in your website link. It'll be good exposure for you—pun intended." She smiled.

His brow lifted. "Do you think you can add in there that I shot a hole-in-one at Augusta?"

"Would you like to teach a second folk school course on golf?"

"Would anyone come?"

"Don't know until we try."

"Sure! I could teach putting on a carpet in the building, driving over at the school ball field, and for the finale, we could spend a day on the course at Superior Bay."

"Sounds like a plan! Now, why don't you get busy with your camera and take some shots of the men. Then come inside. I'll explain to the gals what you're going to do and give Patsy a heads-up so she can stay out of your viewfinder."

"I'll get my camera." He set off for his SUV at a brisk pace.

Betty headed to the east end of the building. Maybe Wayne would have the water on soon, save her a trip to the campground. He was kneeling next to the pump and punching an old-fashioned on-off switch, coaxing barely a groan from it.

"What's up, Wayne?"

He stood and pushed back the brim of his Green Bay Packers cap. "Not the water from this well, that's for sure. I think we can write the epitaph for this well pump."

"That bad, eh?"

"Afraid so."

Betty's stomach clenched. A new one would cost hundreds. "You'd better go find Thad. Maybe he has some ideas, or even some spare parts."

"I'll go talk to him, but it'll take a new unit, I'm afraid, unless I can rebuild this one."

"Thanks, Wayne. Let me know what you find out."

"Will do." He headed for his truck.

Betty gazed heavenward. The clouds over the lake had opened one pinhole of sunshine that spotlighted the surface of the gray-green water miles offshore. "Is that a sign, Lord? Is there hope for that old motor?"

A blue jay scolded from a nearby red pine, sending a squirrel scampering in the opposite direction.

Scolding and scampering. Betty had played the jay's part; now she needed to scamper back to work.

The moment Betty walked in the door, Patsy dropped her squeegee in a bucket and approached her. "Betty, how will I get the outside of these windows clean with no ladder?"

Betty grinned. "Problem solved! I'll back my truck up to the window and you can stand on the bed. You'll want to wait until the fellows are done wire brushing and staining, though."

Karen let out a hoot. "Thought ya was out there goofin' off. Turns out yous guys was problem-solvin'."

"Steve thought of it. Now listen up everyone; I have some news."

Doris set down her mop, ran a hand through her unruly henna hair, and faced Betty. "I hope Wayne's about to turn on the water."

Betty shook her head. "Looks like it will be a while before we get water out of the well."

"So what's the news?" Patsy's gaze searched Betty's.

"I've asked Steve to take pictures of our progress on the building so I can get some coverage with *SuperiorBayJournal dot com* for the folk school. You don't have to be in the photos."

"I don't want to be in them, either." Doris raised her mop to the ceiling. "I've got to lose another twenty pounds before this body shows up online."

"I'll pose for him with a big grin." Karen smiled wide enough to show three gaps in her teeth. "Maybe catch myself a husband."

Doris snickered. "Or an offer of dental work for a price high as the moon, more likely."

Karen planted her hands on her hips, and her focus on Doris. "What? Ya don't think I can lure a man with this be-yoo-tiful mug?"

Doris lowered her mop, faced Karen, and shrugged. "Just sayin'."

Betty chuckled to herself and headed for her mop. At least she wouldn't be the only female in Steve's photos.

Several minutes later, Wayne's truck pulled up, followed by Thad's. Betty set her mop in a bucket and headed outside.

Wayne hopped out and started for Thad's tailgate. "Hey, Betty, good news! Thad gave us a well pump. Years ago they replaced this one that was on the campground well."

"Hallelujah!"

Thad joined them. "The pump leaked, but the motor still works. A new gasket ought to fix 'er up. You might as well make use of it."

Betty smiled. "You just made my day a whole lot brighter!"

They lifted the well pump off Thad's truck, carried it to the pump house, and set it on the ground.

Carlos approached. "Hey, Gram, can I borrow the keys to your truck? We finished the north side at ground level."

Thad's gaze narrowed on Betty. "Do I have a waiver for him?"

She gasped. "I'm sorry! With all that's happened, I plumb forgot! I'll get it to you right after lunch."

He nodded, his gaze shifting to Carlos. "So you're the grandson from California. Janna's been telling me about you."

Carlos blushed. "Nothing bad, I hope."

"No, just her memories of your visits to Mossy Point when you were kids." He nodded in the campground's direction. "Got to run. Still have lots to do before the opening day." He took off for his truck.

"Wait up!" Camera in hand, Steve headed for Thad. "I'd like to get a shot of you with Betty, Wayne, and Carlos. Good PR, the park working with volunteers to repurpose a defunct building."

"Okay, but make it quick. I've got more work to do than you can shake a camera at."

"Come over here by the pump house. Why don't you bend with one hand on your knee, the other pointing to the replacement pump. Wayne, you're kneeling by the old pump, wrench in hand, listening like Thad's the great oracle. Betty and Carlos, you're focused on Thad to hear his pronouncement. Good. Perfect. Hold that position while I get two shots." He clicked the shutter twice and checked the view panel. "Great! Thanks everyone!" He turned to go.

"Steve, wait! I've got an idea." Betty approached him.

"I'm listening." He wiggled his ears and grinned.

She fought the urge to smile at the seventh grader in a man's body and lost.

Carlos joined them. "How do you do that, Steve?"

"Easy!" He wiggled his ears again.

"Can you teach me?"

"Practice in front of a mirror, Carlos. If you've got the gene, your ears will be wiggling in no time. If not, it will take a looong time to train them."

Betty waved her hand in dismissal. "Enough about silly ear wiggling. Don't you have work to do, Carlos?"

He held out his hand, palm up. "Truck keys?"

She fished them out of her jeans pocket. "Be careful. You *do* have a driver's license, don't you?"

"In my wallet." He took off at a jog.

"Nice kid." Steve watched him go and then focused on Betty. "Now what was it you wanted to talk to me about?"

"I'd like a shot of our group for our own records, not for the paper. I think all but Patsy will go along. We could have her take the picture, if you'll show her how to use your camera."

"Sure. Let's do it."

CHAPTER 8

"Say 'Cheese!' everyone." Steve gave the order from the back row of the group as they stood in front of the old Lahti cabin.

Patsy clicked the shutter.

"Everyone stay where you are until I check the shot." Steve headed for Patsy and his camera, reviewed the photo, and smiled at Patsy. "Good job!"

She ducked out of the camera strap and made a beeline inside.

"Back to work!" Karen turned and followed Patsy. Doris trailed behind.

"You mean it's not time for lunch yet?" Steve put on an exaggerated frown.

"Lunch?" Betty's voice joined Lee's in unison.

Lee checked his watch. "We can get another side of the building wire brushed before lunch."

Thad's truck pulled up, Janna driving. She backed in and hopped out. "Thad asked me to haul this picnic table over here for yous. Needs a little paint, but it's solid. I just finished replacing the broken bench. Someone want to help me unload it?"

Carlos headed for her tailgate at a sprint.

Lee and Steve joined him.

Together, they slid the table off the truck and set it on the ground.

Janna slammed the tailgate shut. "Thanks, guys! See yous later." She hopped into the driver's seat and leaned out her window. "Mrs. Hanson, I almost forgot. Thad said to ask if you have a fire extinguisher and smoke alarm for the building."

"No. Hadn't thought of it."

"He said you'll need them before you start your folk school. It's code."

"Tell Thad I'll make sure we get them."

Janna nodded, started the ignition, and pulled away.

Carlos watched her go.

Lee ran his hand over the weathered tabletop. "Where do you want this, Betty?"

"Lakeside, don't you think?"

Carlos continued staring down the road, although Janna was out of sight.

Steve tapped him on the shoulder. "Time to stop Janna-dreaming and put your muscles to work."

"Sure, sorry."

Betty led the way around the east end of the building, past Wayne, who was hard at work on the pump replacement, to a grassy patch overlooking Lake Superior. Carlos, Steve, and Lee set the table down and Betty studied it. *Needs a little paint* was an understatement. The new bench was raw wood and the rest of the boards were peeling.

Patsy emerged from the lakeside door and joined them. "I'd like to paint this table for you, Betty, if that's all right."

"Sure! That'd be great!"

Carlos turned to Patsy. "I'll wire brush it and sand it for you first, if you'd like."

Patsy smiled. "That would be so nice of you, Carlos." Her gaze shifted to Betty. "What color should I use? Do you have a color scheme for Mossy Point Folk School?"

"A color scheme? I never gave it any thought."

"What about a logo? It could go right here." Patsy traced a circle with her hands on the center of the table.

"Haven't given that a thought, either. Are you good at drawing? Could you design one?"

Patsy shrugged. "I'm only a hobby artist but I could give it a try."

"Why don't you do that. In fact, why don't you come up with three different concepts and color schemes and we'll vote on them."

"When?" Patsy chewed on her lower lip.

"If you work on them tonight, we'll vote tomorrow."

"Tomorrow?" Steve stepped beside Patsy. "Are we working here tomorrow, too?"

Patsy took off.

Steve's gaze followed her into the building and then shifted to Betty. "Did I say something wrong? What is it with that woman, anyway?"

Betty chuckled. "Maybe she's just impervious to your charm."

"That's a first."

"Your ex-wives might disagree."

"There's no accounting for poor taste."

"Theirs, or yours?"

Steve's cheeks flushed.

"As for your earlier question, yes, we're working here tomorrow and Saturday and every day but Sundays until this place is ready for students. Now, I've got work to do and so do you." Betty nodded in the direction of Carlos and Lee who were wire brushing the upper portion of the siding from her truck bed.

Steve's shoulders slumped. He shuffled toward the fellows.

Betty took one last look at the picnic table. An image popped into her mind and she hurried inside to find Patsy, who was vigorously scrubbing the west window with the scratcher side of her squeegee. "Patsy, could you include a flying turtle in one of your designs?"

Patsy set her squeegee in a bucket, her gaze narrowing on Betty. "A flying turtle?"

"It's kind of a joke between me and Mr. Engstrom. He said this park has about as good a chance of running in the black as a turtle has of flying. I told him it would happen this year."

A smile crept over Patsy. "A turtle will fly this year, guaranteed!"

"Great! Can't wait to see what you come up with!"

Betty headed to the center of the room, wrung out the mop she'd left standing in her bucket, and looked for a place to start. Karen and Doris had finished with the ceiling and were working their way around the walls of the room, cleaning the upper portion on the north and east sides. Betty set to work on the south wall while a vision of a turtle flying hovered in her mind.

"Patsy, what if the turtle is flying over a mossy point?"

"Good idea! I could make it look sort of like a sea turtle with flipper-like legs spread out as if they were wings."

Betty laughed. "That's us, Patsy. Mossy Point Folk School is a turtle stretching its flipper legs, believing it can fly."

"What's all this nonsense about a flying turtle?" Karen wanted to know.

"I asked Patsy to design a logo for us with a flying turtle. She's going to paint it on the picnic table."

Doris set her mop in a bucket and turned to Betty. "We need T-shirts with 'Mossy Point Folk School' across the bosom and a flying turtle beneath—or maybe it should be the other way around. The turtle flying across the bosom and the words beneath."

Betty chuckled, but dollar signs formed a question mark in her mind. "We'll talk about it after lunch. I'll call Superior Bay Custom Designs and get a quote." As Betty lifted her mop to the wall, she envisioned a triple extra-large shirt on Mr. Engstrom with a flying turtle stretched across his belly, a walking billboard for the folk school. But would he wear it?

Wayne stepped through the open door. "Smells clean in here. Starting to look clean, too."

"Hey, Wayne, what's the prognosis on the well?" Betty leaned on her mop.

"That's what I came to tell you. I'm making a run to Superior Bay for a new seal. Then we'll have water."

"Yahoo! I'm all pumped up about that!" Karen gave a thumb up and continued mopping.

Wayne smiled. "Anything else we need while I'm at the building supply?"

"Yeah, a new set of muscles." Doris rubbed her shoulder.

"Got it. One set of Doris-sized shoulder muscles. Anything else, honey? Maybe you want to ride along, give those shoulder muscles a break?"

Betty cringed inwardly. Doris may have sore muscles, but she powered through when there was work to do, and plenty more needed to be done before this day was over.

Doris shook her head. "You go on without me, Wayne. I can't abandon Betty and Karen and Patsy right now. We're just getting a good start in here."

"See you all after lunch, then. Could one of you ladies please give Doris a ride home at lunchtime?"

"She can eat at my place," said Betty.

"Or mine, if she likes venison chili," said Karen.

"Love it," said Doris. "Haven't tasted venison in I can't remember when."

"I'm on my way, then." Wayne turned to go.

Betty's memory clicked. "Wait! Could you please pick up a new fire extinguisher and smoke detector? Thad says it's code. Bring me the receipt for them, and the seal, and I'll reimburse you."

"Will do."

"Oh, and one more thing."

"What's that?" Wayne paused on the threshold.

"Would you mind terribly stopping by the hospital to see how Frank is doing? I kind of promised his daughter I'd check in on him every now and then and report back to her."

"No problem. See you all later."

Work resumed until shortly before lunch when Karen set down her mop and walked around the room checking the water in each of the half-dozen buckets. "I can't get nothin' clean anymore. The water in every bucket is filthy. I'm gonna toss it all into the woods and drive over to the administration building for a fresh supply. Anybody want to help?" She lifted two buckets and headed for the door.

"I'll help." Doris reached for her bucket.

Patsy set down her squeegee. "Me, too."

Betty grabbed the handle of her bucket and followed the others out the door.

o0o

Early in the afternoon, when everyone had returned from lunch, Betty called a meeting around the picnic table. She stood at one end with her clipboard, calendar, and notes. The men filled one bench, the women the other. Steve sat across from Patsy on the far end, his camera hanging from his neck.

"Thanks, everyone, for the hard work you put in this morning. The place is slowly shaping up. Now, we have some business to attend to before we can get Mossy Point Folk School off the ground." An image of a turtle flapping its wings, struggling awkwardly to take off from dry land, flashed through her mind.

She continued. "Patsy has offered to develop a logo. She'll bring three designs tomorrow, and we'll vote on them. I've checked into getting T-shirts printed with 'Mossy Point Folk School' and the logo, and it will cost about twenty dollars per shirt. How many would be interested in buying a shirt?"

All but Steve's hand went up.

"Great! I'm passing around a sign-up sheet. Put your name and shirt size on it, and I'll get back to you for the payment when I know the exact amount." She handed the clipboard and pen to Lee.

"Next item of business is class schedule. I've brought a calendar. Steve, are you available to teach on Memorial Day weekend? I thought that would be a super time for photographers to catch the spring wildflowers."

"Sure, on one condition."

Lee sighed. "Now what, fancy pants?"

Steve ignored Lee. "I'll teach if you all sign up for my class."

"What?" Wayne scowled at Steve.

"That's preposterous," said Doris.

Karen folded her arms on her chest. "I ain't signin' up for no photography class. I ain't even got a camera."

Steve's focus settled on Patsy. "I just want to make sure I've got some paying students to make my time worthwhile for the park."

Patsy lowered her gaze.

"The best way to find paying students is to get on the phone or the computer," said Wayne. "Put the word out to all your contacts. We need to draw people and money from outside the area."

"Wayne's right," said Betty. "We all need to do that. Now back to my original question, Steve. Photography on Memorial Day weekend, and golf on the first weekend of June?"

"I suppose."

"Lee, can you teach fly-tying the second weekend in June?"

"Can do."

Betty wrote their names on the calendar. "And Wayne, how about decoy carving on the third weekend in June?"

"Sure thing."

Steve's gaze swept in the women. "What about you ladies? What are *you* going to teach? So far it's the men doing all the work."

Patsy raised her hand halfway. "I could teach moccasin making and bead embroidery in the Ojibway style if you think anyone would be interested. It would take three days to finish a pair of beaded moccasins."

Betty's spirit soared. "Patsy, that's a wonderful idea! I took a class like that years ago at North Country Folk School and loved it. I wore my moccasins every day until they gave out, they were so comfortable. How about teaching your class on the fourth weekend in June, Friday through Sunday?"

"Sure."

Betty wrote Patsy's name on the calendar. "We have five Saturdays in June this year. Anybody want to teach on the fifth one?"

"I'll teach birding," said Doris. "It's a great family activity, and I'll bet not one in a hundred can recognize even ten of the most common bird calls in the north woods."

"Good idea, Doris. I'm putting you down. And I'll put myself down for a writers' workshop on the second weekend in July. Now, we need something special for Independence Day weekend. Does anyone have an idea?"

Karen's hand shot up. "I got the perfect thing. A fish boil. We'll hold a fish boil on Saturday night, and I'll teach folks how it's done."

"Great idea, Karen! I'm putting it on the schedule."

Lee shifted his gaze to Karen. "You'll need lots of fish for a fish boil."

Wayne turned to Lee. "You planning to haul in a big catch?"

"Gettin' fish ain't no problem," said Karen. "I can get Ahlberg Brothers over in Superior Bay to donate the whitefish. Nick's a second cousin of mine on my father's side, unofficially."

"Unofficially?" Steve's brow rose.

"You know what I mean. While Nick's papa was out fishing, his mama got too friendly with my papa's cousin Ollie and nine months later, out came Nick."

Steve gazed heavenward.

"Back to the schedule," said Betty. "We've filled the calendar through the second weekend in July. We need lots more teachers and classes to fill out the season. Anyone got ideas?"

"I'd think you could find teachers through that arts and crafts cooperative over in Superior Bay," said Lee.

"Good idea. I'll give them a call." Betty made a note. "Any other suggestions?"

"We could have a pizza party night with a little history of Italian cuisine thrown in," said Wayne. "Mossy Point Pizza could cater the food, and my daughter could do the teaching."

"Drumming up a little profit for your kid, eh?" said Steve.

"I bet she'll charge us her cost," said Wayne. "We could make good money for the park."

"Anything involving food ought to go over well with the campers," said Doris. "I'm getting hungry just thinking about it."

Betty focused on Wayne. "Would you please talk to Zoe and have her call me if she's interested?"

He nodded.

Betty wrote "pizza party?" down. "So far we've got possibilities for a pizza party and for finding teachers through the arts and crafts cooperative. Any more ideas?"

Patsy raised her hand. "I might be able to find some teachers. I'll talk to my people."

"Your people?" Steve smirked. "Did you hear that, Betty? Patsy will have her people talk to your people and get the rest of the schedule filled in."

"Stuff it, Taylor," said Lee.

Patsy's gaze lasered Steve. "If you knew who my people were, you'd be more careful what you say."

"Whoa. Now she's threatening me. Did you all hear that?"

Karen straightened and turned toward Steve. "You turkey. I'll tar your feathers if ya keep on with that wise-acre mouth of yours."

"I'll heat the tar." Wayne grinned.

Steve put his hands up. "No need. I'll behave myself." He raised his camera and aimed it at Wayne.

He put on an exaggerated smile.

Steve clicked the shutter.

"Back to business," said Betty, "and Steve, try not to sound so much like the students in your camera club. Speaking of students, we need lots of them to make this work. I'll write up a press release for the *Superior Bay Journal* and the other newspapers in the region. And I'll run off some fliers at the office supply store. Maybe Thad can get our release posted on the state park web-site."

"Gram?"

"Yes, Carlos?"

"We need a website of our own. And a Facebook page, Twitter account, Pinterest account, PayPal account, and email address. Then we can blog about classes and set up payments for them online. It wouldn't cost us a cent."

"Would you like to set all that up, Carlos?"

"Sure!"

"Anybody else have an idea?"

"Yeah," said Wayne. "I'd like to get back to work. I'm pretty sure I can have water running by the end of the day."

"Meeting adjourned." Betty collected her clipboard, stuck her notes under the clip on top of the T-shirt list, and headed for her truck to leave it on the dashboard. Maybe this Mossy Point Folk School idea would work after all.

Wayne approached her. "Hey, Betty, I stopped by the hospital to see Frank."

"How's he doing?"

"He seems to be recovering pretty fast for someone who just had surgery a couple days ago, but there's something you ought to know."

"What's that?"

Wayne pulled off his Packers cap and ran a hand over his brush cut. "He's talking about getting a lawyer and naming you and the park in a lawsuit."

Betty's stomach clenched. "Maybe it's just talk."

"Maybe he won't be able to find a lawyer to take the case."

"I'd put money on a turtle flying before I'd bet on that."

A smile darted across Wayne's lips and quickly turned upside down. "The accident was his own dumb fault. Everybody who was there knows it." He slapped his cap back on his head and took off for the pump house.

Betty headed inside, her gut churning. She certainly was *not* going to call Frank's daughter to report on his condition, not with the possibility of a lawsuit in the air. What was this all about, anyway? Was she trying to punish her because she'd spurned his advances years ago after Harry died? If only she'd known Frank was going to show up, then maybe she could have gotten his signature on a waiver.

CHAPTER 9

The following Sunday afternoon, with the lunch dishes rinsed and placed in the dishwasher, Betty went to Carlos's room, expecting to find him glued to the computer. Instead, he was standing in front of the dresser mirror.

"What's up, Carlos?"

"Trying to wiggle my ears. I can't get them to move. How does Steve do it?"

"He said it's genetic." She stood beside him and tried to move her ears. "I can't get my ears to budge, and I'm making a guess your parents can't move theirs, either. Why would you even *want* to wiggle your ears?"

"Girls. I read online it's a real magnet for chicks."

"Maybe you'll have to find something else to be your 'magnet,' like your natural good looks and charismatic personality. Now, how about working on a website for Mossy Point Folk School?"

He nodded and carried her laptop to the kitchen counter. She sat beside him while he established email and blog accounts and wrote up descriptions of the classes. Then she helped him write a press release encouraging readers to sign up for the classes. He uploaded the release along with Steve's photos to the *Superior Bay Journal* and several other online newspapers across the state. By the time he finished, the afternoon was nearly over.

"Thanks a million for your help on this, Carlos. I really appreciate your putting in so much time on it." She hugged his shoulders.

He flashed a smile and unplugged the computer. "I didn't mind. It was kind of fun. And I sure learned a lot about good writing. Guess I'll go out to the shop now. I can get a little more done on the shutters before it's time for supper."

Gratitude filled her heart. He'd spent the entire day helping her without a single word of complaint. She rose and started toward the great room in search of her Kindle.

"Gram?"

She turned toward him. His bright smile had disappeared, and lines wrinkled his forehead.

"Did you mean what you said earlier about my looks and personality?"

"Did I mean it?" She cocked her brow. "Does the sun rise in the east? Does day follow night? Does death follow taxes? Oops. Forget that last one. You get my drift. Your looks and personality are enough to win any girl worth having. Guaranteed. Ear-wiggling won't help. Believing in yourself will." She sighed. "Sorry for the lecture."

"I didn't mind." He headed out the door.

As Betty relaxed in her recliner with her Kindle, she found it impossible to concentrate on the romance story she'd been reading. Tomorrow would be a work session at the Lahti cabin, but she really needed to make a trip to Superior Bay during business hours. The folk school needed an online bank account to collect payments from students, and she had to run off flyers and distribute them to as many of the downtown businesses as possible. While she was there, she could stop by the arts and crafts co-operative and recruit teachers. She went to the phone, punched in Lee's number, and explained her dilemma.

"No problem, Betty. I'll supervise the work session; you go to Superior Bay and don't give it another thought."

"Are you sure?"

"What are friends for? I'll stop by and pick up the keys a little before nine."

She drew a deep breath and released her tension. "Thanks, Lee. You're a doll. I don't know what I'd do without you. See you in the morning."

That night, when she slipped beneath the covers, she whispered a prayer. "Thank You, Lord, for the progress we made today on folk school business. Be with me tomorrow in Superior Bay, and with Lee at the Lahti cabin. And if it's not too much to ask, could You please send some students and teachers our way?"

oOo

Three days later, as Carlos sat at the kitchen counter checking email, Betty cracked eggs into the cast-iron frying pan for breakfast, a prayer running through her head. *Lord, I hate to sound like a nag, but I could sure use more teachers and students for the folk school—*

The phone rang. Could it be someone from the arts and crafts co-operative? She reached for the handset. Caller I.D. displayed "Mossy Point Pizza."

"Good morning. This is Betty."

"Zoe Reed-Garvey here. Mom and Dad said you'd like me to put on an Italian cuisine night and pizza party at the park. How about July 20th?"

Betty's heart soared. "That would be great!"

"Let me know the numbers about two days ahead. I can handle up to fifty."

"Will do. Thanks, Zoe! I look forward to it!" She clicked off and turned the eggs. *Thank you, Lord! We're making progress. But we still have a long way to go. Could You send me some students?*

"Hey, Gram, come look at this!" Carlos gazed up from the computer. "Somebody signed up for the photography class!"

Betty stepped behind Carlos to focus on the screen.

He pointed to the email notification and read. "Hello, Mossy Point Folk School. You have received payment of $150.00 from wryfellow at superiorbay dot edu."

"Whoohoo! We did it, Carlos! We have our first student!" She gave him a high-five and headed for the phone. "I've got to tell Lee."

"Gram, what about the eggs?"

She hurried back to the stove, turned off the burner, slid the pan to the side, and then made her call.

Lee answered on the third ring. "Good morning, Betty."

"Lee, we've got our first student. $150!"

"Great! Now we need about a dozen more to make Steve happy."

"I know, I know. Just thought I'd celebrate the moment."

"Betty, with money coming in, you really need to file paperwork to make Mossy Point Folk School a nonprofit organization."

"You're right, but I've been too busy getting the building ready and working online to set aside the mountains of time that task will take."

"I'll help you. Why don't we work on it tonight?"

"Tonight? I thought you and Carlos were going fishing to-night."

"Not tonight, Gram. I'm meeting Janna for pizza."

"That's right; I forgot. Okay, Lee, tonight. But first we've got siding to stain, shutters to hang, windows to caulk, and a roof to coat. Have you found a licensed contractor who will do the roof work in exchange for free classes?"

"Not yet. I'm still working on it."

"Good. Got to get back to my eggs. See you over there at nine."

She served up the eggs, toast, and coffee, and sat beside Carlos. "We've got one more activity to add to the folk school website. The Italian Cuisine and Pizza Party night will be held on July 20th."

"I'll list it as soon as I finish eating." He jammed an entire egg yolk into his mouth.

A scolding was on the tip of her tongue. She managed to bite it back and rephrase. "No need to rush through breakfast."

"Who's rushing? I'm just plain *hungry*." He grinned and stabbed into the egg white.

o0o

After breakfast, Betty helped Carlos load his newly completed shutters into her truck. When they arrived at the old Lahti cabin a few minutes before nine, she wasn't one bit surprised to find Lee standing in the bed of his truck, applying stain to the gable on the west end. No matter how hard she tried, she'd learned in the past week that she simply couldn't beat him to the punch when it came to working on the building. He came early, stayed late, never complained, and kept the others on task. Money couldn't buy that kind of friendship, not that she had any cash left to spend. She pushed aside money worries, shifted the truck into park, and got out.

Lee set down his roller, jumped off his truck, and headed toward them. Running a hand over the freshly dried black paint on a new shutter, he let out a low whistle. "Nice job, Carlos. I can see now why you said you didn't need my help."

Carlos beamed. "Thanks, Mr. Nylund."

They unloaded the shutters while Betty unlocked the door, stepped inside, and turned on the light switch. The three new overhead fixtures Wayne had hung yesterday from the newly painted ceiling flooded the room with full-spectrum light. Now she could really see to paint the walls and floor.

Her gaze shifted to one of the windows. It sparkled. They all did. Patsy sure knew how to make them shine. Too bad they'd soon be smudged with caulk. Lee and Wayne insisted they needed it; said they'd do it today. Why hadn't they mentioned it before Patsy spent all that time cleaning glass? Good thing she was leaving this morning to visit her friends for a few days.

Steve wouldn't be here either. Going golfing. At least that's what he'd said right after Patsy had said she'd be gone. Was it his love of golf or Patsy's absence that caused him to skip out?

Betty tucked that question away as she unlocked and opened the lakeside door. A cool breeze off Lake Superior prompted her to zip her sweatshirt. Clouds hovered near the horizon. It wasn't supposed to rain today. That's what the online weather report said last night. She *hoped* it wouldn't rain, at least not until the stain dried.

To her right, the picnic table lured her for one more admiring glance at the flying turtle logo Patsy had painted. She'd captured the whimsy perfectly. And it had come out great on the T-shirts she'd picked up from the custom design shop two days ago.

Enough woolgathering. So much needed doing. She headed inside.

The walls and floor screamed for repairs and paint. The porcelain on the sink and toilet stool held on stubbornly to their rust stains despite Carlos's efforts. At least partitions and a door at the east end of the room now enclosed the stool, the toilet flushed properly, and the old sink that stood just outside the lavatory didn't leak.

But what would she do about the rest of the room? It was bare. Tables and chairs had to be built or bought—another big expense. Where would the money come from?

Vehicles pulled up. Doors slammed. Karen and Doris stepped inside, Karen carrying a toolbox.

Betty greeted them with a smile. "Hey, you two, good news. Someone signed up online for Steve's photography class!"

"That's encouraging." Doris shrugged off her jacket.

"Man or woman?" Karen set her toolbox down with a clunk.

"Man."

"Married or single?"

"Don't know. He goes by the name wryfellow at superiorbay dot edu."

"Least he's got a sense of humor. He'll need it with Steve for a teacher." Karen took a look around the room, her gaze settling on the west wall. "Thought I'd fix the holes and loose panels so we can get paint on in here. The fellas've got their hands full outside."

"Great idea," said Betty. "What can we do to help?"

"I'll hold boards while you pound nails," said Doris. "Wayne says I'm the best carpenter's assistant he ever had. I always tell him I'd better be the *only* carpenter's assistant he ever had, if you know what I mean."

"Thanks for the offer, Doris, but I don't need no help. Not for now, anyway. Why don't you and Betty start painting the lavatory? I'll have the old walls fixed up by the time you're done." She lugged her toolbox to the west end of the room.

Betty pried the top off the half-full can of white paint left over from yesterday's work on the ceiling. The latex odor pricked her nose as she stirred. When she had poured some into a pan, she picked up a roller, filled it with paint, and began applying it to the exterior of the lavatory.

Doris dipped a brush into the paint. "I'll work on the corners. That's the job Wayne always gives me when we paint. Corners and trim."

"We'll make a good team," said Betty. "I'd much rather roll than brush."

"And I'd much rather pound nails," said Karen.

Betty rolled out the paint and dipped her roller into the pan to soak up another load. Something whirred, and then a gunshot-like blast exploded in the room.

Startled, she whirled around.

Paint flew off her roller, spattering Doris across her behind.

Doris laughed. "I thought you were rolling, not spatter painting."

"Nice speckle job on Doris's backside, Betty." Karen positioned her nail gun. Another whir and blast cut the air.

Betty winced. She'd go deaf by morning's end. "So sorry, Doris. Do you want me to wipe . . . ?"

"Wipe my butt? Nah. These are my old painting jeans. A few white spatters just make them more interesting."

Betty evened out the paint on her roller and applied it to the bare partition, wishing she were anywhere but in the same room with a nail gunner. As the bare wall turned white, she more easily blocked out the annoying pops and focused on getting the job done.

Two hours later, when Karen put away her nail gun and started painting on the west end of the room, Betty heaved a sigh of relief. The whoosh of wind in the pines, gulls calling across the water, and the men's conversation and laughter as they applied stain to the exterior, calmed her nerves.

Tires crunched on the gravel road out front. Was Steve coming to work today after all? She turned to look out the front window. A state SUV pulled up. Whose could it be?

The driver door opened, and Mr. Engstrom emerged with his pregnant-like paunch in the lead. A much younger fellow stepped out of the passenger's side. Tall, tanned, slim, dirty blond hair casually combed back in a wave.

Betty set aside her roller and headed outdoors. "Hello, Mr. Engstrom. What brings you to these parts?"

"Just showing my friend around. He's looking for a summer place. Chip Landers, this is Mrs. Hanson."

Chip's mouth opened in a drop-dead-handsome smile, revealing teeth bright enough to shame the sun. "Pleased to meet you, Mrs. Hanson."

Arrested by his blinding smile, she almost forgot to offer her hand. "Welcome to Mossy Point Folk School, Chip, or the makings of it anyway.

His hand wrapped around hers like a warm cocoon. "Thad was just telling Ray and me a little about your project. Sounds interesting."

Their hands parted, and with some effort, she recovered her focus. "It's still under development, but we'll be ready to open on Memorial Day weekend with a photography class. Why don't you join us?"

"I'd love to, but I'm afraid I'll be out of the area then."

"I'll bet you're a golfer, eh?"

He nodded.

"We're having a golf outing the weekend after Memorial Day. You can sign up online. Just go to mossypointfolkschool dot com." Oops. She'd just morphed Steve's golf class into an outing. Sounded like a better idea anyway for raising funds. She'd discuss it with the others later.

"Not sure I can make it back here then, but I'll take a look at my calendar."

Lee wandered over, and Karen emerged from inside, a paint smudge on her cheek. Betty introduced them to Mr. Engstrom and Chip.

Karen offered a wide smile. "We're havin' a fish boil the first Saturday in July—whitefish from Ahlberg Brothers. Better sign up quick. It's fillin' up fast."

Chip returned the smile. "Thanks for the info. I'll keep it in mind."

"Chip is looking for a summer place," said Betty.

"You single or married?" Karen asked.

Betty stifled a gasp.

"Single, but—"

"Me too. We could hitch up; then you'd have your summer place—mine! Ain't much for sale in these parts right now 'cept for a deer camp or two that ain't got plumbing or electric."

"Thanks for the offer, but—"

"You think it over."

"Come on, Chip; we've got more to see." Mr. Engstrom took a backward step toward the SUV, lost his balance, and started to fall.

Chip reached out to steady Mr. Engstrom.

CHAPTER 10

Mr. Engstrom and Chip teetered near a fall. In the greatest display of fancy footwork and miraculous leveraging Betty had ever seen, Chip remained upright and steadied Mr. Engstrom.

The head of the General Land Office recovered quickly, a skill he'd evidently perfected from decades as a state employee. He flashed a cigar-stained smile. "Nice talking to you again, Mrs. Hanson." His gaze darted to Lee and Karen and back again. "Best of luck to you with the folk school. To tell the truth, I'm surprised at how good this place looks. Last time I saw it—some twenty years ago or more—it was looking pretty shabby."

"Thanks, Mr. Engstrom. We're doing our best to make the folk school attractive. See you at the end of the season when this park is profitable. And I'll show you my flying turtle."

"That'll be the day." Mr. Engstrom squeezed himself into the driver's seat of the SUV.

Chip quickly tucked himself into the passenger's seat. Mr. Engstrom backed out and gunned the SUV toward the campground, raising a cloud of dust.

Lee moved closer. "What do you suppose that was about?"

Betty waved the dust away, trying hard not to sneeze as she watched them go. "Chip's looking for property."

"With the head of the General Land Office for a realtor?"

Betty turned and faced Lee. "Maybe they're old friends."

He wrinkled his nose. "Something doesn't smell right."

o0o

Betty was stashing the last of the supper dishes in the dishwasher when Lee arrived to work on the forms for nonprofit status. He carried a fistful of papers in one hand, which he tossed on the counter, and a bouquet of trillium in the other.

"Blossoms to brighten your day. Or evening, I should say."

"Thank you, but you shouldn't have picked—"

"I know you don't believe in picking them, but I have hundreds of thousands of them in my woods, and you love them, so why not bring a few of them indoors? There will be plenty left to propagate for next season."

She smiled. "I'll trim off the ends and put them in water so they won't wilt."

By the time she had finished with the trillium, Lee had removed his jacket, revealing his white Mossy Point Folk School T-shirt. She set the vase of trillium on the counter and gave him a good looking over. "Goll', you look nice in that shirt."

Lee turned and posed, hand on hip like a model. "Blame it on Patsy. She's one genius of an artist." He paused and stared at Betty's Oxford shirt. "Why aren't you wearing yours?"

"Saving it for when I'm out in public and can be a walking advertisement for the school."

He nodded and pulled out two stools. "We'd better get started. This is going to take all night and then some."

"Coffee?" Betty reached for the new one-cup coffeemaker Carlos had insisted on buying when they were in Superior Bay three days ago. She had balked at the price, and especially at the cost of the one-cup portions of café con leche he picked out to go with it. But when he had bargained for it with a promise to start work on his GED this weekend, she had made the purchase.

Lee interrupted her reflection. "Coffee sounds good, but forget that one-cup gizmo. We'll probably go through a pot before this is done."

She pulled her coffeepot out of the cabinet and started it brewing, then took a seat on the stool beside Lee. A gentle hint of his spicy aftershave drifted to her, spreading warmth within. He leaned her way. His arm brushed hers, sending tingles through her as he placed a set of stapled forms in front of her. His tender gaze met hers and held, the moment suspended in time. Was he feeling as drawn to her as she was to him?

She pushed the question aside and focused on the set of stapled forms. "Articles of incorporation for the state?"

He nodded. "We'll start with those. We need them before we can file anything with the IRS. It's not too complicated, but we have to write a mission statement that will be acceptable to both the IRS and the state. It must include this statement right here." He handed her another printout.

"This is going to call for a computer. I need to look up the North Country Folk School mission statement in order to get an idea what we're aiming for." She retrieved her laptop from the other end of the counter, plugged it into a nearby socket, and hit the power switch. While she waited for it to boot, she looked again at the form for the state. "I see there's a twenty dollar fee for filing the articles of incorporation with the state. What kind of fee will we owe the IRS?"

"Plenty. But you needn't worry—"

"How much?" Betty's gaze held his.

The laptop beeped and Lee pointed to her computer. "It's on. Why don't you look up that mission statement?"

"Why won't you tell me how much?"

He sighed. "Four hundred dollars."

"Four hundred dollars?" Her stomach soured. "Where am I going to get four hundred dollars? I'm way overspent as it is."

"Students. By the time you're ready to file, you'll have enough student tuition to pay the fee, so stop worrying."

"I hope you're right." She opened her Internet search engine, typed "North Country Folk School," and hit "Enter."

Lee began to hum, "If I Were a Rich Man."

She couldn't help giggling. Ignoring the search engine results, she turned to him, warmed by the impish smile he beamed at her. His sense of humor was spot on, its timing impeccable, and his confidence was just what she needed. Most of all, his friendship was priceless—more than she deserved. She rested her hand on his forearm.

"I couldn't do this without you, Lee. You know that, don't you?"

He placed his left hand, the one that still bore a wedding ring, over hers and fiddled with the wedding and engagement rings she continued to wear. "I learned years ago never to underestimate Betty Hanson. Once you set your mind to something, it happens."

"Then why am I such a failure with my daughter?" She searched his blue eyes.

"You're way too hard on yourself. Things will work out with Angie. Give it time."

"It's been two years since she's spoken to me."

"She'll talk to you again, more likely sooner than later, now that her son is here."

If only she had his confidence. She withdrew her hand from his, turned to the computer, and clicked on the mission statement link. While she copied, pasted, and revised the wording, Lee poured coffee for both of them and then began studying some of the papers he'd brought.

Step by step, with the help of a "how-to" booklet he'd bought online, Lee guided her through the form. Half an hour later, when their coffee cups were empty, she reached the field asking for the names and addresses of the incorporators.

Lee pointed to the instructions. "It says here, 'Educational corporations need at least three incorporators.'"

"There's me, and you, and who else?"

He went to her kitchen desk and returned with the portable phone. "Give Wayne and Doris a call. Invite them over if they're home. We'll need to form a board of directors before we can file with the IRS anyway."

A cup of coffee was all the enticement needed to lure Wayne and Doris into the organizational meeting. Within minutes of their arrival, the papers for the state were complete, and discussion of the IRS form began. A board of directors had to be chosen, budget estimates drawn up, a conflict of interest policy adopted, and a myriad of other details filled in.

Two hours later, while they were still wrangling with the specifics, Doris reached for the portable phone. "I've got a craving for pizza. What do you say I order one before my daughter closes up?"

"There goes your diet." Wayne wagged his finger at her.

"Oh, hush. Betty, Lee, how about it? You up for pizza?"

"Sure, why not," said Betty. "Might as well wreck two diets for the price of one pizza."

"I want pepperoni on my quarter," said Lee.

"Mine, too," said Betty.

Doris placed the order for half pepperoni and half anchovy, and the work resumed until her daughter called to say the pizza was ready. While Lee and Wayne made the run to pick it up, Betty prepared to make another pot of coffee and Doris tidied up the countertop.

"So how are things between you and Lee?" Doris jogged a stack of papers together.

"Good." Betty added water and soap to the coffeepot, hoping her brief, casual reply would be satisfactory.

Doris moved the computer aside and laid out napkins. "Seems like the two of you are getting closer since Wayne and I left for Florida last fall."

"Maybe it's the folk school work. He's been a real soldier. I couldn't do it without him . . . and you and Wayne and the others. But especially Lee." Betty rinsed the pot and started filling it with fresh water.

"Are you sure there isn't something more bringing the two of you closer? A little, dare I say, romantic attraction starting to bud?"

"What do you mean?" Betty turned off the water and set the stem and basket in place.

Doris pointed to the trillium bouquet. "I bet Lee brought you those, didn't he? I know very well *you* never pick wildflowers."

Betty smiled. "You know me too well." She filled the basket with coffee and plugged in the pot.

Doris set out plates and approached Betty. "So tell me the truth. There's more to you and Lee than folk school work, isn't there?"

A car door slammed in the driveway.

"They're back," said Betty, thankful to lay aside that subject. She opened the door to let the men in. The aroma of spicy tomato sauce filled the kitchen, sparking Betty's appetite. One slice. She'd eat one slice and send any leftovers home with the others, or save them for Carlos.

Lee set the box on the countertop and flipped open the lid. "Mmm mmm. That daughter of yours sure knows how to make a pizza. Looks great. The aroma drove me crazy all the way home."

Home? Had Betty heard right? Was Lee calling her place home?

Doris winked at Betty behind his back. Had she also caught the slip?

Betty ignored her. "Sit down, everyone. Help yourselves. The coffee will be ready in a couple of minutes."

Lee managed to pull a slice free from the gooey cheese and bite off the point. Sauce slobbered onto his chin. He wiped it off with his finger, licked it clean, and grinned at Betty.

His boyish zest made Betty smile. She helped herself to a slice and instantly understood his zeal. The pizza tasted even better than it smelled and looked. One slice? Did she really have the willpower?

"Saw Carlos and Janna and some of her friends," said Wayne.

Betty swallowed her first bite. "I hope they didn't think we were checking up on them."

Lee wiped his chin with his napkin. "I made a point of telling him we weren't. He said he'd be home soon. Janna has to be to work early tomorrow. Looked like they were having a good time. Lots of laughter and teasing while we were there."

"Good. I was hoping Carlos would connect with some people his own age." Betty headed to the coffeepot to fill a thermal pitcher with the fresh brew.

"Just one more reason to keep the park open and businesses running," said Doris. "The kids won't have any place to hang out if our daughter can't make a go of it."

"More incentive to get this paperwork done." Wayne tapped his finger against the stack of forms beside him.

"Pizza first. Those forms will still be waiting when we're done." Lee reached for another piece.

Betty poured coffee into Lee's cup and hers and passed the pitcher down to Doris and Wayne. "I kind of overstepped my bounds today when Mr. Engstrom and his friend Chip stopped by. I said we were having a golf outing in June when really it's just Steve teaching beginners. Then I got to thinking that an outing would probably raise lots more money than classes. What do you all think?"

"I bet Steve would love that idea," said Doris.

Wayne nodded. "Instead of griping about teaching for no pay, he'd be golfing."

Lee reached for the portable phone and handed it to Betty. "Call him and see if he thinks we could schedule an outing at Superior Bay Golf Course."

"Now? It's getting kind of late to make a phone call, don't you think?"

"He'll still be up. Might not be home, but you could leave a message."

Betty headed for the phone list on her kitchen desk, found Steve's number, and punched in the digits. When he didn't answer, she left a message about the golf outing suggestion and returned to her stool with the phone.

"More pizza?" Lee pushed the carton toward her. "There's another slice waiting for you."

She shook her head. "I think I'll save it for Carlos, unless you want it?"

The phone rang. Betty checked caller I.D. "Hi, Steve. Thanks for calling back."

"Hi, Betty. Great idea to hold a golf outing!"

"Glad you like it. I'm going to put you on speaker so Lee, Doris, and Wayne can hear you. Do you think we could get Superior Bay Golf Course to schedule us on a Saturday this summer?"

"I'm sure of it. I'll be over there tomorrow and see what dates the manager has available. How'd it go at the work session today? Got that building ready?"

"Soon. I assume you won't be coming tomorrow if you're going to the golf course."

"Right, you are. But I'll be there on folk school business. That ought to count for something."

"It counts a lot. Thanks, Steve. Talk to you later."

"Bye."

"Steve, wait! I just remembered something. Somebody signed up online for your photography class. We have our very first student!"

"Blonde, beautiful, and single?"

"Not likely. Goes by the email wryfellow at superiorbay dot edu.

"Wryfellow? I know him! Of all the . . . . He's the photography teacher over at the community college. He ought to be teaching *me*!"

"Should make class time interesting for you."

"No kidding. Now I'm worried. What could I possibly teach an award-winning photo artist?"

Wayne leaned toward the phone. "What's this I hear? Does the emperor of egos doubt himself?"

"Go chomp on some cheddar, Cheesehead. Betty, I'll ping you after I set up a golf date." Steve clicked off.

Betty slid back onto her stool. "I sure hope Steve knows how to organize a golf outing because I certainly don't. I've never played a round of golf in my life." Her gaze slid past Lee to Doris and Wayne.

"Don't look at us," said Doris. "We're probably the only snowbirds in Florida who don't golf."

"Steve will know what to do," said Lee.

Wayne chuckled. "And then it will be up to the rest of us to make sure the work gets done."

The door opened and Carlos walked in.

"Hey, Carlos, we saved some pizza for you." Lee pointed to the leftover slice.

"No, thanks, Mr. Nylund. I'm stuffed. I ate four slices over at the pizza shop." He exchanged greetings with Doris and Wayne and headed for the laptop. "You all mind if I use this? Thought I'd check email and get a head start on my GED."

"By all means, take it," said Betty.

He unplugged it and headed down the hall.

Wayne picked up the stack of forms and instructions. "Time to get back to these, don't you think?"

With Doris's help, Betty cleared away the plates and pizza and refilled the coffee cups. Work resumed on the unfinished financial details, leading to a discussion of future operating expenses. Betty's mind spun with the numbers Lee and Wayne tossed up for consideration.

"Gram!" Carlos jogged down the hall and into the kitchen in his bare feet. His dark eyes sparkled. "You'll never guess what happened!"

"Did we get another student?" Betty crossed her fingers.

Carlos beamed. "Not one, Gram. Nine! We've got nine more students in the photography class!"

Betty gasped. "Ten in one day?"

"How'd that happen?" Lee asked.

"I checked out comments on our Facebook page. That first student, wryfellow, is a teacher over at the college."

Betty nodded. "Steve told us that when we called him earlier."

Carlos continued. "He's teaching a photography course over there this summer, and as a prerequisite, he's making all his students sign up for Steve's class. He says they'll get the basics from Steve, and then he won't have to waste time on them when classes start up in June."

Betty gave him a high five. "Nice job, Carlos! Your work online really paid off. Now, weren't you going to start studying for that GED?"

He aimed both forefingers at her like pistols. "Right! I'm outta here."

Thank you, Lord! Ten students and Carlos ready to study. Betty couldn't ask for more.

"That sheds a whole new light on budget numbers," said Wayne.

Doris nodded. "Better increase your estimates."

At midnight, with Wayne and Doris gone, Betty saw Lee to the door. "Thanks so much—for the flowers, the forms, and the help filling them out."

Cradling her face in his hands, Lee tenderly kissed her forehead. "My pleasure." His voice was quiet, husky, as his gaze and his touch lingered on her.

Warmth radiated through Betty. She slipped her arms about his neck and closed her eyes.

His lips met hers briefly, exquisitely, and then he stepped away. "See you at the work session tomorrow morning."

The door closed behind him, and as he drove off, a piece of her heart went with him.

"Hey, Gram?"

Betty jumped and turned to face Carlos.

He stood by the coffee pot, an impish smile on his face. "Looks like you and Mr. Nylund are an item."

Warmth flooded her cheeks. "How's the studying going, Carlos?"

"Probably not as good as your friendship with Mr. Nylund, but I'll get there. Thought I'd grab a cup of coffee and get back to it." He opened the cupboard and pulled out a mug.

"Don't stay up too late. We've got a work session starting at nine tomorrow. I'm going to bed. Good night."

"'Night Gram. Sweet dreams." He winked.

CHAPTER 11

Eight days later, on her way to a work session at the folk school, Betty dropped the application for nonprofit status into the mail. It had really irked her to pull $400 out of the account and send it to the IRS, but Lee was right; she had no choice but to pay the filing fee.

At the cabin, the gas company installed a propane tank and hooked it up to the stove Thad had put in a few days ago. Good thing Wayne had enlisted his brick-laying buddy to fix the chimney last weekend, and convinced his electrician friend to update the electrical service.

The roof contractor, who had started to apply a coating to the metal roof earlier in the week, finished his job by late afternoon. Betty stood a few yards back and gazed up at the results. Too bad Lee had gone to Michigan four days ago for his daughter's appendectomy and wasn't here to see how his idea came out—wide white and black stripes running from the peak to the eaves. Lee would be back tonight, but probably too late to get a good look at the roof in daylight. It looked like something out of a cartoon, but she'd never tell him that. Maybe she'd get used to it.

The contractor stowed his ladder on his truck and approached Betty. "Lee said to leave this with you." He pulled a folded paper from his pocket, handed it to her, and high-tailed it to his truck.

She'd been expecting an invoice. Lee had tried and tried to find a contractor who would barter in exchange for classes. With time running out, the board had been forced to hire. She studied the bottom line. Her heart skipped a beat. So far, student tuitions didn't come close to covering expenses. "There's still time." She muttered to herself and headed for her truck to toss the invoice on the dashboard.

"Hey, Gram, come look." Carlos beckoned to her from the door.

She headed inside where he'd been staining a table he'd built.

"What do you think, Gram?"

Carlos's dark walnut stain contrasted nicely with the white walls and ceiling and gray floor. "Very attractive, Carlos. What if we ask Patsy to paint the logo in the center like she did on our picnic table?"

"Perfect!" He tossed his stain-soaked rag into a white plastic bucket beneath the table and headed for the sink to wash up.

The park truck pulled up and Janna stepped inside. "Hi, Mrs. Hanson. I see yous got the roof done today."

"What do you think of those stripes, Janna?"

"Bold." She turned to Carlos. "Hey, Carlos, ready to go? The others are waiting for us down at the parking lot."

He wiped his hands on a paper towel, his focus shifting to Betty. "We're heading into Superior Bay for tacos and a movie," he said. "Would you please take that bucket of rags home and fill it with water?"

She checked her watch. "Five o'clock already? I've got to get a move on. Lee's coming back from his daughter's today, and I promised to have supper ready at six." She headed for the lakeside door to close up.

Carlos started for the south door with Janna. "Don't wait up for me, Gram. And don't forget the rags."

"Got it. Have a good time, you two." She struggled with the door. Damp weather had warped the wood, making it hard to shut the double doors tight.

Gravel crunched beneath an approaching vehicle. Maybe Lee was back early from Michigan and could help her lock up.

A car door slammed, heels clicked on the wooden floor, and a familiar female voice addressed her.

"Hello, Mrs. Hanson."

Vicky Quinn. All decked out in a designer dress and stiletto heels. What was Frank Schram's daughter doing here?

"Hello, Vicky. How's your father?" Betty had steered clear of hospital visits since Wayne's warning of a lawsuit fifteen days ago.

"Grumpy. He's not happy at the long-term care facility over at Superior Bay. He'd rather recover at home, but who would be there to help him?" She dismissed the possibility with a shake of her head. "Mrs. Hanson, I came to see exactly where my father took his fall. Could you please show me?" The sweetness in her voice and her smile carried no hint of a planned lawsuit.

"He fell outside." Betty led Vicky to the spot near the building west of the door where she had discovered Frank lying on his back, moaning.

"So he climbed a ladder that was leaning against the building, broke through a rung, and landed on the ground here?" Vicky marked the spot with the toe of her patent leather shoe.

"No ladder was leaning against the building when Frank got here. He took an old decrepit ladder off my truck, a ladder that I was planning to haul to the landfill."

"And you saw him take it off your truck?" Vicky's gaze pinned her.

"No. But how else—"

"Did anyone see him take the ladder off your truck, or fall?"

"No. We were all working inside, except for Wayne. He was cutting brush on the north side of the building."

"I see. Thank you, Mrs. Hanson. You'll be hearing from our lawyer." She got into her Shelby Mustang, backed onto the road, and spit gravel, leaving a cloud of dust.

Betty's thoughts spun faster than Vicky's wheels. Lawyer. Wayne was right. Frank's suing. A brick landed in the pit of Betty's stomach. She'd need a lawyer. They cost money. Lots of money. Where would it come from? Her extra cash was gone. Worse yet, a lawsuit could shut down the folk school and the park. All for something that was Frank's own fault.

There had to be a way around this. If only Lee were here. She checked her watch. In forty minutes, he'd be at her house. She padlocked the south door, climbed into her truck, and headed for home. Not much time to cook. She'd pull some pre-prepared chicken breasts out of the freezer. Lee liked them last time she'd served them. Those and some steamed vegetables with rice would be quick to fix.

o0o

Twenty minutes past six. Where was Lee? The chicken breasts, steamed broccoli, and rice were ready and waiting in the oven on warm. Betty paced to the kitchen window.

While she watched for Lee to pull into the driveway, her mind churned about a possible lawsuit. She closed her eyes and bowed her head. "Lord, you'll have to help me with this. I know life's not fair. But couldn't you bring a little justice into this situation for the sake of the park and the folk school?"

She opened her eyes. Lee was pulling into the driveway. She stepped out onto the porch. The moment he emerged from his truck, she greeted him with a smile. Was it only four days ago that he'd left? Seemed more like a week. "About time you showed up. Dinner's ready."

"Good because I'm plenty hungry." He pecked her on the cheek. "Sorry I'm late. Ran into road work about half an hour north of Rapid River. Tried to call while I was stopped dead along with about a hundred other cars, but my cell phone couldn't find a signal. How'd it go at the folk school today?"

Betty opened the door and he followed her into the kitchen. "I'll tell you about it over supper. How's your daughter? Still sore from the appendectomy?"

"Sore, but mending fast." He sniffed the air. "Is that broccoli I smell?"

Betty nodded. "We're having chicken breast in pineapple sauce, and rice, too."

"What? No tacos, no burritos, no enchiladas, no pizza?"

"No Carlos. He went with Janna and her friends to Superior Bay for supper and a movie. With him gone, I thought I'd take a break from the steady diet of Mexican and Italian cuisine we've been on." She opened the oven and removed the two covered dinner plates she'd kept warm.

Lee washed his hands and carried his plate to the dining table.

Betty joined him there, and Lee reached for her hand and bowed his head.

"Father God, thank You for the food we are about to eat and the strength we will gain from it. Thank You for Betty's efforts to prepare this meal, and for her work at the folk school. And thank You for bringing me home safely. In Jesus's name. Amen."

"Amen."

Lee uncovered his plate, cut a piece of chicken, and popped it into his mouth. "Mmm. Really hits the spot. You're a great cook."

"You flatterer. You know the chicken came pre-prepared from Glutton Food Service."

"Glutton? Glidden, you mean."

"Glutton, Glidden, whatever. Anyhow, they cooked the chicken. I steamed the broccoli and cooked the rice."

He grinned. "It's all good, no matter who cooked what. So tell me about the folk school. What did I miss? Is the roof done yet?"

Betty nodded and swallowed her first bite of chicken. Lee was right. She'd forgotten how well the zingy pineapple sauce perked up the chicken breast. "The roof is done. Big, fat, black and white stripes, exactly like you suggested, and a big fat bill to go with them."

"Pay it out of the student tuitions. Did more people sign up for classes while I was gone?"

"A few. But I'm worried."

"The camping season hasn't even started yet. There's plenty of time to beat the bushes for new students."

"I know. There's something else I'm worried about, though. Something that could kill our chances of saving the park, no matter how many students we get."

Lee put down his fork and pinned her with a narrowed gaze. "Spill, Betty."

She took a sip of water to wash down the bile rising from her gut. "Frank Schram's daughter came by the folk school just before I left. She asked a lot of questions about Frank's fall. When she was all done, she said we'd be hearing from their lawyer. Then she got into her Mustang and cleaned the gravel off the road with that heavy foot of hers."

Lee leaned back and pushed his plate away, color rising in his cheeks. "That dirty, rotten . . . . He doesn't stand a chance with a lawsuit. Some ambulance-chasing contingency lawyer probably got to him."

Betty lowered her gaze. "I shouldn't have talked to Vicky. She's going to take what I said and twist it to their advantage." Betty squeezed her eyes shut to hold back tears.

Lee's hand covered hers. "We'll win this, Betty. We'll save the park, and we'll beat Frank in court if it comes to that."

"But—"

"No 'but' about it. The truth will prevail. Besides, he's got six months to wait before he can even begin to file. That's the law when it comes to suing for injuries. By then the camping season will be over, the park will be in the black, and Frank will be all healed and back to normal. Maybe he'll drop his case."

"Do you think?"

"No, but no sense worrying about something you don't control. Focus on what you *can* do." He pulled his plate closer, cut a sizeable chunk of chicken, and popped it into his mouth.

"Maybe after dinner, we could work on some public service announcements for the June classes."

"Or . . . we could go fishing. It'd do you good to get away from folk school work for a few hours. You've been pretty intense about it since this all started."

"You're right. A little time on the water will be soothing."

"You're on. Soon as dinner is over, we'll launch my boat and head for my favorite fishing spot."

o0o

Darkness was closing in fast by the time Lee pulled his boat out of the water and drove Betty home. He eased onto the shoulder in front of her house, put his truck in "park," and left the motor running.

She opened her door far enough to turn on the cab light. "Thanks, Lee. I'm definitely more relaxed than when we started out. See you tomorrow?"

"I'll be there."

She slid her foot onto the running board.

"Say, Betty, you wouldn't have some coffee you're trying to get rid of, would you?"

"Only if you're willing to come in and help."

He killed the motor and hopped out.

She unlocked the front door and Lee followed her into the kitchen. The red blinking light on the answering machine at her desk screamed for attention. She pressed Play.

"Betty, this is Thad. Give me a call ASAP. There's a problem at the folk school."

His curt message sent a shiver up her spine. She brought up his number on the display, hit Enter, and waited through three rings.

"Thad here."

"Thad, it's Betty."

"You ought to get over to the park. There's been a fire at the school—"

"Oh my goodness! Be right there." Her heart raced and a boulder thudded to the bottom of her stomach.

CHAPTER 12

Betty dug in her purse for her truck keys and pulled them out. Her hand trembled so badly, the keys fell on the kitchen floor.

Lee picked them up. "I'll leave my truck and boat out front and drive you over in your truck."

Less than a minute later, he backed out of the garage. Betty got into the passenger seat, her stomach souring. What could have gone wrong? Was the entire school nothing but a heap of ashes? She chewed her lower lip. *Thy will be done, Lord.*

Lee drove cautiously through the campground. A handful of sites were occupied with pre-season campers. Campfire smoke tinged the air. On the road to the folk school, Betty's headlights caught Thad's truck a short distance ahead. He pulled off where the school should be. When Lee pulled in next to him, the headlights of both vehicles showed that the school looked just as it had when she'd left it, except that the windows were wide open. Betty took a deep breath and got out of her truck just as Thad was getting out of his.

"I thought you said there was a fire."

"Inside."

Lee joined them and Thad led by flashlight to the lakeside door.

"This door wasn't locked. Did you know that?"

Events of late afternoon flooded her mind. The struggle with the warped door. The conversation with Vicky. "I tried to lock it, got distracted, then forgot. Sorry, Thad. I'll be more careful."

"Probably a good thing you forgot; otherwise the whole place might have burned down. When I drove over here about half-past eight to check the place out, the smoke alarm was beeping. I could see through the window that a bucket under a table was on fire."

Carlos's oily rags! He'd asked her to take the bucket home and put water in it. After Vicky's visit, she'd totally forgotten about the bucket and the unlocked door. Spontaneous combustion had caused the fire.

Thad continued. "I didn't have the folk school keys on me, so I came around to this door to see if by some chance I could get inside. The door pulled right open, so I grabbed the fire extinguisher. The rest is history, so they say. I opened the windows to air the place out."

Lee patted Thad on the back. "Good job, man. You really saved the day."

Thad opened the door and flipped on the light. "There's a lot of smoke damage, and a hole in the floor where the bucket was. That table's done for, too. But the building's still standing."

Betty's heart landed on her feet. The pristine white walls and ceiling were now covered with an oily, smoky film that stank so bad that she could hardly breathe. The same for the lectern Carlos had polished so carefully. There was no way the place could be cleaned up in time for the first class. All she'd worked for, paid for, planned—ruined. And it was all her fault. Her stomach turned.

She rushed outside and headed for the bushes in case her gut emptied. *Inhale to the count of two. Exhale to the count of eight.*

Footsteps approached. "You all right, Betty?"

It was Lee. If she talked, she'd throw up for sure.

He drew closer. "Betty?"

She put one hand on her gut and one hand palm out.

"Look, I know you're upset, but—"

Her stomach heaved and she lost its contents in the bushes. Her nausea subsided and she turned to Lee. "Take me home."

He nodded, placed his arm about her waist, and walked her to the truck.

As Lee drove, Betty thought out loud. "I'll have to cancel the photography class, refund all the students' money. But . . . " Heat seared her veins. "I've already spent a good chunk of it on the nonprofit application fee! There's no way I can give it back! They'll arrest me for fraud!"

Lee reached for her hand. "Don't panic."

She jerked her hand free. "Easy for *you* to say."

"Listen to me, Betty. You don't need to cancel. We can clean up the smoke damage and make the repairs before next Friday."

She was still trying to wrap her mind around the situation as he pulled into her garage and ushered her inside.

He checked his watch. "I think I'll pass on that cup of coffee. Can I make you some herbal tea? Do you have any chamomile? It'll calm your nerves and your stomach."

"You'd do that for me?"

He smiled. "Show me where to find it, and then go and re-acquaint yourself with your recliner."

She pointed to the cupboard and then headed off to the great room, plopped into her easy chair, and extended the foot-rest. When she pulled on the table lamp, Zeb, Harry's ten-point buck, stared down at her from above the fireplace man-tle. "Not a good day, Zeb. I blew it, and it's going to take a miracle to make things right."

"What say?" Lee's voice drifted from the kitchen. "I didn't quite catch that."

"Just mumbling to myself."

A few minutes later, Lee brought a mug of tea for her and one for himself and sat kitty-corner from her on the sofa. "Now don't go having nightmares about this. It's all fixable. We can get the folk school ready before Steve starts the pho-tography class."

"I hope you're right." She sipped the hot brew. "Do you have any idea how to go about cleaning up soot?"

Lee shook his head. "We'll look it up online tomorrow. Probably have to go to Superior Bay to get what we need. Or we could call a professional service to do it."

Betty shook her head. "Too expensive. I'm afraid we'll just have to apply elbow grease to get the job done. Carlos will be so disappointed. He just finished staining that table this after-noon, and now it's ruined." She squeezed her eyes shut. A tear leaked down her cheek.

Lee reached for her hand and gave it a squeeze. "Every-body makes mistakes. Give yourself another ten minutes to mourn the loss, and then press on."

"Easier said than done."

"You're an overcomer, Betty. Something knocks you on your can, and next thing I know, you're up again and running. It happened when your daughter moved to California. It happened when Harry died. It will happen now. I know it."

She gazed into his blue eyes and read there the truth of his words. A plan sprang to mind. "Tomorrow morning, I'll make calls to the Reeds, Karen, Steve, and Patsy. She ought to be back from her trip. I'll tell them what happened and ask them to come for a work session at one o'clock. In the morning, you and I will go to Superior Bay and pick up cleaning supplies."

"That's the Betty I know." He smiled and winked.

When their tea mugs were empty, he took them to the kitchen and then returned. Tenderness shown in his eyes as he gazed down at her. "Are you going to be okay? I'll stay the night, if you want."

She shook her head and reached for his hand. "I'm all right. You'd better go."

He bent down, his lips meeting hers briefly. Then he straightened, squeezed her hand, and stepped back. "See you tomorrow. I'll let myself out."

She nodded, turned off the table lamp, and closed her eyes. Sooty images jumbled together in her mind as she dozed off. She woke to the sound of Carlos's return.

"Hey, Carlos, how was the movie?"

"Gram? Why are you sitting in the dark? I thought you'd be in bed."

She switched on the table lamp. "Normally, I would be, but I've got something to tell you. I didn't want to wait until tomorrow."

He sat on the sofa where Lee had been earlier, a questioning look in his dark eyes. "What's up? A bunch more students signed up for classes?"

"I wish. Remember that bucket of oily rags you asked me to bring home?"

"Yeah?"

"I forgot. It caught on fire. Your table is ruined, and the lectern is a mess. I'm so sorry, Carlos."

"What? I can't believe it! I slaved over that table and the lectern for hours!" He got up and paced across the room.

"That's not all. There's smoke damage all over the inside of the building, and a hole in the floor where the bucket melted and burned through. I'm calling a work session for tomorrow afternoon at one o'clock. We're going to need all the help we can get."

He returned to the sofa. "I'm so sorry, Gram. I should've put water in the bucket before I left."

"It wasn't your fault. I promised you I'd take care of it. Then I got distracted and forgot. It's a good thing Thad checked on the building when he did; otherwise, the folk school would've burned down." Her thoughts turned in a new direction. "Say, Carlos, would you mind checking the balance in our online account? Lee and I are going over to Superior Bay in the morning to pick up cleaning supplies. You're welcome to come with us if you want."

"I'll wake up the computer and report back."

As he headed down the hall to his room, Betty prayed. "Lord, show us the way through this mess. We need money. We need to clean up and repair. But You already know all that. Help us to serve You through the folk school project, and to save Mossy Point State Park. Thank You. Amen."

Carlos returned with a smile. "Good news. Two more students signed up. One for Lee's class and one for Wayne's. There's a couple hundred dollars more in the account."

"Thanks, Carlos. Maybe that will be enough to cover the clean-up supplies."

"What do you need to buy?"

"Don't know yet. I was going to do an online search to find out."

"I'll do it for you right now."

o0o

The next morning, Betty's phone calls to round up help brought positive responses from Doris, Wayne, and Karen. Steve's answering service said he was golfing and his cell phone was turned off. Patsy didn't answer, so Betty left a message about the fire and need for help cleaning up.

When Betty, Lee, and Carlos arrived at the folk school a few minutes before one o'clock, Thad's truck was parked in front.

Betty turned to Lee. "Thad must be airing the place out. Will you and Carlos please unload the cleaning supplies so we can get started? I'm sure the others will soon be here."

Lee and Carlos got out and headed for the tailgate while Betty approached the open door. She paused at the threshold. The stench and ugliness of last night engulfed her like a tidal wave. Inside, a short, burly, middle-aged woman wearing a park uniform and a butch haircut stood beside Thad in the center of the room, staring down at the hole burned into the floor. As Betty drew near, Thad made introductions.

"Betty, this is my boss, Eva Underwood. Eva, Betty Hanson, head of the Mossy Point Folk School project."

Betty ignored the chill coursing through her and extended her hand. "Pleased to meet you. We're here to make repairs and clean up."

Eva's tight grip nearly made Betty wince. "Thad tells me you're the one responsible for this."

Nausea surged within. "The fire was my fault. But I promise—"

Eva placed her hands on her hips. "I'm tempted to close down this operation. The fire here could have spread through the entire park and beyond, if Thad hadn't caught it in time."

"I know, but—"

"It tells me something about the leadership here."

Betty's heart raced. "I'm sorry about the fire. It was a mistake. We all make mistakes."

Carlos and Lee carried in the cleaning supplies.

Eva's focus shifted to them and back to Betty. "If you were me, how would you convince me not to shut you down?"

Betty took a deep breath. "Because I'm going to make sure nothing like this happens again; because the folk school is going to put this park in the black for the first time ever; because if you close the park, the entire community of Mossy Point will dwindle down to a ghost town; because you don't want to lose more residents and tax dollars from the State of Sup—"

"Not sure I'm buying into your logic, but go ahead and clean up. And remember this: I'm putting you on notice. If anything else goes wrong here, you're done. This building will be closed, and there will be no folk school. Do you understand?"

Betty nodded.

As Eva and Thad exited the building, a black van with an Ojibway Indian logo pulled in beside Lee's truck. Patsy and several other adults piled out of the van. If the tribal logo hadn't identified them as Ojibways, the long, blue-black hair of both men and women, and their olive skin certainly would have marked them as American Indians.

Betty headed outside. Why, of all days, did this have to be the one when Patsy would bring her people to see the folk school?

Patsy made introductions. "Betty, this is my father, Eugene, my mother, Leona, my Uncle Gordon, my Aunt Marlene, and our friend, Arthur. We're ready to start the cleanup."

Betty's heart soared. "Thank you all for coming! I can't tell you how much I appreciate your willingness to help!" She led them inside.

Greetings and handshakes were exchanged all around, and then Lee and Carlos handed out the cleaning solutions, chemical sponges, rags, goggles, face masks, and rubber gloves.

Like a surgical team, Patsy and her kin set to work, some tackling the ceiling, others scrubbing walls, and Patsy and her mother cleaning windows. Betty pitched in, soon joined by Wayne, Doris, and Karen, while Lee and Carlos tended to replacing burnt flooring. It was probably just as well that Steve was spending his day at the golf course. With the number of adults working inside, there wasn't room for one more.

After an unusually quiet stretch, Karen began singing a familiar childhood tune with her own twist on the lyrics.

"Ninety-nine square feet of soot on the wall, ninety-nine square feet of soot. Wipe one off, what've you got? Ninety-eight square feet of soot on the wall."

Doris chimed in on the next verse, and then Betty and Patsy. By the time they had reached ninety-five, Patsy let out a loud whistle.

"Since you are singing about numbers, let me teach them to you in our language." She sang a verse in her tribal tongue.

Karen chuckled. "You're gonna have to take that a little bit at a time if I'm gonna learn it your way."

Patsy started at the beginning and word by word, phrase by phrase, led the others through the song. As Betty concentrated on the Ojibway words, patches of white slowly expanded on the walls and ceiling. Her spirit lifted. Like the design painted on the picnic table out front, the cleaning process was a figurative flying turtle spreading its wings.

By mid-afternoon, with the clean-up about half-done, everyone gathered at the picnic table out front for a break. Patsy's flying turtle design brought smiles and words of approval from her relatives, and especially from Arthur, who hovered close to Patsy. Was Betty imagining it, or did he consider Patsy to be more than a friend? If so, the feeling was evidently not mutual. Patsy seldom made eye contact with him, and she purposely sat between her mother and aunt on the bench rather than beside him as he had suggested.

Small talk flowed for a few minutes, and then Eugene turned to Betty. "My daughter tells us you need teachers."

Betty nodded. "We have several weekends unscheduled this summer. In fact, no one is scheduled for the month of August. Do you want to teach?"

His gaze shifted to Leona and Gordon. They each gave a nod, and Eugene focused again on Betty. "We could fill all five weekends of August with Ojibway crafts and culture—if you agree."

Had Betty heard right? The entire month of August? "That would be incredible!"

Leona's gaze caught Betty's. "I could teach black ash basketry. It would be a beginner's class lasting two days."

Karen's palm hit the table. "I'd sign up for that one. I love baskets. 'Sides, I gotta prove my sister wrong. She says I don't have enough brains to pass basket weaving, let alone the underwater kind they teach in college."

Betty suppressed a snicker and focused on Leona. "We'd be extremely grateful to have you teach basket making."

Leona turned to Karen. "If you take my class, you will be able to tell your sister that you have passed underwater basket weaving. The black ash splints must be soaked in water before they are woven."

Karen's gap-tooth smile opened wide. "Hot diggity! Put me down for that class, Betty!"

"Will do, Karen." She shifted her gaze to Leona. "Which weekend in August do you want to teach?"

Leona shrugged and looked at Eugene.

He turned to Betty. "We'll discuss the August schedule tonight and Patsy will let you know." He rose. "We should get back to work. In a couple of hours, we'll be done."

His words lifted Betty's spirits. But at the end of this day, would she really be able to put the sooty nightmare behind her?

CHAPTER 13

True to Eugene's words, the folk school walls, ceiling, and floor glistened by suppertime.

As the others hauled cleaning supplies to Lee's truck and the Ojibway van, Betty stood alone in the center of the room and did a slow pirouette. Not a spot had been missed, and only the slightest odor of stale smoke remained. Her heart soared.

At the sound of van doors closing, she hurried out to the driver's side of the vehicle where Eugene was seated, his window open. "Thank you for your hard work! I don't know how I could possibly repay you all." Her gaze swept the others in the van.

Eugene gave a nod. "Your gratitude is payment enough." He started the ignition.

Betty stepped clear and waved as he slowly backed out and crept toward the campground. *Thank you, Lord! You sure plucked me out of a mess today.*

o0o

Six days later, Betty pulled on her "Mossy Point Folk School" T-shirt and checked her watch. Four o'clock. An hour to go before Steve's students would start arriving for the very first class.

She headed to the kitchen, picked up the list on her desk, and compared it with the supplies strewn across her kitchen counter. Lemonade, bottled water, cookies, napkins, paper plates. Lee would pick up the sub sandwiches from Mossy Point Pizza a little later. She shoved the bottled lemonade and water into the ice chest sitting on the floor and shut the lid. Time to load the truck and haul everything to the park.

A car door slammed. Who could it be? Lee and Carlos had already headed to the park with a load of chairs they'd made in Harry's workshop. She turned to gaze out the window.

A tall blonde stepped out of a Chevy Impala that looked like it was ready for the scrapyard. Angie. What was she doing here?

Betty drew a sharp breath. Her heart pounded in an uneven rhythm. Two years of silence from her only child and now she was here, unannounced, heading for the front door at the worst possible time.

The doorbell rang. Betty's feet refused to budge. The bell rang again, several times in quick succession. She nearly tripped over the ice chest on her way to answer it.

Through the screen on the storm door, Angie's tired blue eyes gazed down into Betty's.

"Mom, can I come in?"

Angie's unsteady voice tugged at Betty's heartstrings. She nodded and swung the screen door open.

Angie stepped inside, moisture welling in her eyes. "Oh, Mom, my life is such a mess!" Her face crumpled.

Betty wrapped her arms about her, the embrace melting the tension from two years of silence. Angie hugged her so tightly she could barely breathe. Forcing air into her lungs, she managed to whisper. "You're going to be all right. I promise."

Angie released her, a tentative smile forming as she swiped tears away with the back of her hand.

Betty pulled tissues from her pocket and handed them to Angie. If only she could stop time, sit down with Angie, and hear her story. According to Carlos, it wouldn't be pretty, and she'd have a difficult time refraining from judgment, but it would have to wait. The folk school needed her.

"I'm sorry for your trouble, Angie." She kept her voice soft and soothing. "I've got a million questions for you, but they'll have to wait. I was just about to load up the truck with some supplies, and I could sure use your help." She stepped toward the kitchen.

Angie let out a huff. "I've just come two thousand miles to see you, and all you have time for is a hug and a tissue? You're the same workaholic mother I grew up with, even in retirement!"

A knife twisted in Betty's heart. She turned to face Angie again. "I'm sorry you've never resolved your issues with the past. It's time to move on. You popped in here out of nowhere. You can't expect me to drop everything I'm doing when I have two dozen people depending on me right now. If I'd known you were coming—"

"What? You would've baked me a cake?"

Betty smiled. "You know I'm no good at cakes. I would've killed the fatted calf, put my best robe on you, and celebrated. As it is, I've got to get over to the park with some refreshments, and I've got to go right now. You can help, or stay here and get some rest."

Angie sighed. "No party for the prodigal daughter." She followed Betty into the kitchen. "What's all this stuff?"

"Food for the folk school we started at the park."

"There's a folk school at the park?"

"It opens today. The students will be showing up for the very first class at five o'clock. I've got to set up. Could you please help me carry this ice chest to the truck?" She reached for a handle.

Angie picked up the other end of the chest. "We can go in my car."

"Are you sure?"

"What do you mean, am I sure?"

"No offense, but your car doesn't look very dependable. Besides, you look like you need some sleep. I'll be back in an hour or so."

Angie headed for the front door. "I'm not staying here alone. Besides, my car got me all the way here from California. I'm sure it will go another mile over to the park." She pushed through the front door.

Betty followed, and together they managed to set the ice chest on the threadbare backseat. With another trip inside for the remaining supplies, Betty grabbed her student registration list, name tags, and house keys, locked the door behind her, and headed for the passenger side of the car.

Angie got into the driver's side, started the ignition, and backed out. "How is it that a folk school is starting up over at the park?"

"My idea. Long story."

"Give me the Reader's Digest condensed version." Angie's gaze flicked her way, brow lifted.

"Why is it you're afraid to stay home alone?"

"Long story."

"Give me the Reader's Digest condensed version."

"I'm trying to stay one step ahead of a pesky follower. I think I lost him back in Wisconsin, but I'm not sure."

"Is someone stalking you?"

"Sort of. I'll explain it all later."

"You'll explain it now. I don't want some nasty, dangerous troublemaker showing up at my house while we're gone."

Angie chuckled. "This stalker is a nuisance, but he's not dangerous. Now tell me about the folk school."

Betty held back her tongue from asking more questions. Time for that later. "I got the idea for it about a month ago when I learned that the State of Superior plans to close Mossy Point State Park if it doesn't make enough money to cover its expenses this season. That would be a real disaster for the village, so I got to thinking how we could increase the park's revenue, called up some friends, and the rest is history, so they say."

"I'll never forget the vacation we took over at North Country Folk School when I was a teen. I didn't want to go, but you and Dad made me. I was so glad you did. That's when I fell in love with jewelry." Angie turned into the park entrance.

"Mossy Point Folk School is similar to North Country with a few extras thrown in, like a golfing weekend, a pizza party night, and a fish boil. In June, we're teaching fly-tying, decoy carving, beaded moccasins, and birding. In July, I'm holding a writers' retreat and your friend, Zoe, is teaching Italian cuisine. The month of August is going to feature American Indian crafts and culture every weekend."

"How did you manage that?"

"One of the volunteers has relatives who are part of the Keweenaw Bay Indian Community."

Angie slowed as if to turn into the parking lot near the administration building.

Betty pointed straight ahead. "Keep going on through the campground and out the other side. We fixed up the old Lahti cabin as a classroom."

"No kidding? I bet that was a lot of hard work."

"You don't know the half of it." Visions of the smoke-stained walls flashed in Betty's mind, but she wasn't about to tell that story right now.

Angie proceeded slowly past newly arrived campers settling into their site—two boys about Carlos's age assembling the frame for a small tent. Would they show up for the photography class later? Other sites were occupied with travel trailers, motor homes, and fifth wheels.

Angie slowed down and craned her neck, her gaze sweeping the campground. "Looks like this place is starting to fill up for Memorial Day weekend."

"We need all the campers we can get if we're going to meet expenses and keep this park open."

Angie drove out the other end of the campground. "It would be a real shame for this place to close. I can't imagine the state letting that happen."

"If this were still Michigan, we wouldn't be having this discussion. The State of Superior has a pretty thin budget."

As they approached the folk school, Lee's truck came into view. What would Angie say when she saw Carlos? What would Carlos say? He'd refused to call his mother and tell her where he was in the three-and-a-half weeks since his arrival. Betty prayed their encounter wouldn't result in a verbal battle.

Angie pulled in next to Lee's truck. "This place really looks great, Mom! I love the striped roof and black shutters. How different!"

"Glad you like it!" Betty checked her watch. Half-past four. "We'd better haul this stuff inside and get set up."

She and Angie got out of the car as Lee and Carlos came out of the folk school. Lee headed toward Betty, but Carlos stopped just outside the folk school door, his focus riveted on his mother.

Angie hurried toward him. "Hey, buddy, how are you?" She spread her arms.

"Mom, what are you doing here?" His tone registered disbelief.

"I came to get a hug from my only child." She wrapped her arms about him.

He gave her a brief hug and stepped away. "You knew I was here?"

"I've always known where you are, twenty-four-seven, from the day you were born."

"I don't believe that."

"Believe it, Carlos. You're micro-chipped."

"Mom—"

"Oh, yes. First, when you were a baby, and then when you had your tonsils out at the age of ten."

"Micro-chipped? Me? Where?"

"On your butt."

Carlos ran his hands over his hips.

Angie pointed both index fingers at him. "Gotcha!"

Carlos laughed. "You really had me going there."

"Come on. Help us unload." Angie draped her arm over Carlos's shoulders and walked him to her car.

Betty breathed a sigh of relief and reached for the bag of cookies, paper plates, and napkins on the backseat while Lee grabbed the ice chest.

Carlos took the bag from her. "Gram, why didn't you tell me Mom was coming?"

She gazed into his dark eyes. "I didn't know. I never had her micro-chipped." She grinned and winked.

He smiled.

Angie took one end of the ice chest from Lee. "Hello, Mr. Nylund. Nice to see you again."

"Good to see you, Angie. It's been a long time. Haven't seen you since . . . "

" . . . since Dad passed five years ago. You're looking good, Mr. Nylund. Haven't changed a bit since I saw you last."

Lee smiled and proceeded into the building. He and Angie set the ice chest on one end of the table and then he turned to Betty. "I'd better go pick up the subs."

"I'll come with you." Carlos set the bag on the table and headed outside.

Gravel crunched as a car approached. Betty peered out the window, expecting to see Steve's SUV. Instead, a compact car she didn't recognize came to a stop beside Angie's sedan.

"I can't believe that idiot found me!" Angie took a quick look around, ran into the bathroom, and slammed the door.

The driver of the compact car hopped out, carrying a camcorder. He spoke to Carlos, who pointed to the folk school.

The young man, a few years older than Carlos, hurried toward the door. His sun-streaked brown hair was tied back in a ponytail and his T-shirt and jeans looked like he'd slept in them. The moment he entered the folk school, a pleasant smile broke across his tanned face. His gaze swept the room and landed on Betty. "Good afternoon, ma'am. I'm looking for Angela Martinez. Have you seen her?"

Betty flashed a warning look at Lee and made a reply. "Why are you looking for her?"

"You haven't heard? She's one of the twelve California winners of the four-hundred-million dollar Super Lotto jackpot—the *only* one of the twelve who hasn't given a statement to the press."

Betty gulped air so quickly she nearly choked. Could it be? Angie, a multi-million-dollar lottery winner?

The cameraman continued. "I'm here to get her statement on film. I know she's here somewhere. The fellow outside said so." He looked around the room again and then marched up to the bathroom door and pounded on it. "Come on out, Angela. I know you're in there. No escaping now. Just give me a statement, and I'll leave you alone, I promise."

Lee strode up to the cameraman. "Hey, buddy, move along. She doesn't want to talk to you."

The fellow ignored him and pounded on the bathroom door again.

Lee shouldered in between the cameraman and the door. "Like I said, she doesn't want to talk to you. Now go on, get out of here. Scram. Vamoose." He pointed to the front door.

"Vamoose? I know you northern Michigan people just got your own state, but I didn't know you had your own language, too. The moose up here must be getting to you."

A car engine sprang to life out front. Betty gazed out the window. Angie backed up her Impala and then gunned it toward the campground, spitting gravel and raising a cloud of dust.

The cameraman cussed, ran out the door, and sped after her.

Lee drew a deep breath and let it out in a whoosh. "Angie did a great job getting rid of him for us, didn't she?"

"Yeah, but how will *she* get rid of him?"

"She'll think of something. She was tricky enough to hide in the bathroom and crawl out the window."

Betty went to the closed door and tried to turn the handle. "Locked."

"Got a paperclip?"

Carlos came inside. "What was that all about? One minute, Mom's here, and the next, she's trying to outrun some dude with a camcorder."

Betty shrugged. "When that 'dude' showed up, your mother locked herself in the bathroom and snuck out the window without explaining." No point mentioning the lottery. She went to the table and pulled a paperclip off her stack of registration pages and offered it to Lee.

"Your hand is shaking." He enfolded it with his. "Take a deep breath and release it slowly."

Betty did as told, closing her eyes and counting to eight as she exhaled.

"Good. Now put all that nonsense out of your mind. We've got a folk school to run." Lee squeezed her hand and released it.

She smiled up at him. "Thanks for reminding me." But was the lottery win nonsense, or real?

He straightened the paperclip enough to slip one end of the wire into the center hole of the doorknob. Then he swung the door wide open. "Problem solved."

Betty checked her watch. "You two had better get a move on. I need those sandwiches."

Lee gestured to Carlos. "Come on. You heard the boss."

Betty set out the paper plates, napkins, and cookies, and placed the registration list and name tags at the end nearest the door. Movement outside caught her eye. A camera-laden fellow of about fifty was approaching, his large, crooked nose leading the way.

He stepped inside and looked around. "So this is Mossy Point Folk School. Very nice." He aimed his gaze and smile at Betty. "I'm Izzy Zaminski, 'wryfellow' online."

Betty returned his smile. "Welcome, Izzy. You were the very first student to sign up for our first class. After that, we had about twenty more, your students at the college, I understand." She checked his name off the class roster and handed him the name tag she'd hand-lettered earlier.

He removed the backing and slapped it onto a gray T-shirt printed in black with the words, "Got the bug?" and a cartoon-like figure of an insect holding a camera up to its face.

"Nice shirt, Mr. Zaminski. In case you're interested, I can get you a Mossy Point Folk School T-shirt like mine for $20. Profits go to help with the folk school expenses. Should I order one for you, size large?"

"I'll give it some thought." He gazed out the window as if looking for more arrivals. "I thought Steve would be here. I wanted to talk with him before class starts."

Betty checked her watch. Ten minutes to five. She'd expected Steve to show up by now. "He'll be here any minute, I'm sure. Help yourself to some lemonade and cookies while you're waiting. Sandwiches will be here soon." She opened the lid of the ice chest.

Two young men walked in carrying cameras, the two she'd seen setting up a tent earlier. By the time she'd checked their names off and handed them their name tags, several more students had arrived. She was still checking them in when Lee and Carlos carried in the subs. After they set the tray of sandwiches beside the ice chest, the students helped themselves and took places at the long empty table on the other side of the room. Carlos joined them there, chatting with perfect strangers as if they were old friends.

At ten minutes past five, most of the students had registered, but Steve was nowhere in sight. She mentioned her concern to Lee. "I wish I'd have given him a call this morning to remind him to be here at five."

Lee shook his head. "That wouldn't have been necessary. It's not like him to forget or be late for something as important as this, even if he *did* do a lot of grumbling about the volunteer work. I'll go to the campground phone and give him a call. Do you have his cell phone number?"

Betty tore a corner off a sheet of notebook paper and began to scribble it down from memory.

The roar of an un-muffled four-wheeler sounded out front.

CHAPTER 14

"There's Steve now." Lee pointed.

Betty looked up. Sure enough, Steve was getting off the back of a grungy four-wheeler driven by Angie. Where did she find that thing?

Steve brushed off his khaki pants, said something to Angie, and headed inside while Angie rumbled off to who-knows-where.

"Sorry I'm late. Had a breakdown coming back from the golf course. Wouldn't be here now if Angie hadn't given me a ride."

Izzy approached Steve and extended his hand. "Glad you're here. I wanted to talk to you before you start the class."

The two wandered off and Betty turned to Lee. "How about a sandwich?" She handed him a paper plate.

He put a sub on the plate along with a couple of cookies and sat in one of several chairs behind the refreshment table. Betty placed a sandwich and cookie on her plate, grabbed a bottle of lemonade for Lee and one of water for herself, and sat beside him.

"We did it. We got the first class underway." She took a bite of her sandwich and gazed at the far table. The buzz of students' voices lifted her spirits the way it always had during her teaching days—back when Harry was alive and well and Angie had her life on track in California.

"Looks like Angie lost her stalker." Lee took a sip of lemonade.

Betty sighed. "Lost her stalker and found Steve."

"Sounds like she found a lot more than Steve, if that fellow's claim about her lottery win is true."

Betty's spine tingled. Could it be? "I have to hear it from Angie before I'll believe it. Even then . . . ." The prospect was too much to wrap her mind around right now.

Gravel crunched. Angie's Impala pulled in next to Lee's truck. She strolled into the folk school as if she hadn't a care in the world, helped herself to a sandwich and a bottle of water, and sat beside Betty.

Betty's gaze locked on Angie. "You've got some explaining to do."

"Food first, explanation later." Angie chomped off a large bite of her sandwich and began to chew.

"Just answer me this. Was that reporter telling the truth when he said you were a multi-million-dollar lottery winner?"

Angie leaned close and whispered into her ear. "It's true, but don't get too excited. I'm about out of cash, and I won't see a penny of my winnings for another couple of weeks." She sat back and sipped her water.

Betty's heart raced.

Lee leaned forward, gazing past Betty to focus on Angie. "How'd you lose that camcorder dude?"

She smiled. "On my way out of town, I spotted a four-wheeler behind the pizza shop. I knew it was Zoe's and that she always leaves the key in the ignition, so I borrowed it and made sure the stalker was watching. Then I headed down the two-track that goes back into the state forest until I got his vehicle stuck in the sand."

Lee grinned at Betty. "I told you your daughter was tricky enough to get rid of him."

Angie shook her head. "It's only temporary. Soon as he gets his car unstuck, he'll be back on my tail."

"Maybe you ought to give him what he wants. What would it hurt to do a short interview?" Betty raised her brow.

Angie scowled. "Give him an interview? After what he's put me through?" Her volume rose. "You have no idea how difficult he's made my life for the last two weeks! He practically camped out in front of my house. He followed me everywhere I went. The last thing I want to do is reward him with an interview he can sell to the TV networks."

Betty put a finger to her lips. Too late. The students turned to stare. An awkward silence filled the room.

Carlos glared at his mother and then sprang from his chair. Grabbing his empty plate and bottle, he tossed them out with a thud and headed through the door as if his feet were on fire.

Betty rose and forced a smile as she focused on the students. "We have more sandwiches and cookies here if anyone wants seconds. Feel free to help yourself."

"Don't mind if I do." Izzy wandered over to snag another sandwich, cookie, and bottle of lemonade. Others followed. The buzz of student conversation resumed.

Betty sat down, angling toward Angie, who took another large bite of her sandwich as if nothing out of the ordinary had happened.

"Seems to me the least you could do is send someone out to get that fellow unstuck. Why don't you and Lee go in his truck and drag him out of the sand? Let him catch some film of you helping. That would put a good light on you for the press."

"Nothing doing." She spoke around a mouthful of sandwich.

Betty caught sight of Carlos sitting on the picnic table out front, his elbows on his knees and his chin in his hands as he watched the undulating waves running toward shore. She carried her unfinished sandwich and beverage out through the lakeside door and sat on the table beside him.

"I hate her."

His words pierced Betty's heart. "Pardon?"

Carlos turned to look her straight in the eye. "You heard me, Gram. I hate it when Mom goes ballistic."

"Whew. You had me worried. Hating what she does is different from what you said before. You don't really hate your mother, do you?"

He shook his head and settled his chin in his hands again, gazing at the waves. "After the recession hit, Mom went ballistic on Dad and me all the time. I didn't blame him for taking off. But I was mad at him for leaving me behind. I was the only one left for her to pick on. Now you know why I left home the day I turned eighteen. I just couldn't take it anymore."

"Maybe her finances will improve and she'll go back to being the mom you knew before the recession." Betty took a bite of her sandwich.

"Yeah, right. And maybe Dad will come back."

"It could happen."

"When turtles fly." He quirked a smile at her and winked.

"Don't count me out on turtles flying. We've made a good start here tonight, thanks to you and your work online."

Students wandered outside, setting up tripods and aiming and shooting shoreline images. Betty carried the last of her sandwich and drink inside to the buffet table where Lee and Angie were still seated. Both of them rose as Betty approached.

"We're heading off to rescue a stuck cameraman." Angie picked up her empty plate, stacked it on Lee's, and carried them to the trash can.

Betty turned to Lee. "I'd like to know what you said to her."

He grinned. "Nothing. She talked herself into it."

Angie returned and handed her car keys to Betty. "We'll probably be back before you're done here, but if not, at least you can get home."

Betty tucked the keys into her pants pocket and began cleaning up. A few sandwiches were left over, and some bottles of water. The ice chest with water could stay. She'd have to refrigerate the sandwiches or find some hungry takers.

Carlos came inside, cleaned up the table across the room where a few dirty paper plates and napkins had been left behind, carried them to the trash can, and turned to Betty.

"I'm going to hang around the park until Janna gets off at midnight. She'll bring me home."

"Have a nice time. Say, would you please do me a favor and take these sandwiches over to the breakroom at the Administration Building?" She held out the keys to his mother's car.

"I'm not supposed to drive Mom's car. I'm excluded on her insurance."

"Did you get into an accident?"

"No. I got to be a teen driver, and it was too expensive."

"I won't tell if you don't. You're only going to the break-room and back, ten miles per hour at the most. What's the worst that could happen? A tent could run you down?"

He took the keys and the tray of sandwiches. "Be right back."

With Carlos gone and most of the students outside, Betty sat down to finish her sandwich, thankful for a calm moment after the tension Angie had brought with her from California. By the time she had finished and tossed her paper plate into the trash, Steve, Izzy, and the students had begun to gather inside again.

"Find a seat, everybody." Steve motioned to the far table. "Take a load off your brain and listen up. I'm going to give you some rules about photography. First, does anybody know the best way to make money at photography?"

Izzy raised his hand. "Sell your camera."

A few chuckles rippled through the room, and Steve continued. "Right you are. This class is about making your amateur photography better than that of someone who hasn't taken the class. If you think you'll make a small fortune as a photographer, remember this—you'll have to start with a large one."

Betty smiled. Steve had the rapt attention of his students even if they weren't going wild over his jokes. As he listed the points he'd cover in his lecture and on the photo shoot to follow—how to hold the camera for maximum picture sharpness, how to use selective focus, how to choose shutter speed and F-stop settings—she headed out front to the picnic table to watch the waves breaking onshore.

Questions crowded her mind. How long would Angie stay? What would she do with her fortune? How would it affect her life and Carlos's, and even Manuel's?

If *she'd* won a fortune, the first thing she'd do was make sure the park stayed open. At least the first folk school class was booked solid and off to a good start. Maybe the turtle would fly after all . . . and Angie would change and Manuel would come back. She could hope. And pray.

Half an hour went by with no sign of Carlos. Had he gotten into an accident after all? Maybe she should take a walk in the direction of the Administration Building.

Gravel crunched. She stood and headed around the side of the building. Carlos pulled in. Lee was right behind and parked beside Carlos.

He got out and approached Betty. "I'm in trouble now." He handed her Angie's keys.

Angie hopped out of Lee's truck, slammed the door, and marched toward Carlos. "What do you think you're doing, young man? You know you're not supposed to drive my car! What if you got in—"

"Angie, don't blame him," Betty interrupted. "It's my fault. I asked him to take leftovers to the breakroom in the Administration Building."

Angie's gaze switched from Carlos, to Betty, and back. "Why didn't you tell Mom you're not insured?"

"He *did* tell me. I told him to go ahead."

"You?" Angie's searing gaze bored into Betty. "I can't believe it! After all the times you grounded me for not following your rules, you knowingly encouraged Carlos to break *mine*?"

Betty sighed. "So ground me if it will make you feel any better."

Carlos huffed and said, "Thanks for reminding me why I left California, Mom." He headed inside.

"I can't believe it! I'm gone for less than an hour, and you have my son driving my car uninsured. I can't even trust my own mother!"

"Did you get the camcorder guy pulled out?"

Lee nodded. "Pulled out and on his way to the East Coast."

Angie sighed. "I never could understand why he'd follow me so far. Turns out he was on his way to a summer job at his relatives' resort in Maine. Getting my story was just a lark along the way. Now that he's got it, he'll stop at the first Wi-Fi connection he finds and upload film. By six o'clock Pacific Time, it will be all over the California evening news."

Betty smiled. "It's good that you talked to him. Now, he won't be stalking you."

"I only agreed to talk to him after he accepted my terms."

Lee offered a wry smile. "She drives a hard bargain. He had to promise not to disclose her current location and not to release his film to local news media, or she'd sue him for invasion of privacy."

"Maybe now I'll get some rest and some peace of mind." Angie combed her fingers through her short, blonde hair.

Betty held out Angie's car keys. "Why don't you go on home. Your old room is waiting for you. Lee and I will finish up here."

Angie grabbed the keys. "Good idea. I could use a shower and a good night's sleep." She settled into the driver's seat, backed out, and headed toward the campground a little too fast to suit Betty.

Lee nodded toward the folk school. "How's it going?"

Betty smiled. "Steve's good. He's got the kids right in the palm of his hand. And with his class full, we're earning back some of our start-up expenses. The golf outing next weekend has a lot of interest, too, but I'm worried about your fly-tying class two weeks from now. We've got to find more students for you. Only three are signed up so far, and two of them are me and Carlos."

"We'll think of something." Lee checked his watch. "How about taking a break? We've got another couple of hours be-fore you have to come back and lock up. We could go over to the falls for a little while."

"Good idea. I haven't been over there yet this spring. Let me check inside to make sure everything's okay." She stepped through the door. The kids were gathered around Steve as he explained settings on one of their cameras. Izzy stood in the background, arms folded, and a look of approval on his face. The refreshment table was just as she'd left it, minus a few more bottles of water. No point in her hanging around any longer. She headed for Lee's truck.

He drove through the campground and out the opposite end, following the gravel road to the falls. A minute later, he pulled off to the side and walked Betty to the viewing plat-form, a wooden structure with safety railings and benches. She leaned against the barrier, Lee beside her. White water tum-bled over the hundred-foot sandstone drop. The splash-song soothed her nerves and resurrected memories.

"Harry and I used to love coming over here. So did Mom and Dad. They brought us kids up to the park from Detroit al-most every summer. We'd camp here for a week or two, hike all the trails, fish in the lake, visit these falls. When it came time to pick out a college, I was determined to attend one in the U.P." She gazed up at Lee. "Sorry for rambling on. You knew all that already."

He grinned. "I like hearing it again."

Betty focused once more on the falls. "This place reminds me how important it is to keep the park open. Other families should have the same opportunity mine did. But I'm plumb out of ideas for making the folk school succeed."

"Maybe Angie will think of something." He reached for her hand, enfolding it in his own. "Let's sit for a while and reminisce about the good old days. It will help you unwind." He led her to a bench and sat close beside her, his arm about her shoulders.

She relaxed against him and told the familiar story of how Harry proposed to her here, bringing sandwiches and fries from the Beef Palace, a bottle of Boone's Farm wine, and a diamond ring. "No dinner in a fancy restaurant for us."

"Still, it was better than his first idea—taking you hunting and proposing while you were sitting in the blind. Joan told him in no uncertain terms that he needed a better plan." Lee referred to his late wife.

Betty cocked her brow. "I never knew that."

Lee's cheeks flushed. "I'm sorry. I figured Joan had probably mentioned it years ago. I should've kept my mouth shut." He got up, returned to the barrier, and rested his elbows on the rail, head bowed.

Betty approached him and placed her hand on his arm. "What is it, Lee?"

He let out a sigh. "Harry was my best friend. The last thing I wanted to do was to tarnish his memory."

"You haven't tarnished his memory. You've just given me a new one—one that tickles me inside. Let's face it. We all knew Harry wasn't the most romantic fellow to walk the earth. And we all knew he was passionate about deer hunting. Just ask Zeb!"

Lee glanced out of the corner of his eye. A hint of a smile appeared.

She tugged on his sleeve. "Come, sit with me again. I want to hear the story of your proposal to Joan at the Allumette."

He sat beside Betty, his arm about her shoulders as before, and described his evening with Joan at the fanciest restaurant in Superior Bay. They dined on sirloin-for-two. At the end of the meal, a server rolled the dessert cart to their table. It contained a variety of choices including a prominently displayed chocolate fudge cupcake with a diamond ring on top. "Joan took a close look at the cupcake, said, 'Isn't that interesting?' and with a twinkle in her eye, chose the New York cheesecake instead."

Betty smiled. "Joan always was a big tease." She let a silent moment lapse before offering an observation. "I have a feeling both Harry and Joan would approve of you and I growing closer."

Lee kissed her cheek and then her ear, sending shivers through her. She turned to him. His lips met hers, gently at first and then more insistent. Heat darted through her and her pulse quickened. When the kiss came to an end, she nestled in his arms, her head against his shoulder.

Moments slipped by free of conversation until Lee spoke. "Have you ever considered remarrying?"

Her pulse quickened. "I . . . I suppose the thought has crossed my mind."

"Mine, too."

oOo

It was nearly eleven o'clock when Betty kissed Lee good-night on the front stoop and let herself inside. She smiled at the way he had persuaded her to go to Mossy Point Pizza for a snack after they'd locked up the folk school. She'd balked at the idea of ruining her diet one more time, but Zoe made her a healthy salad to crunch on while Lee ate his personal pizza.

Wayne and Doris had come in and joined them for a while. They had volunteered to serve breakfast at the folk school the next day and had a few questions about the routine. Then they discussed ideas for pumping up folk school enrollment and time had flown by.

She quietly walked down the hall to Angie's bedroom. A gentle breeze ruffled the sheer curtains, cooling her room nicely. Angie lay sound asleep in the center of her queen-sized bed. Thank the Lord she was finally getting some peace of mind after her tiring cross-country drive.

Betty headed for the shower, relaxed under the warm spray, and then dried off and pulled on her favorite cotton jersey pajamas. She plumped the pillows against her headboard and reached for her Kindle. The sparkle of her diamond engagement ring caught her eye, and she paused to study it. With Lee's mention of remarrying, was she ready to take off her engagement and wedding rings and move on?

Decades ago she'd been forced to part with her rings. Harry had been pink-slipped. Angie made her entrance into the world. No matter how carefully they pared expenses, with a new baby, they soon ran through their savings. Just when it seemed certain they'd lose their house, Harry found work. But he wouldn't get his first paycheck until after the bank would foreclose. He came up with a plan to hock their rings at the pawnshop, save the house, and redeem the rings before they could be sold. The day he'd brought their rings home, she'd prayed she'd never have to go without them again.

But times had changed. She'd been a widow for five years. Her heart had healed from the emptiness she'd suffered after Harry passed. She worked her rings past her knuckle, hesitated, and then shoved them back in place. *Soon, but not now.*

She bowed her head and whispered a prayer. "Thank you, Lord, for Harry, for Lee, for memories. You've watched over me through all my years. And thank you for the blessings of this day—for success at the folk school, for the reunion with Angie—for all the help you've given along the way. Thank you for your Holy Word. Let me read it now and take comfort in it. In Jesus's name. Amen."

She opened her Kindle Bible and navigated to Psalm 100.

Make a joyful noise unto the Lord—

The phone rang. Caller I.D. showed Lee's number.

"Lee, what's up?" She kept her voice low, hoping Angie was still asleep.

"Sorry to call so late, Betty, but I thought you'd want to know. Eleven o'clock news ran the interview Angie did with the reporter. Everyone knows she's staying with you in Mossy Point and helping you out at the folk school."

"She said that? About helping me at the folk school?"

"Sure did. Just thought I ought to warn you, word is out."

A rock plummeted to the bottom of Betty's stomach. "Thanks for the heads-up, Lee."

"See you tomorrow. Sweet dreams."

"Yeah, right. Good night, Lee." She hung up the phone and it rang again. Reeds' number displayed. "Hi, Doris."

"Why didn't you tell us about Angie's lottery win? Do I have to watch the eleven o'clock news to find out what's happening with my best friend's kid?"

"Sorry, Doris. I just found out about it today, and I was sworn to secrecy. That interview wasn't supposed to air on local television. Angie had an agreement with the cameraman that it would only go to the California news station."

"What's Angie going to do with all that money?"

"I don't know. I only know that she won't get a penny for another couple of weeks. We'll talk more tomorrow. Don't forget—the students will start showing up for breakfast a little before eight."

"I'll be there."

"Great! Talk to you later." Betty hung up the phone just as Angie stumbled into her room.

"What's up with all the phone calls? Did something happen to Carlos?"

"They weren't about Carlos. They were about you. The Superior Bay television station ran your interview with the camcorder guy. Everyone knows you won the lottery and that you're in Mossy Point, here, at my house."

The phone rang again.

Angie snatched the receiver from the cradle. "County Morgue . . . . Manuel? . . . . You saw me on the news? Where are you? . . . . Tomorrow? . . . . Yes, Carlos is here . . . . No, he can't talk to you. He's out with his friends right now . . . . I'll tell him . . . . Yeah, sure. Me too . . . . Tomorrow. Bye."

Angie set the phone in the cradle and pulled the plug. The kitchen phone rang. She padded down the hall in her bare feet. The ringing stopped, and she returned to Betty's room and plunked down on the edge of the bed. "It's all your fault. If you hadn't told me to do that interview, the phone wouldn't be ringing off the wall."

The blame game. Acid burned in Betty's gut.

Angie grew pensive. "On the other hand, if I hadn't done that interview, Manuel wouldn't have called."

"What did he have to say?"

"He'll be here tomorrow night." She shook her head. "I knew that was going to happen. He blamed me for the breakup and wouldn't talk to me when I tried to get back together with him. Now that he knows I won the lottery, he can't get to me soon enough. It appears to me that money is more powerful than truth."

"Probably depends on whose money and whose truth. Are you two still married, then?"

Angie nodded. "Neither of us ever filed for divorce. He's legally entitled to half my winnings."

"And what about love? Sounded to me like you were glad he called just now."

Angie shrugged. "He told me he loves me just before he hung up. I brushed it off. I'll believe that, if he'll believe I never cheated on him. Either way, he's coming tomorrow."

Betty grinned. "Look on the bright side. He'll keep the gold-diggers and pesky press people at a distance. He was always very protective of you."

Angie offered a thin smile. "That's what I love about you, Mom. The glass is always half-full." She rose and headed for the door.

CHAPTER 15

Betty drifted off to sleep, visions of the folk school and Angie jumbling together in her mind. Several hours later, she awoke fully rested. Memories of the successful folk school opening put a smile on her face as she pulled on a pair of Capris and her folk school T-shirt. Thankfully, Doris, Wayne, Patsy, Karen, and Zoe were handling the meals for the students today. Good thing, with Angie here and Manuel coming in tonight. Carlos would be glad to see his dad.

Carlos. She hadn't heard him come in last night. Had she slept through it? Her heart lurched. She stepped across the hall and peeked into his room. He lay on his bed sound asleep. Taking a deep, relaxing breath, she closed his door and headed for the kitchen.

She switched on the one-cup coffeemaker, set the frying pan on the burner, and pulled the bread and eggs out of the refrigerator. As she was cracking eggs into the pan, Carlos wandered into the kitchen still wearing his pajama bottoms.

"'Morning, Gram. Coffee sure smells good. You making me breakfast?"

"Sure thing. It will be ready by the time you're dressed."

"I'll be back in a few." He disappeared down the hall.

She cracked two more eggs into the pan. While she waited for them to cook, she plugged in the phone and called Lee. He answered on the first ring.

"Good morning, Betty."

"Hi, Lee. I was thinking. I need to go to Superior Bay this afternoon for some groceries. With Angie here and Manuel coming in tonight, the pantry needs restocking. And I'll need supplies for the folk school meals tomorrow. Want to go along?"

"Manuel is coming? Are they reconciling?"

"He's coming. Reconciling is a question mark."

"How about if I pick you up at half-past eleven and treat you to lunch?"

"You don't have to do that."

"I *want* to do it."

"Then it's a date. See you at half-past eleven." She hung up the phone and unplugged it.

The sizzle of the eggs caught her attention. She flipped them and put two slices of bread in the toaster. Carlos returned dressed in his Superior Bay Community College T-shirt and blue jeans. As he set places on the countertop, worry wrinkles marred his forehead.

Betty refilled the coffeemaker, served up the eggs and toast, and said a blessing over the food. As Carlos ate, he re-mained quiet—too quiet. She broke the silence.

"You're up early for a Saturday."

"Thought I'd study for the GED. Got to get into college come fall."

"How are things with Janna?" Could she be the source of his troubled brow?

"Fine, as long as I'm studying. She's always on my case about it—in a good way."

"Smart girl."

He smiled and shoveled a forkful of egg into his mouth. Then his sullen look returned.

"Something bothering you, Carlos?" She crunched on her toast.

He took a sip of coffee and turned to her. "Last night at the park, some kids from the folk school were saying Mom was on the late news talking about winning millions of dollars in a lottery. I told them they must be wrong, but they insisted. One of them even called her a "rich bitch." I almost got into a fight. Why would they make something like that up?"

Betty drew a long breath. *Lord, should I tell Carlos about Angie's good fortune, or leave it for her to do when she gets up?* An answer came to mind.

"I wish your mother were awake so you could tell her what happened. I'm sure she has a logical explanation." She retrieved her cup of coffee from the coffeemaker and sat beside him again. "For now, let's put it aside because I have something very important to share."

"Good news?"

"I think so. Your father will be here tonight."

He paused, fork midway to his mouth. "Dad? Here? Does Mom know?"

"He called her last night and told her. He knows you're here and is looking forward to seeing you."

Carlos lowered his fork to his plate. "Not sure I want to see him."

"Why not? I thought you'd be pleased."

Carlos shrugged.

"Are you angry at him?"

"I'm afraid he and Mom will just start fighting again."

"Maybe they'll iron out their differences. We could pray about it."

"Would you do that, Gram?"

"Sure. Let's bow our heads." She reached for Carlos's hand and he wrapped his fingers firmly around hers. "Lord, Angie and Manuel have had their problems, and a long separation. We ask your guidance for them to reconcile their differences and restore their marriage. And help Carlos to move ahead with his studies for the GED exam. Thank you, Lord. In Jesus's name. Amen.

"Amen."

She squeezed his hand and let go. "Lee and I are going to Superior Bay later on for lunch and to pick up some groceries. Want to come?"

He shook his head. "GED. I promised Janna I'd work on it all day."

"Good plan." She sipped her coffee.

Carlos appeared lost in thought, saying nothing more until he had carried his empty plate to the sink and started the coffeemaker again. "I'm going to start studying now. I'll be back for my coffee."

Betty nodded and headed to the radio to tune in the Superior Bay station, hoping to catch local news while she finished her eggs and toast. A reporter's tenor voice drifted softly from the speakers.

"It seems we have a multi-million-dollar lottery winner in our midst. Angela Hanson Martinez, who grew up in Mossy Point and moved to California twenty-two years ago, was one of twelve winners of California's Super Lotto this month. She is currently in Mossy Point visiting her mother.

"Speaking of millions of dollars, the State of Superior is looking to cut about $500 million in order to balance the budget. Parks, state police, and Secretary of State Offices are some of the areas that may get the ax . . . ."

Betty switched off the radio, mumbling to herself. "Did you really have to tell about Angie? And as for the parks, I'm not about to let Mossy Point close. We're going to make money this year. Turtles will fly, just like I promised Mr. Engstrom."

Carlos returned for his coffee mug. "You talking to me, Gram?"

Betty chuckled. "No. Just responding out loud to some news on the radio."

He smiled and headed off to his room.

Betty swallowed down the last of her coffee, rinsed the dishes, and filled the dishwasher. At the kitchen desk, she sat down and opened the latest credit card bill. The list of expenses was longer than she'd anticipated, and the bottom line was larger. Start-up costs for the folk school and purchases for Carlos amounted to much more than she'd thought. She needed reimbursement for folk school expenses soon in order to avoid huge interest charges. But that wouldn't cover the extra costs since Carlos moved in.

And now Angie was here and Manuel would arrive tonight. If the lottery money had come in, she'd ask Angie to help out, but that wouldn't happen for several more days. With the power bill and telephone bill, her checking account would be down to nothing. Retirement and Social Security wouldn't pay out again until next month. But she needed groceries and she needed them today. There must be a way.

She fingered her wedding and engagement rings and bowed her head. *Lord, what do I do? You know my circumstances. Got any advice for me?*

As if spoken aloud, one word came to mind.

Trust.

She pulled an envelope full of folk school receipts from a pigeonhole, tallied them up, then returned them to their place and began tidying up the great room. If Angie stuck to her guns, Manuel would be sleeping on the pull-out sofa tonight. She collected old newspapers and magazines and tossed them in the recycle bin, then dusted the furniture and hardwood floor while Zeb looked on.

Betty paused to gaze up at him. "It's getting interesting around here. Things are changing fast. But you never change, Zeb, always looking down at me with that same benevolent gaze."

"Mom, who are you talking to?" Angie stood at the end of the hallway still in her nightgown and bare feet.

"Zeb. He never argues back."

Angie chuckled and stepped closer. "Unlike me. I'll never forget the time I was arguing with you when I was about sixteen and you said to me, 'Why can't you be more like Zeb?'"

Betty giggled. "And you said, 'That old beast? You want me to grow hair on my face and antlers on my head?' And I said—"

"You said, 'No. Just learn how to keep your mouth shut.' Guess I'll never get that one down, will I?"

Betty slipped her arm around Angie's waist. "Guess not. Did you get a good night's sleep?"

Angie shrugged. "Good as it could be considering the circumstances."

"Worried about Manuel coming tonight?"

Angie gave Betty a quick hug and stepped out of her embrace. "I guess. He kept popping up in my dreams, and I kept sending him away, never sure if he was pursuing me for money or for love." A thoughtful moment lapsed. "I'm going to get dressed and eat some breakfast. Then I want to know all about this folk school you've got going."

"Can I get you some coffee, eggs, and toast?"

"Just cereal and coffee." Angie headed for her room.

Betty continued her clean-up efforts until Angie returned. In the kitchen, Betty put the coffee on and set out the cereal and milk. Angie found a mug, bowl, spoon, and napkin, pulled out a stool, and sat down to eat.

Betty sat beside her. "Carlos was up early. Said he wanted to spend the day studying for the GED."

Angie swallowed a mouthful of cereal. "I thought he'd be in bed. You mean he's in his room studying? How'd you manage that?"

"He's been hanging around Janna Jarvis. She told him to spend the day studying."

"Yay, Janna. I'll have to give that girl a bonus when my check comes in." Angie winked.

"If you did, she'd use it for her college expenses. Now, on a different subject, I told Carlos about Manuel coming in tonight. I hope you don't mind."

Angie shook her head.

"When will you tell him about your lottery win? Some folk school students staying at the park saw you on TV last night and told Carlos about it. He didn't believe them—told them it must have been someone else. I said you'd have a logical explanation for him when you got up."

Angie sipped coffee and swiveled her stool toward Betty. "I've given a lot of thought to this—how it will affect his thinking, his choices in life, his incentive to stand on his own two feet in this world. I'd like him to get a college education and find success in his own right. Here's what I came up with . . . ."

As Angie's plan unfolded—help Carlos with college until he graduates or drops out—Betty's heart soared. At least in the area of wealth management, wisdom appeared to be the ruling force.

"What do you think, Mom?"

Betty gave two thumbs up. "I think you've nailed it. I'll be right by your side to back you up if he argues or complains."

"Thanks. Now, if I only knew how to handle Manuel." She chewed her lower lip.

"When is he coming in? I was wondering whether to count on him for dinner tonight."

Angie shook her head. "I'm picking him up at the airport at six, and then he's taking me to the Allumette for dinner."

Betty cocked an eyebrow. "The Allumette, eh? Can't do better than that in these parts. Sounds like Manuel's really serious about getting back together."

"Yeah, but . . . ." She lowered her gaze and fiddled with the napkin in her lap.

"But what?"

Angie's gaze appeared uncertain as it met Betty's. "You know me. My unruly tongue gets me into trouble. I'm afraid I'll blurt something out that I'll regret and sabotage my chance to make things right again."

"Why don't we pray about it?"

Angie sighed. "God's probably listening to *you*. But *I've* messed up so many times I doubt He'd hear me. Or even recognize my voice. But if He did, He'd say, 'Angie, I worked it out so you could be a millionaire. Isn't that enough?'"

Betty shook her head. "I'm sure God will hear you if you lift your voice to Him. I'll pray first." She wrapped her fingers around Angie's long, slender ones. "Almighty God, Angie and Manuel need your help to reconcile their differences. Please give them wisdom and love to heal the rift and mend their marriage, and help Angie to control her tongue." She squeezed Angie's hand.

"Hello, God; it's Angie. Do you remember me? I know it's been a long time since I've talked to you. I'm sorry for that. I'll do better from now on, I promise. Now, God, please answer Mom's prayer. Help Manuel and me to put our troubles behind us. But if he's only coming here for money and not for love, then send him away. And one more thing. Help me to do what's right with the lottery money. Thanks, God. Talk to you later, I promise."

"Amen." Betty released Angie's hand.

"Amen." Carlos's voice echoed from the hallway. His gaze held Angie's as he approached her. "So it's true then, what the kids said about you winning the lottery. Why didn't you tell me?"

"I'm sorry. I wanted to explain it to you last night, but I was too tired to wait up for you. I never dreamed I'd be on local TV. I had an agreement with the fellow who filmed me that he wouldn't release the news here, but he obviously ignored it."

Carlos moved his head slowly from side to side. "Wow. I've got a millionaire mom. I can't believe it." He pulled up a stool beside his mother and rested his hand on her forearm.

"Ouch!" Angie jerked her arm away. "You pinched me! Why did you do that?"

Carlos grinned. "Just had to make sure you were real, and this wasn't a dream."

Betty suppressed a chuckle and headed to the dining area to dust the table and chairs, keeping her ear tuned to the ongoing conversation.

Carlos continued. "Does this mean you and Dad are getting back together?"

Angie answered with her mouth full. "Maybe. We'll see."

"So, Mom, now that you're a millionaire, how about buying me a new pickup truck?"

Angie's coffee mug clanked against the counter. "Absolutely not!"

"Why not? What's the good of having a lot of money if you don't buy some nice stuff?"

"The good of having a lot of money is that I can help you pay your college expenses. I thought you were in your room studying for the GED so you could go to college this fall."

"I was, but what's the point? With all that money—"

"*My* money. I will not have it depriving you of a college education or the will to make a success of yourself. *Me comprendes?*"

"Yeah, but—"

"No buts. You need an education."

"I'll need wheels."

"Wheels and a new pickup truck are not exactly inter-changeable in my vocabulary. Wheels could be a nice older car like my Chevy Impala."

Carlos groaned.

Betty stepped up to the counter. "Or an older truck like your grandfather's '51 Studebaker. You could fix it up, Car-los. You always liked that old thing. With a little work, it will get you to and from classes, and no one else will be driving anything like that old Stude."

"You'd let me use Grampa's old truck?" Carlos's brow lift-ed.

She nodded. "I can't think of a more noble purpose for that old thing than to get you to and from college. And when you graduate with your four-year degree, I'll sign the title over to you."

Carlos shot up from his stool and raised his arms in a victo-ry gesture. "Whoohoo! Thanks, Gram!" He hurried to Betty, gave her a quick hug, and then headed for the door. "I'm go-ing out to the barn and take a look at it. Maybe Dad will help me fix it up."

"Carlos, wait." Angie called after him, but he ignored her.

Betty turned to Angie. "I hope I didn't overstep my bounds, offering Harry's antique truck."

"Not at all. Are you sure you want Carlos to have it? I mean, he's young, and you know what can happen when young drivers get behind the wheel."

"I raised *you*, didn't I?"

Angie laughed. "I had my share of fender-benders, didn't I? Carlos is a better driver than I was at his age, thank goodness, but insurance costs were too high in California to put him on my policy. It was hard enough just meeting the mortgage payment and keeping the lights on, once Manuel was out of work. I guess I'll never have to worry about that again."

Betty sat down beside her. "I'm sorry you were having such a difficult time. Why didn't you tell me? I would have helped you out. You know that, don't you?"

Angie turned away. A moment later, her teary-eyed gaze met Betty's. "I know. I didn't want your help . . . . I didn't want you to know my life was a dismal failure . . . marriage on the rocks, too many bills to pay, standing in line at a food pantry just to put meals on the table."

A Superior-sized boulder crushed Betty's heart. She reached for the tissue box at the end of the counter, helped herself, and slid the box to Angie. "And that's why you didn't speak to me for two years?"

Angie nodded and dabbed at her tears. "Pride. And I didn't want a lecture about how I'd screwed up."

The words sliced Betty to the core. Had she been too controlling? Too critical? Too much a perfectionist with her only child? No wonder Angie had talked so easily with Harry. He'd been none of those things. With him gone . . . .

"I'm sorry, Angie."

"For what?"

"That my lecturing ways kept us apart. I shouldn't have—"

Angie grasped Betty's hand. "I forgive you. Now let's put that behind us. We've got bigger fish to fry. I want to know all about this folk school, what classes you've got planned, how many students have signed up, who's helping you with the work."

"Carlos—"

He came through the garage door. "Hey, Gram, when was the last time you ran the Stude?"

"Lee starts it up about once a month. It's probably due to be run again. I'll get the keys." She headed to the kitchen desk drawer.

"Is it okay if I back it out of the barn? I can get a better look at it in the sunshine."

"Sure, go ahead. Do you know how to put the old stick shift into reverse?" She handed him the keys.

"Piece of cake." He headed for the door.

"Be careful letting out the clutch."

"Don't worry." The door banged shut behind him.

Betty turned to Angie with fingers crossed.

Angie grinned. "Don't worry. He'll do fine. Like I said, he's a better driver than I was at his age. Now, you were about to tell me who's helping you with the folk school."

Betty sat down beside her again. "Carlos and Lee have helped the most; the Reeds, Steve Taylor, Karen Baker, Patsy Webb. And one day, Patsy's relatives from Baraga helped out, too. Patsy's fairly new here. She just moved to Mossy Point from Baraga last year."

In the distance, the Stude engine revved, and then idled.

Angie nodded toward the sound. "Carlos got the truck running and managed to back it out without hitting anything."

He popped in through the garage door. "Gram have you got a pad and pen? I'll make a list for Superior Bay. Mr. Nylund can help you get some things at the auto parts store."

She headed to the kitchen desk. How would she pay for auto parts? Angie would reimburse her later, but the credit card was way overspent already. She handed a pad and pen to Carlos. He thanked her and disappeared.

Angie carried her dish to the sink. "Sounds like you have a lot of helping hands for the folk school. Do you have a website?"

"Carlos built one for us. MossyPointFolkSchool dot com. Students can sign up and pay for classes online. We have a bank account and PayPal account, too."

"I think I'll check those out while Carlos is fiddling with the truck." She started toward the hallway.

"Angie, I'm going to Superior Bay later with Lee for lunch, and to buy groceries—and auto parts, evidently. Anything you need?"

She grinned. "Nothing that money can buy."

CHAPTER 16

Lee pulled up promptly at half-past eleven. Betty grabbed her purse and fabric shopping bags and headed out the door. Carlos rounded the corner of the garage, list in hand, and made a beeline for Lee's truck, reaching it ahead of her. So much for Carlos studying for the GED this morning. He'd spent the entire time fiddling with the old Stude. Oh well. He probably couldn't have concentrated on his studies anyway, with his mother's good fortune on his mind. Maybe this afternoon, he would get some studying done.

Carlos was still standing beside Lee's truck, discussing his auto parts list, when Betty climbed into the passenger seat, and it was starting to sound expensive. Oil, lube grease, transmission fluid. Thank goodness air for the tires was still free. Gas wasn't, but that would be Angie's responsibility. Carlos thanked Lee and trotted off in the direction of the barn.

Lee tucked the list into his denim shirt pocket and turned to her with a smile. "How's it going with Angie in residence?"

"Better than I expected, mostly."

"Mostly?"

"House guests cost money. Add those expenses to the ones for starting the folk school, and I'm tapped out. If only I could make the total on my bank account swap places with the total on my credit card bill . . . ."

"The board will reimburse you for folk school expenses. Is there enough money in the account?"

"No, but it will help. We need to have a meeting and vote on it."

"Call the Reeds and take a telephone vote. You can count me as being in favor. As for the other, won't Angie help you out? After all, you've taken care of Carlos for nearly a month now."

"I'm sure she'll help when she gets her payout a couple of weeks from now, but I'll exceed my credit card limit and overdraw my bank account before then if I'm not careful." Acid gurgled in her gut. She needed to change the subject before it became heartburn. "Where are you taking me for lunch?"

"You name the place."

"How about that little tea room over on Third Street. I haven't been there in—I don't remember when."

"The tea room, it is."

"And Lee?"

"Yes?"

"Before we go to the tea room, would you please stop by that pawnshop on the corner?"

"Pawnshop? Are things that bad?" He flashed an inquiring glance her way.

"I'm afraid so."

Thirty minutes later, Lee pulled up in front of the pawnshop, helped her out of the truck, and followed her inside. A middle-aged fellow in a pinstripe suit greeted them.

"How may I help you?"

Stomach souring, Betty worked the engagement and wedding rings off her finger and set them on the glass countertop with a shaky hand. "What can I get for these? And how long would I have to redeem them?"

"Let me take a look." He pulled a loupe out of his pocket and inspected the rings, weighed them on small scales, and then named an amount far smaller than their actual value, but much higher than Harry had paid forty-two years ago.

"What happens if I take your offer?"

"You can redeem them anytime within the next one to four months by paying back the loan plus fees and interest." He punched numbers into a computer, wrote four amounts down on a pad, one for each of the next four months, and showed them to her. The redemption amount was a good bit higher than the loan, even if she came in next month. But a month was long enough, and the transaction wouldn't affect her credit rating.

"I'll take your offer, sir."

He smiled. "Very well. I'll write up your ticket."

Lee put his palm out. "Wait just a minute, please." He twisted his wedding ring off his finger and set it on the counter. "What would you give for that?"

The pawnbroker inspected and weighed the ring and named a price.

"Add that amount to her loan."

Betty gasped. "Oh, Lee, are you sure?"

His head jerked in a nod.

She blinked back tears and tried to swallow past the lump in her throat, managing to clear it by the time the pawnbroker had handed her the pawn ticket and counted out the cash.

She stuffed the bills into her wallet. "Thank you, sir. I'll be back before the month is out."

"Thank you, ma'am, sir. I look forward to seeing you again. Have a nice day."

Lee nodded. His hand on Betty's elbow, he ushered her out of the shop and opened the truck passenger door.

She turned to him, searching his blue eyes for any sign of regret, finding them dry and clear. "Why did you pawn your ring?"

He shrugged. "Seemed like the right thing to do. Now let's get lunch. I'm hungry."

"Bank first. I don't want to carry this much cash around."

"It's a deal."

o0o

Lee's truck radio played '50s music as he pulled up in front of Betty's house late that afternoon. She checked her watch. Half-past five. Where had the day gone?

He came around to the passenger side and opened the door. "I'll haul the stuff from the auto parts back to the barn." He reached for the bags behind the seats.

Carlos bounded out of the house. "I'll help you with those things, Mr. Nylund."

The two of them headed for the barn.

Angie emerged from the front door wearing a short black dress with a low-cut neckline that showed her cleavage and long, shapely legs to her best advantage. Around her neck hung a stunning art deco necklace of diamond-like gems that sparkled in the late afternoon sun. Her stiletto heels clicked against the sidewalk as she hurried toward her car.

"I'm off now, Mom. Wish me luck."

Betty smiled. "You look marvelous, Angie. I thought you'd be gone by now. Better get a move on, if you plan to be at the airport in time to meet Manuel's plane."

"Leave the door unlocked for us, will you? We might be late getting in." She slid into the driver's seat of her Impala, slammed the door, revved the engine, and backed out so fast she spit gravel and raised dust.

Betty shook her head. Why was Angie always pushing the deadline, or missing it completely? Would she ever understand that girl?

She reached into the storage area behind the seat, grabbed two of the grocery bags, carried them inside, returned to the truck, and pulled out two more bags.

Carlos and Lee reappeared. Carlos took the bags from her while Lee hauled the remaining groceries from the back and slammed the door.

"Thanks for getting the stuff for the truck, Gram. I owe you."

"I'm keeping track. Did you get any studying done today?"

He shook his head. "Mom was on my computer all afternoon until just a little while before she left. Janna will kill me."

Inside, they set the groceries on the kitchen counter and Lee turned to go. "See you later. Tomorrow at church?"

"Don't you want to stay for supper?"

He grinned. "I could be convinced."

She pulled the package of ground beef out of the grocery bag. "Great! I need a grill cook for the burgers."

Carlos turned to Lee. "Since you're staying, maybe you could help me with the Stude after supper?"

"Your father will help you with it when he gets here. I thought I'd do some fishing. Want to come?"

Betty wagged her finger at Carlos. "You've got to study. Your mother's gone now, so there's no reason why you can't get on the computer tonight, at least until Janna's off work."

"Yeah, but—"

"You owe me, remember? The truck and the fish will still be there tomorrow after church. Besides, when you see Janna later, you'll be able to tell her you did some studying."

"Good thinking, Gram."

Lee nudged Betty with his shoulder. "Want to go fishing with me while Carlos studies?"

She shook her head. "I thought I'd drive over to the folk school and catch the Reeds before they finish serving the kids' supper. There's that little matter of reimbursement."

"I'll take you over, and we can go fishing afterward."

Betty gazed up into Lee's eyes, so hopeful, and nodded. How could she turn him down after what he'd done for her today?

o0o

At the dinner table, Lee asked a blessing over the burgers, salads, and baked fries; then Betty focused on Carlos. "So tell me. Why was your mother on the computer for so long?"

Carlos sighed and rolled his eyes. "It all started when she asked me to show her the folk school website. After that, she started an online conference with some website designer she knows in California. I hung around for about fifteen minutes waiting for her to finish, but she told me to go work on the Stude. Said she'd come get me when she was done, but she never did."

"Is she getting the designer to redo our website?"

"I think so."

Lee tucked his fork into his salad and then focused on Carlos. "Did you happen to see whether anyone else signed up for my fly-tying class?"

"No new sign-ups. Not just for you, but for anything."

Betty's gaze met Lee's. The lines between his brows reflected her concern. "We'll have to think up some ways to spark interest if we're ever going to exceed the start-up expenses and put this park in the black for the season. The turtle has to fly—in more than just the logo on the picnic table and the T-shirts."

Lee nodded. "Maybe the Reeds will have some ideas."

oOo

Betty held the lines to Lee's fishing boat while he slowly backed the trailer down the launch ramp. The boat floated free and he pulled up into a parking spot.

She wrapped the lines around the dock pilings and zipped the personal floatation device he'd given her to wear. Why did she always feel like such a blimp in this thing? *Stick to your diet.*

Lee danced a jig on his way from the truck to the dock, the words to "Little Bitty Pretty One" drifting to her on the mild offshore breeze. Tonight, he didn't miss a step, and the smile he flashed at her lit his face, putting a sparkle in his blue eyes.

"Thanks for coming with me tonight, Betty."

His buoyant mood put a smile on her face despite the money worries. Yes, the Reeds had agreed to the board reimbursing her receipts, but ongoing folk school expenses coupled with a lack of new students spelled trouble, and no one seemed to know how to increase enrollment.

Lee knelt to hold the boat steady, motioning with the sweep of his hand for her to get in. He tossed in the lines, stepped into the stern, and started the old Johnson motor with one pull.

As he backed away from the pier and maneuvered toward the mouth of the river, her gaze landed on a vintage fishing tackle box with a fresh coat of olive green paint. "Lee, where did you get that tackle box? I don't remember ever seeing it before."

"It came out of the Lahti cabin. Remember?"

"You're kidding! How did you get rid of all the rust?"

He grinned. "Apple cider vinegar. I thought I'd take it to the fly-tying class to show what can be done to restore an old tackle box. I took some 'before' photos to display with it."

"Good idea!"

A few minutes later, when he reached the mouth of the Mossy Point River, he dropped anchor, baited a hook with a night crawler, and handed her a pole. She adjusted the bobber and dropped the line over the port side.

He did the same over the starboard side and started to hum "Come Softly to Me."

She giggled. "Do you think the fish know that tune?"

His bobber jiggled and then disappeared.

"Evidently." He jerked his line to set the hook and reeled in an eight-inch rock bass. Carefully, he worked the hook out of its mouth and lowered the bass to the water's surface. "Back you go, little fella. Send your mama or papa this way." He baited his hook again and tossed it overboard.

Betty's gaze shifted from her bobber to her bare ring finger. She wiggled it against the other fingers, missing the metal bands and the sparkle of the small diamond she'd worn for so many years. *I'll get them back, Harry; I promise.*

"Pawnshop remorse?"

Lee's question sent warmth to her cheeks. She shrugged. "How about you?"

A moment lapsed and then he shook his head.

"Will you be sorry if I can't come up with the redemption fee?"

He drew a breath and exhaled slowly. "The ring served its purpose when I was married. It served a new purpose today, an important one. I can let it go." A smile crept across his face. "Besides, I hardly think the mother of a millionaire daughter is unlikely to redeem her pawn ticket."

She poked him in the chest and pinned a scowl on him. "Not a word of this to Angie. Promise?"

"Promise. I won't have to tell her. She's a jewelry addict. She'll notice your rings are missing and dig into the reason. And you'll tell her the truth because you never lie."

"I don't wear a halo."

"Sure you do. You're the guardian angel of Mossy Point State Park, the mentoring grandmother of Carlos, the concerned mother of Angela. You even named your daughter 'angel' with an 'a'."

"Hush. You're scaring away the fish."

He leaned close and whispered. "You're an angel."

She shook her head and whispered back. "Not."

He grinned. "Your bobber's moving. Even the fish recognize an angel."

The fish nibbled and ran with her line. She set the hook and started to reel in. The fish fought her, bending the tip of her pole beneath the surface. "Must be a small-mouth bass."

"A fighter like you. Need help?" Lee reeled his line in, set his pole down, and reached for the net.

"I always need help. You know that." She continued reeling in.

He grabbed her line and worked the net around a decent-sized small-mouth bass. It flopped so hard she was sure it would jump back in the lake. Lee grabbed hold of the wiggly fish, removed the hook, and measured it.

"Fourteen inches, right on the line. Want to keep it? Today's the first day of the season for keeping bass. You're not required to throw him back."

Betty shook her head. "Do you want him?"

He stared at it a moment and then sent it back.

Betty baited her hook again and tossed it over the side. Lee flung his line out. A few minutes later, with no action on either line, he pulled anchor and headed down the shoreline to a reef. There, Lee hooked a couple of bass too small to keep, and then, with the sun sinking below the horizon, motored back to the launch.

Twenty minutes later, Lee parked in front of Betty's house, got out, and walked her to the door.

She gazed up into his placid eyes and smiled. "Thanks for taking me fishing. Coming in? I'll make coffee."

He shook his head. "What time are you leaving tomorrow morning to serve breakfast to the kids? I'll pick you up, and take you to church afterward."

"Better be here by quarter-past seven so we can load the things into your truck."

"I'll be here." He bent to kiss her, wrapping his arms about her and holding her tight. Warmth radiated deep within, spreading through every inch of her.

When he released her and drove away, a big slice of her heart went with him.

CHAPTER 17

Betty headed inside and down the hall to Carlos's room.

He gazed up from the computer. "Catch any fish?"

"Sure did. A fourteen-inch small-mouth. The rascal fought like a champ."

He put two thumbs up. "When you gonna grill it?"

"I'm not. He's swimming in the lake." She nodded toward the computer. "How's the studying coming?"

He sighed. "This math is killing me."

"Wish I could help, but that was my weakest subject. Nearly didn't graduate college because of the math requirement. Maybe Janna can help you. I'll be in the kitchen working at my desk."

"How about bringing me a cup of coffee?"

"Sure. It'll only take a minute, thanks to the coffeemaker you're so fond of." She turned to go.

"Gram, almost forgot."

She looked back and lifted her brow.

"Mom called a few minutes ago. Said to tell you she and Dad aren't coming home tonight. They've checked into a hotel room." He grinned.

She raised crossed fingers. "Sounds like they might work things out after all. I'll get your coffee."

Minutes later, she delivered a fresh cup of café con leche to Carlos and then returned to the kitchen to tackle the unpaid bills. How had she let her household spending get so out-of-control? Carlos. From the coffeemaker to the online GED studies, nothing was cheap—except the clothes from the thrift shop.

She wrote out checks to the energy company, the phone company, and the credit card company. Pulling cash from her wallet and a church donation envelope from a pigeonhole, she prepared her offering for church. Thanks to Lee, she had some money left in her wallet and her bank account—enough to tide her over until Angie's windfall came in. She stuffed her checkbook and church envelope into her purse and headed for the shower.

Refreshed, relaxed, and ready for a little escape until bedtime, she leaned back on the pillows plumped against her headboard and grabbed her Kindle. Maybe tonight she'd get to the happily-ever-after ending of the romance she'd been reading in brief snatches for the last three weeks. But what about her own real-life romance?

o0o

In mid-afternoon the following day, Betty headed off to her bedroom for a nap. Serving breakfast and lunch at the folk school and attending church in between had caught up with her. She sat down on her bed, kicked off her loafers, and lay back. She'd heard nothing from Angie and Manuel, and prayed no news was good news. Then her thoughts drifted to Lee and she fell asleep.

Sometime later, she awoke to the ringing of the phone. She reached for the handset and checked the caller I.D.

"Angie?"

"Hi, Mom. You sound like you just woke up."

Betty stifled a yawn. "I was napping. Where are you? Is everything okay with you and Manuel?"

"We're at the Hotel Amour. Things couldn't be better! Listen, I need to talk to you about the park. You know how fond I am of that place—playing there all summer long when I was a kid, and working there when I was a teen. That park is part of my DNA! Anyway, I told Manuel how important it is to me to help you with the folk school so we can keep the park from closing. I came up with a plan . . . ."

For several minutes, Betty listened, responding with "Great!" or "Good thinking" when Angie invited her opinion.

" . . . So Manuel and I will see you at the folk school at half-past eight tomorrow morning for the press conference. Be sure and wear your flying turtle T-shirt, and get the Reeds and Mr. Nylund and the others who've been helping you to do the same."

"Got it. But Angie, are you sure about this? Is Manuel onboard?"

"Sure as I'm sitting here." There was a shuffling sound on the other end.

"Don't you worry, *Isabelita*." Manuel's deep voice resonated in her ear. "I'm backing *mi angelita* one hundred and fifty percent. See you tomorrow. Tell Carlos we'll work on that old Stude, and it will be *perfecto!*"

"I'll tell him. See you in the morning."

The line went dead. She clicked off and headed for the bathroom to dash cold water on her face. Had she really heard right, or was she dreaming? Yes, the folk school needed more students, teachers, and publicity, but she never in her wildest dreams would have come up with a plan like Angie's.

She dried her face, returned to the bedroom, and picked up the phone. Lee and the Reeds needed to know about the plan and the press conference. Steve, Karen, and Patsy would hear her news in person when supper was served at the folk school. She'd overstepped her bounds, giving approval to Angie's plan without a vote from the board officers—Lee and the Reeds—but how could they possibly oppose it?

o0o

Early the next morning—Memorial Day—Lee helped Betty set up for breakfast at the folk school: coffee or tea, orange juice, bagels, sweet rolls, donuts, cold cereal, and fresh fruit. A TV news van pulled up beside Lee's truck just as the coffee finished percolating. A young female reporter, her long blonde hair pulled back into a ponytail, entered the building.

"Good morning. I'm Ursula Carlyle, TV 6 News."

Betty extended her hand. "I'm Betty Hanson, and this is Lee Nylund."

Ursula shook their hands, her focus returning to Betty. "Mrs. Martinez isn't here yet?"

"She'll be here by half-past eight. Help yourself to some coffee and something to eat. The students will be here soon."

Ursula shook her head. "Maybe later. I need to set up my equipment right now. Maybe I can talk with a couple of your students, see how they like their experience here while I'm waiting for Mrs. Martinez."

"Sure." Betty prayed the students would give a good report.

Ursula hauled in her tripod and camera and set them up in the corner at the end of the buffet table.

Two students wandered in.

Lee greeted them. "Help yourself to some breakfast, gentlemen."

"Gentlemen?" The taller, blond fellow looked around. "You talking to us?"

His chubby, dark-haired friend chuckled. "Yeah, stupid. We're the only males in the place besides him." He turned his attention to Betty. "Is it true your daughter won millions in a lottery?"

Betty grinned. "Evidently."

He jabbed his friend, slopping coffee onto the blond fellow's shirt. "Told you so!"

"Hey, watch it! This was the only clean shirt I had. Now what'll I do?"

Ursula approached the young men. "Say, how would one of you like to be on TV 6 News and tell about your experience here at the folk school?"

The dark-haired student smiled. "I'll do it!"

"Follow me." Ursula stepped off toward her camera and tripod. The young man followed.

His friend tagged along. "You sure you want him? He's a real comedian in front of a camera."

Betty chewed on her lip. Just what she needed. A jerky student in front of a TV camera to represent the Mossy Point Folk School experience. At least he didn't have a stain on his shirt.

Several more students wandered in, and she focused on keeping the table stocked with food and beverages. Steve and Izzy arrived and the dining table was soon filled with young people. The buzz of conversation peppered with laughter warmed Betty's heart and almost made her miss her teaching days.

At twenty minutes past eight, Steve began giving instructions for the morning shoot. As he talked, Doris, Wayne, Patsy, and Karen wandered in to wait with Betty and Lee for the eight-thirty press conference. Their excitement was nearly palpable. A young male stringer for the *Superior Bay Journal* arrived with a camera slung over his shoulder and a notebook in his hand.

But where was Angie?

Steve dismissed the class with instructions to wait with him outside for the press conference; then Lee and Wayne moved the lectern outdoors in front of the building as Angie had requested in her phone conversation.

Ursula approached Betty. "I got some good footage of the students." Her gaze swept the others and returned to Betty. "Mrs. Martinez isn't here yet?"

"I'm sure she'll be here any second." Gravel crunched as Angie's old Impala came to a halt beside the news van. Betty pointed. "There she is now." She and the others headed out the door.

Angela got out of the passenger seat wearing a navy blue pant suit and carrying a portfolio that looked all business. Manuel wore a red polo shirt and a pair of black twill pants that made the most of his olive skin and buff physique. Carlos emerged from the backseat wearing his Mossy Point Folk School shirt and jeans.

Ursula beamed a smile and extended her hand to Angie. "Mrs. Martinez, I'm Ursula Carlyle, TV 6 News. I'm looking forward to hearing your announcement about the folk school."

"Great! I'm ready to talk!"

"When you've finished your announcement and start taking questions, I'll pack up so I can get to my next assignment. Now, just give me a minute to haul my equipment outside and get set up."

While Ursula moved her camera and tripod, Angie and Manuel introduced themselves to Patsy and the newspaper reporter from the *Superior Bay Journal,* renewed their acquaintance with the Reeds and Karen, and engaged in conversation with some of the students. Thad and Janna drove up in the park truck and joined the throng. Lively chatter filled the air.

With the camera in place and ready to roll, Angie stepped behind the podium.

Manuel let out a whistle so loud it made Betty's ears ring— and gained immediate silence.

Angela smiled. "I'm Angela Hanson Martinez, the daughter of Betty Hanson, who had the wonderful idea to start Mossy Point Folk School here at Mossy Point State Park. The goal of the folk school is to raise enough revenue to keep Mossy Point State Park from closing at the end of the season, but in order to do that, we need more teachers and students.

"As some of you may know, I'm a Super-Lotto Jackpot winner from California. That money will help the new State of Superior keep Mossy Point State Park open. Here's how. Listen up, because you could be a big winner, too.

"Today, I'm announcing a new contest. One student chosen randomly from each class offered this season at Mossy Point Folk School will win $10,000."

A student gasped.

"You heard right. One student from each class will win $10,000, including someone from the photography class that is standing in front of me right now."

Students erupted in cheers and applause.

Angie beamed and put her palm out. Voices died down.

The dark-haired boy who'd done the interview with Ursula raised his hand. "You mean somebody standing here right now will win $10,000?"

Angie nodded. "That's exactly right. It could be you!"

His blond buddy jostled him. Others murmured excitedly.

Angie continued. "Listen up, because there's more. And please save further questions until the end.

"Class sizes are limited, so your chances of winning are good. But for those of you watching at home, here's how to enter for a chance to win. You must sign up and attend a class. I'll tell you how in a minute.

"In addition to the student winners, one teacher from this season will win $10,000. We need volunteer teachers for September.

"Now listen closely. Here's how to enroll as a student or volunteer as a teacher. Starting tomorrow morning, go to MossyPointFolkSchool dot com to pick out the class you want to attend or to sign up to teach using the teacher application form.

"Let me repeat. Students and teachers can sign up at MossyPointFolkSchool dot com starting tomorrow. The website is not online today due to the modifications being made to accommodate this contest.

"Once again, one student in each class and one teacher from this season will win $10,000. Sign up starting tomorrow morning, and good luck! You could be a big winner! Now, I'll take questions."

Ursula shut off her camera and retrieved her mike from Angie. "Thank you, Mrs. Martinez, and good luck with your giveaways."

"Thanks for giving me the opportunity to tell about my contest. I'll be watching for your report on the evening news." Her focus shifted to Karen, whose hand was waving wildly. "Go ahead with your question, Karen."

"Am I eligible to win? I mean, just 'cause I've been a volunteer here since day one with your ma, that don't rule me out, right?"

"You're eligible. Only family members are ineligible. You could definitely be a winner, Karen."

She grinned. "I think I'm gonna sign up for a few more classes, increase my chances! That's legal, ain't it?"

"Yes, but remember, you also have to attend. Just signing up isn't enough. Any other questions?"

Steve raised his hand and Angie gave him a nod. "When will you be announcing the winners and awarding the money?"

"Student winners between now and the end of June will be announced on the first of July and checks awarded the following week. Thereafter, checks will be awarded within a week of the end of each class. The winning teacher for the season will be chosen randomly and awarded his or her check on the last Saturday of September. Any other questions?"

A female student raised her hand. "Exactly how much money did you win, anyway? And what are you going to do with it besides give it away in this contest?"

Angie smiled. "The amount of money I won would be the total lottery amount divided by twelve since there were a dozen of us in a pool who split the winnings. What I'm going to do with it besides running this contest is still undecided."

The red-haired fellow next to her spoke up. "Why don't you offer a contest for the best photo from this class instead of just having a random drawing? Seems like that would make more sense."

"Good question. My goal with this contest is to encourage more students and teachers to engage with the Mossy Point Folk School experience, not to foster competition among students, which would run counter to the folk school concept. Any other questions?"

Lee raised his hand. "How are you going to determine the winners? Throw names into a hat? Spin a roulette wheel? Toss darts at a board?"

"Great question. Thanks for asking. I want everyone to know that I will not personally pick any winners. An accounting firm has been hired to keep track of all the participating students and teachers and will randomly pick winners and issue the checks. Anyone else have a question?"

Steve raised his hand. "Are you going to pick a winner from the golf outing next week? Technically, it's not a class; there's no teaching; it's just a fundraiser."

"Thanks for bringing that up. If there are no more questions about the student and teacher contest, I'll move on to the fundraiser incentives. There are two events that are not classes: the golf outing next weekend and the fish boil on the first Saturday in July. For each of these, one ticket-holder attending the event will be chosen for a $5,000 cash award. You must be present to win, and the check will be presented on the spot. So get your tickets starting tomorrow at MossyPointFolkSchool dot com and show up! Tickets are limited for the golf outing and fish boil; first come, first served. More questions?"

Wayne Reed raised his hand. "Can an individual win more than once?"

"Absolutely! Does anyone else have a question?"

Silence reigned.

"Thank you all for coming, and good luck!"

Steve raised his hand. "Photography students, follow me!"

En masse, they migrated in the direction of the shoreline, abuzz with chatter about the contest.

Manuel headed for Angie, a wide smile on his face. "You looked and sounded great!" He grabbed her hand and raised it to his lips.

Carlos headed for his folks. "Hey, Dad, can we go home now and work on the Stude?"

"You bet, son." He wrapped one arm around his wife's waist and the other around his son's shoulders and guided them toward the Impala.

As Manuel held the front passenger door for Angie, her gaze sought Betty's. "See you at home, Mom."

Betty nodded. "I'll be there soon."

Lee approached her. "Looks like the reconciliation was successful."

"Angie glows. I'm so happy for her and Manuel." She gave a nod toward the folk school. "I'd better go and clean up."

Lee followed her. "Say, what are you doing the rest of the day?"

"How about a good old-fashioned cook-out with the kids? Got to make use of the ground beef and hot dogs I bought yesterday."

"Need a grill cook?"

"You're hired!"

CHAPTER 18

As Betty prepared a tray of burger patties for the grill, Angie worked alongside her arranging a selection of fresh veggies and dip.

"Great idea you had, Mom, for a cook-out. I can't remember the last time we grilled good old hamburgers and hot dogs right from the package. In California, our friends were either vegetarians or too sophisticated for plain fare."

"I'm glad you and Manuel are here to enjoy it with us." Betty placed a patty on the tray. As she withdrew her hand, Angie grabbed ahold of her left wrist.

"Mom, you're not wearing your rings. I've never known you to take them off, not even for kitchen work, and I'm sure I saw them on your finger a couple of days ago."

Betty drew a deep breath and met her daughter's gaze. "I'll be perfectly honest with you—"

Angie grinned. "It's Lee, isn't it? You and he are thinking of tying the knot, right? Time to put off the old and put on the new." She gently squeezed Betty's wrist and let go.

"Yes, and no. It's true my friendship with Lee is getting more serious, but that doesn't have anything to do with my missing rings." Betty flattened a lump of burger between her palms.

"What, then?" Angie's gaze drilled into her.

Betty set the patty on the tray and reached for more burger. After all the lectures she'd given Angie in past years about sticking to a budget and watching her discretionary spending, how could she admit she'd failed to follow her own advice? She drew a breath and gazed into Angie's questioning blue eyes.

"The fact is, my finances have been really stressed lately, first with some major home maintenance bills, then with Carlos coming to live here. After that, I paid the start-up expenses for the folk school. I ran really short of cash, and instead of going deeper into credit card debt, I pawned my rings."

Angie gasped. "Oh, Mom. I'm so sorry. Why didn't you say something? Not that I—"

"Bingo. You won't have any extra cash until the lottery payment comes in. I knew that. I did what I had to do. 'Nuff said."

Angie shook her head vigorously. "When my lottery payment comes in, we'll redeem your rings, and I'll reimburse you for every penny you've spent on Carlos since he showed up here."

"That would be wonderful!" Betty's heart soared. Movement outside the back window caught her attention. "Lee's headed this way. That means the grill is hot and he's ready to cook. And look at me. I'm only halfway done making patties."

Angie reached for some burger. "I'd better help you. Can't keep the cook waiting!"

oOo

"Mom, come look at this!"

Angie's voice floated from Carlos's room to the kitchen as Betty rinsed breakfast dishes and loaded the dishwasher the next morning. She turned off the water and headed down the hall.

Manuel and Angie were looking over Carlos's shoulder at the computer. He was on the PayPal page for Mossy Point Folk School and the four-figure amount showing in the account made her gasp. "This is great news, Angie!"

She beamed. "Twenty-five people signed up for classes overnight—or should I say we had twenty-five enrollments. It seems some of them signed up for more than one class."

Carlos glanced over his shoulder. "We sold tickets to the fish boil, too."

Manuel slipped his arm around Angie's waist and pulled her close. "You'll have all the tickets sold and classes filled in no time, *mi angelita*, with your press conference, newspaper article, and ad in the shopper guide."

oOo

That evening, with Manuel and Carlos in the garage tinkering with the Stude, and Angie working on the computer in her bedroom, Betty grabbed her Kindle, leaned back in her recliner, and began to read. She was starting to doze off when approaching footsteps and Angie's voice cut through her drowsiness.

"Mom, guess what? Loads more people signed up for classes today!" She glided buoyantly into the great room, her face lit with a smile as she came to a halt in front of Betty. "I'd say your money worries are over. Your folk school bank account is looking positively fat!"

Betty started to smile, and then a dreadful thought assailed her, making her gasp.

"Mom, what's the matter? You ought to be jumping up and down for joy. Instead, you look as if I just told you that the Grinch has stolen Christmas."

Betty pointed to the couch. "You'd better sit down. There's something I've been meaning to tell you."

"This sounds serious." She perched on the edge of the sofa.

Betty lowered the footrest of her recliner and gazed into Angela's narrowed blue eyes. "It could be, or I might be stewing over nothing. Do you remember Frank Schram?"

Angie nodded. "Vicky's father, old Schram the grump man—at least that's what us kids called him. What about him?"

"He's threatened to sue me."

"You're kidding!"

"I wish I were." Betty rehearsed the story in detail.

When she finished, Angie shook her head slowly from side to side. "What a lousy, rotten shame that he's putting you through all this worry when the blame for his troubles rightfully falls on *him*."

Betty shrugged. "It is what it is, and there's nothing more to do . . . except wait and pray."

Angie reached for Betty's hand. "Then we'd better do it—pray, that is. Lord knows you're already waiting." Angie wrapped her long fingers around Betty's hand and bowed her head. "God, it's me again, Angie. You know about the trouble Mom's having with Frank Schram. Why, Lord? Why would you let that cantankerous old coot do this to her? You've got to make him stop. That's all there is to it. Amen . . . and thanks!"

Betty couldn't help smiling. "I feel better already. You really tell it like it is, don't you?"

"Have you ever known me to be any different?" Angie's brow rose.

Betty shook her head. Now, if only God would answer her precocious daughter's petition.

CHAPTER 19

On the eighth day after the television interview, as Betty fried eggs for breakfast, Angie sang her way from her bedroom to the kitchen.

"For I'm a jolly good lady, for I'm a jolly good lady, for I'm a jolly good l-a-a-dy . . . 'cause I'm rich as the mint today!"

Carlos and Manuel, who were sitting at the counter sipping coffee, smiled and shook their heads.

Angie hugged Betty's shoulders. "Today's the day, Mom! The lottery money will magically appear in my account, and we'll be set for life!"

Betty smiled up at her. "You're sure?"

"That's what they told me after they validated my winnings. Just to make sure, I'm going to call the bank the minute they open up and get my account balance from a real person."

Carlos sipped his café con leche and set down his mug. "What time do they open, Mom?"

"Nine o'clock, noon our time." She checked her watch. "Pooh. Four hours to wait."

Manuel rose and demanded a good-morning hug and kiss, then held her loosely in his arms. "Can't you just look online, or call the automated teller and get the balance, *angelita*?"

"This account will never be accessible online. I'm not taking that kind of risk with the amount of money that will be on deposit. As for automated teller calls, they're okay for normal purposes, but I want to get it straight from a live human being this time." She stepped out of his embrace to grab the pot of coffee from the coffeemaker and fill a mug. "Then, I have to transfer most of it to my financial adviser's account for investment."

Carlos grumbled. "What about the Stude? I thought you were going to pay for parts?"

Angie waltzed over to him and rested her hand on his shoulder. "Fear not, my son. I shall keep a king's—make that queen's—ransom available for a shopping spree so that you, young prince, can drive to college in a finely restored chariot."

o0o

On the stroke of twelve noon, Angie commandeered the portable phone and sequestered herself in her bedroom to call her California bank.

Betty prayed while wiping off the shelves in the refrigerator. *Lord, let the lottery money be in her account like they promised.*

As Betty cleaned up the stovetop and oven, and Manuel and Carlos sat on stools at the kitchen counter studying the latest copy of *Vintage Truck*, several minutes passed. What could be keeping Angie? Surely it didn't take this long to get a balance on an account.

A bedroom door opened. Betty gazed down the hall.

Angie emerged from her room, stepped quickly toward the kitchen, and placed the phone in the charger. Then she pirouetted toward Manuel and Carlos, her hands held high and wav-waving while her feet did a happy dance.

"Whoohoo! We're going shopping! The lottery money is in my account and available for immediate expenditures!"

Manuel sprang from his stool, whisked her off her feet, and whirled her around.

When her feet touched down, she gazed up at him, brow raised. "How about lunch in Superior Bay, then shopping?"

He grinned, his even white teeth sparkling against the backdrop of his dark complexion. "Whatever you say, *mi angelita!*"

Carlos padded on bare feet toward his parents. "Mom, Dad, can we go to the auto parts store and order what we need for the old Stude?"

Manuel released Angie, his gaze on Carlos. "You bet, son! We're going to the Toyota dealership, too, and buy a Lexus."

Angie wrapped one arm about Manuel's waist and the other around Carlos. "Tell you what, fellows. While you two are ordering truck parts and shopping for a Lexus, Mom and I have a couple of stops to make; then we'll meet you at the Toyota dealer's. But first, we've got to eat." She turned to Betty. "Can you be ready in ten minutes?"

"I can be ready in five!"

"We'd better take two vehicles."

Manuel pulled keys from his pocket. "You ladies take the Impala. Carlos and I will take the truck, if that's okay. We'll meet you at Jose's Grill in . . . " he checked his watch " . . . forty minutes?"

Angie aimed both index fingers at him. "You're on! Let me get you the bank card." She hurried off to the bedroom, returning half-a-minute later and handing it to Manuel. "Do you remember the PIN I gave you?"

"I'll never forget it, *mi angelita*." He rattled off four numbers.

She chuckled. "Now, if I can get you to remember my birthday."

Manuel scowled. "I know your birthday. It's October sixteenth."

Betty winced.

Angie sighed, eyes looking heavenward.

"October eighteenth?" Manuel's brow rose.

Betty laughed. "At least if he thinks it's the sixteenth, he won't be late."

"Speaking of late," Angie headed for the hall, "I've got to get ready or we won't be at the restaurant in forty minutes."

oOo

A few minutes after two o'clock, Betty followed Angie out the door of Jose's Grill. Carlos and Manuel joined them on the sidewalk in front. Angie giggled as she wrapped her arm around Manuel's waist, evidently showing the effects of the two celebratory cocktails she'd consumed.

Manuel checked his watch, and then he gazed affectionately at Angie. "Meet you in a couple hours? Four o'clock at the Toyota dealer's?"

"Four o'clock."

He kissed her cheek and took off down the street with Carlos.

She watched them go and then offered her car keys to Betty. "You'd better drive. Bank and pawnshop! I've got to reimburse you for Carlos's expenses, and then we'll get your rings out of hock. After that," a grin wide as Superior Bay split her face, "shopping!"

At the bank, Angie arranged for a generous reimbursement to be instantly transferred into Betty's account. Betty took a deep, cleansing breath, expelling all her money worries as she exhaled.

At the pawnshop a few minutes later, the same middle-aged gentleman who had waited on Betty during her first visit greeted them from behind the counter. Even his pinstripe suit was the same.

"May I help you, ladies?" His focus settled on Angie and his smile grew a little larger. "I saw you on T.V., didn't I? Angela Martinez, lottery winner?"

Angie pointed both index fingers at him. "Bingo!"

"Congratulations, Mrs. Martinez. How may I help you today?"

"My mother and I are here to redeem her rings."

"Certainly." His gaze shifted to Betty. "Do you have the ticket?"

Betty dug into her purse for her wallet, pulled out the ticket, and handed it to him.

"Ah, yes. I'll be right back." He stepped into the room behind the counter.

Angie gazed down into the glass case, studied the jewelry displayed there, and pointed to a vintage multi-strand seed pearl necklace. "That's a beauty. It would go perfectly with my hot pink suit. What do you think?"

"I haven't seen your suit, but I do like the necklace. I've always favored pearls. So classy and versatile. But is it worth that price?"

The gentleman returned with the three rings and set them aside on a velvet pad. "May I show you something from the display case?" He slid the door open.

Angie pointed to the necklace. "That one."

"Ah, yes. This is a Guld Kedjan necklace from Sweden, vintage 1970 to 1980. I don't normally accept costume jewelry, but this is an exceptionally fine piece with great value." He laid it on the velvet pad and opened the clasp. "Care to try it on?"

Angie took it from him, turned toward a countertop mirror, and held it up against the opening of her scoop-neck T-shirt, covering the black diamond pendant she was wearing.

The pawnbroker smiled. "It looks lovely on you, ma'am."

She laid it on the pad next to the rings. "I'll take it."

He nodded. "And do you wish to redeem all three rings at this time?"

Angie glanced at the rings and then at Betty. "You pawned Dad's wedding ring, too?"

Betty shook her head. "It's Lee's. He contributed it to the cause."

Angie's eyes widened; then she focused on the pawnbroker. "Yes, sir. We wish to redeem all three rings."

"Very well." He totaled up the amount.

Angie handed him her bank card and then nudged Betty. "Put your rings on, Mom. Better wear Lee's, too, until you get home. Wouldn't want to lose it . . . again." She winked.

Betty slipped Lee's ring onto her left fourth finger. It swam on her. Would it even stay on behind her rings? She quickly slid on her wedding ring and engagement ring. They clinked against Lee's. Her mind flashed back to the day Harry had re-deemed their rings all those years ago, filling her heart with gratitude. Moisture welled in her eyes.

"Mom? Are you all right?"

She smiled. "Couldn't be better, thanks to you."

The pawnbroker placed Angie's bank card, receipt, and a pen on the countertop.

Angie signed the store receipt and then tucked the bank card and her copy of the receipt into her purse.

He carefully arranged the necklace in a jewelry box and slipped it into a small paper bag along with his business card. "Thank you very much, ladies. Come again. Our selection is always changing." He focused on Angie. "If you'd like to leave your phone number and a list of preferences, I can call you when something becomes available that I believe would be of interest to you."

Angie smiled. "Thanks, but no. I'm too much of a jewelry hound as it is."

He grinned. "Very well. You have a nice day now. And good luck with that contest for Mossy Point Folk School."

"Thanks!" She took Betty by the elbow. "We'd better get moving. We've got more stops to make before we meet up with the guys." In the car once again, she reached for her seat-belt. "What's the best jewelry store in town?"

Betty narrowed her gaze on Angie. "Jewelry store? But you just told the pawn broker you were too much of a jewelry hound."

"I'm not looking for jewelry, exactly. Manuel and I need new watches. Who sells fine timepieces?"

Betty shrugged. "The jeweler out at the mall on the highway, I suppose."

"Let's go there."

A few minutes later, they walked through the doors at the main mall entrance and down the long corridor past clothing stores, gift shops, a shoe store, and an electronics store, finally reaching the jewelry store.

Angie paused at the window, gazing at the watches. "Movado. Citizen. Shinola?" She turned to Betty. "Ever heard of a Shinola watch?"

Betty shook her head. "Who would want a watch made by a company named 'Shinola'? And who would name a company that? Back in my day, if you weren't very smart, someone would ask, 'Don't you know hit-with-an-s-in-front from Shinola?'"

"Hit-with-an-s-in-front?" Angie chuckled. "I like your alternative wording, Mom. But what should I expect from a vintage English teacher?"

"And I like yours. 'Vintage' is better than 'old' or 'retired'."

Angie stepped inside the store and Betty followed.

A petite, bottle-blonde woman of about fifty greeted them with a ruby-red smile. "May I help you, ladies?" As her gaze settled on Angie, her eyes widened and she drew a sharp breath. "You're Angela Martinez, the lottery winner! Oh, my! It must be so exciting, all that money, and now you're out shopping!" Her hand fluttered against her chest.

Angie smiled. "I've come to look at watches."

The woman drew a long breath as if to compose herself. "Watches? Of course. Anything in particular I can show you?"

"I'd like to see that Movado with the diamonds around the face."

"Certainly." The woman removed it from the display case and draped it over her wrist.

The price tag dangling from the metal watchband said $2395. Betty stifled a gasp.

Angie seemed not to notice. "Perfect. I'll take it!" She turned to Betty. "Need a new watch, Mom? My treat."

She shook her head and held out her Bulova-clad wrist. "The one the school gave me when I retired is working just fine and didn't cost me a cent—except for a quarter century in front of a classroom."

"You're sure you don't want a new one?"

"Positive. This one has sentimental value, of sorts."

Angie grinned, her gaze shifting to the clerk. "I'll need a gentleman's watch for my husband. Something practical and tough."

She chose a Movado watch with a stainless steel case and black rubber strap for Manuel. Two thousand dollars for a watch that had absolutely no precious metals or gems? When did recycled tires become so chic and expensive?

Angie wore her watch out of the store and handed the bag containing Manuel's to Betty. "Would you mind holding onto this for me? I'd like to visit that shoe store we passed earlier. I could use some new treads. How about you?"

Betty shook her head. "I'll hold the watch. You shop."

Betty kept a tight grasp on Manuel's watch and followed Angie to the shoe store, two clothing stores, the electronics shop, and a gift shop.

As Angie tried to decide between two collectible figurines, Betty checked her Bulova. "Angie, how's that new watch of yours working?"

She glanced at the diamond-studded face. "The watch is keeping good time. The wearer is oblivious. We'd better get a move on if we're going to meet the fellas at four."

CHAPTER 20

Betty pulled into the Toyota dealer's lot, parked the Impala next to her truck, and followed Angie into the showroom. Manuel and Carlos were already studying the finer points of a burgundy Lexus SUV with the aid of a salesman.

Manuel beckoned to Angie. "Come see. I think I've found our new car."

Angie cupped her hand around Betty's elbow. "Let's go see, Mom. It should be interesting."

Manuel introduced them to the salesman named Bob before he ushered Angie to the driver's seat.

"Look at this! It's got fourteen adjustments for the front seat plus heat for the seat and the steering wheel. Get in. See how you like it."

Angie slid onto the parchment leather seat and leaned back. "This *is* comfortable."

Carlos moved close. "It's got plenty of power, too, Mom. The paparazzi will never catch you. It does zero to sixty in seven-and-a-half seconds."

"Sounds like a speeding ticket." Angie winked.

Bob slid into the passenger seat and pointed to the electronic panel. "You've got four-zone climate control, an app suite for emergency services, dinner reservations, or movie tickets; front and side monitor cameras; a pre-collision system for added braking; and adaptive front lighting on curves."

Carlos opened the rear door and sat behind Angie. "I can play movies back here, Mom. There's a screen on the back of your seat."

Betty peered into the third row of seats. "There's another screen on the back of Carlos's seat. Looks like all the passengers will get the entertainment they want."

Her gaze caught sight of the price sticker on the rear window. The bottom line nearly made her gasp. She could find three suitable cars for the price of this one SUV.

Bob stepped out. "Why don't we take her for a test drive? If you give me just a minute, I'll move her out of the showroom."

In the parking lot, Manuel took the driver's seat, Angie the front passenger seat, Betty and Carlos the second row, and Bob a third-row seat. Betty leaned back into the well-padded leather, enveloped in its organic scent and surrounded by soft classical music.

Bob's voice rose above the string lullaby of *Clair de Lune*. "She's got VGRS—variable gear ratio steering—making her more stable at high speeds and requiring less rotation of the wheel at slow speeds; there's TRC, a traction control system; and VSC, vehicle stability control; the SRS . . . ."

oOo

Someone jostled Betty's arm. "Gram, wake up. We're back."

She opened her eyes to find Carlos grinning at her. Angie and Manuel were getting out of the Lexus. She checked her watch. Had she really been asleep for half an hour?

Manuel opened her door. "What do you think, *Isabelita*? Should we buy it?"

She shrugged. "That's up to you and Angie." With some effort, she left the embrace of her leather seat and refrained from expressing an opinion on price.

Bob climbed out of the third seat. "Come on into my office, everyone, and we'll talk."

Betty shook her head. "I think I'll go home and leave the wheeling and dealing up to the rest of you. Angie, should I count on you and Manuel and Carlos for supper?"

"Better not. See you later, Mom. And don't fall asleep on the drive home."

"I won't." She exchanged keys with Manuel, climbed into her truck, pulled her cell phone out of her purse, and speed-dialed Lee. He answered on the third ring.

"Hey, Betty. What's up?"

"What are you doing for supper?"

"I was just about to go over to Mossy Point Pizza and order an Italian sub. Where are you?"

"At the Toyota dealer's. I'm heading home now. I've got something to give you."

"A Lexus? Gee, that was thoughtful of you."

"Ha, ha. Angie and Manuel are dickering on a Lexus right now. They don't need my help, and they're not coming home for supper, so I thought maybe we could eat together."

"Should I order a salad for you? Do you want to eat at Mossy Point Pizza, or at your place, or at the falls, or where?"

"So many choices . . . salad is fine, and let's eat at your place."

He grumbled.

"What's the matter? Haven't you done your dishes lately?"

"I'm sure we did them the last time you were here."

"I don't even remember the last time I was there, it was so long ago. Get started on those dishes right now. I'll call in our order and pick it up on my way to your house."

"I'll reimburse you."

"No need. Angie fattened up my bank account today. I'm celebrating. See you in a bit." She called in their order for a sub and a salad, turned off her cell phone, dropped it into her bag, and headed for Mossy Point.

Forty-five minutes later, she pulled into Lee's long, winding driveway, taking the gravel two-track slowly so as not to jar the sub and salad. She loved this quarter-mile stretch of road thick with cedars on either side. Inhaling deeply of their scent, she released the cleansing breath slowly.

A doe followed by two spindly-legged fawns no more than a couple of weeks old skittered across the road a hundred feet in front of her. The sight put a smile on her face and gratefulness in her heart for the marvelous wonders God had created in the north woods.

She pulled to a stop in front of Lee's log home. He came bounding off the front porch as she stepped out of the truck.

"Dishes are done and the table is set." He grinned as he opened the passenger door and grabbed the bag of food. He peered into the storage area behind the seats. "Wow. Looks to me like you've done some heavy duty shopping."

"Carlos and Manuel bought some things for the Stude."

He nodded and led the way to the front door, holding it open for her as she stepped into the kitchen.

The place was neater than she'd seen it in years—glass canisters all in a row and sparkling clean, granite countertop polished to a shine, cherry cabinets wearing a patina and emitting a hint of lemon oil, and no dirty dishes in the sink. Even Joan hadn't kept things this tidy.

Lee set the bag on the counter and began to remove its contents. "Sandwich for me, salad for you. Did you say you had something to give me? I mean, besides supper?"

"Close your eyes and hold out your hand." She worked her rings off her finger and removed his. Making sure his eyes were still shut, she placed his ring in the palm of his hand.

He opened his eyes and blinked. "Thanks, Betty."

"No. Thank Angie."

He smiled. "See? I told you there wasn't much chance of our rings not being redeemed, you with your jewelry hound daughter who just happened to win millions." He set his ring on the granite countertop.

The gold circle blended in with the busy stone pattern. "Don't you think you should wear it? It's hard to even see it on this countertop. You could easily lose it."

He pulled a white saucer from the cabinet, set his ring in the indentation, picked up his sub and her salad, and headed for the dining table. "Say, how about some fishing after supper? I made a new lure I want to try out before I teach that fly-tying class this weekend."

Betty started to slip her rings back on her finger, paused, placed them with Lee's on the saucer, and joined him at the table. "Sure, we could go fishing. You've got a full class. Can't disappoint the students."

oOo

Lee's new lure worked like a miracle. Or maybe it was just a hungry school of large-mouth bass that passed their way because Betty's worms got an equal number of hits and together they hauled in enough for tomorrow's dinner.

Back at Lee's, she stood beside him in the fish shed dressing her share of the catch. Minutes later, they carried the fillets into the kitchen to wrap them in plastic. As they worked, his gaze strayed to the saucer where their three rings were clustered together.

With the fish all wrapped and stored in the refrigerator, Betty reached for her purse. "I'd better get home. You know how I hate driving after dark. Too many deer to freeze in the headlights."

"Should I bring the fish over tomorrow for supper and grill them for you all?"

"You bet! Angie, Manuel, and Carlos will love it, assuming they're home and not out tooling around the countryside in a brand new Lexus." She took her rings from the saucer, tucked them into the zippered change section of her wallet, and pulled out her keys.

Lee followed her outside and opened the driver's door of her truck. "Thanks for everything, Betty. The sub, going fishing, cleaning your catch . . . ." He kissed her briefly.

She set her purse on the seat and turned to gaze up at him. "You left one item off your list of thanks. Your ring."

" . . . and my ring. You really didn't have to redeem it, you know." He took her left hand in his, raised it to his lips, and brushed a kiss against her bare ring finger. "I notice you aren't wearing yours."

She looked up into his questioning blue eyes and shrugged. "Got used to going without, I guess."

He reached for her other hand and enveloped both of hers within his. "When I saw your rings with mine on that saucer, I thought . . . " His words were soft, his gaze wistful.

"Go on. Tell me what you thought."

"I'd better not say."

Betty rose on tiptoe and brushed a kiss against his lips. "Please tell me."

He slipped his arms gently about her. "I had this vision that one day soon we'd take our three rings to a jeweler and have them made into two new rings."

"Wedding rings?"

He nodded.

She wrapped her arms about his neck and smiled. "First, we have to get through this folk school season." *And avoid a lawsuit by Frank Schram* went unsaid. She pushed the thought from her mind and pulled Lee closer until their lips met, gently at first, and then the kiss deepened, sending tingles through every inch of her.

Their lips parted and he held her close, her cheek pressed against his chest, his chin resting atop her head. His heart pounded in her ear, syncopating the rhythm of her own. In her mind, she tossed the last shovelful of dirt over Harry's grave and his spirit rose, smiling down on her and Lee as it vanished into the heavens above.

She leaned back, her gaze meeting Lee's. "I'd better hit the road now, or I might just stay here all night."

He began to sing "Stay," a tune she recognized from the '50s. Tightening his embrace, he moved his feet in a slow dance. She couldn't remember the last time she'd danced. It wasn't with Harry. He'd never danced with her in the entire forty-five years she'd known him.

She easily followed Lee's lead, shuffling across the gravel driveway and around her truck, ending by the driver's door, right where they'd started. If she didn't step out of his embrace right now, she really *would* stay.

Smiling up at him, she pressed free of his touch and climbed into her truck. "See you tomorrow for supper. Thanks for the song and dance."

He leaned in her open window and kissed her again. "Tomorrow."

She drove away, watching him watch her in the rearview mirror as she fought the urge to stay.

o0o

A couple of weeks later, Betty returned home in late afternoon from a clean-up session at the folk school, parked her truck in the driveway, and headed for the mailbox.

"How much junk mail did I get today?" she asked herself as she strode down the driveway. Inside the box was a stack of solicitations along with a large catalog envelope addressed to Carlos. "McPherson College" was printed on the upper left corner with a Kansas address.

The pole barn doors were wide open, and Manuel and Carlos were bent over the engine of the Stude truck, their backs to her as they revved the motor. She headed straight for them, exhaust fumes nearly making her cough.

"Carlos!" she shouted above the noise.

The engine slowed to idle as he spun around to face her, dirt smudged on his cheek.

"The mailman brought you an envelope from McPherson College."

"Great! Let me see it!" He extended a grimy hand.

"Uh, maybe you'd better clean up a little."

"Here, son." Manuel offered him a container of orange hand cleaner and a relatively clean rag.

Carlos swiftly wiped his hands clean, grabbed the envelope, and ripped it open.

"What's McPherson College?" Betty asked. "I thought you were planning to attend Superior Bay Community College."

Carlos pulled out the catalog and tossed the envelope into the trash can. "I am. After that, I'm going to McPherson. They have the only Automotive Restoration Degree program in the country. Look here." He opened the catalog and began paging through while Betty and Manuel looked on.

She pointed to a photo. "Isn't that Jay Leno?"

"Sure is. He and *Popular Mechanics* sponsor a full scholarship for a sophomore student each year."

Manuel chuckled. "I guess you won't need that."

"I know. I think it's neat, though, that some kid gets a break. It costs over $30,000 a year to attend McPherson."

"How did you find out about this place?" Betty asked.

"Vintage Truck. I noticed their ad the day Dad and I were reading the magazine; then I went online and ordered this catalog."

"Seems like you're getting a little ahead of yourself. First, you've got to get your GED. How's your review coming? Did Janna help you with math?"

"Sure did. I'll be ready to take the test next month. Do you think we can get a test date in . . . say . . . three weeks?"

"I'll look into it."

Carlos handed her the catalog. "Better take this inside. It will just get ruined out here. Would you please put it in my room?"

"Sure." She slipped it under the stack of junk mail, turned to go, and then spun around. "I almost forgot to ask. How's your work coming on the Stude?"

Manuel flashed a bright white smile. "Carlos is doing great! He'll have her running and looking like new real soon."

Carlos gazed admiringly at his father. "Couldn't do it without you, Dad. You taught me everything I know about auto mechanics."

Manuel punched Carlos playfully in the shoulder. "Back to work, kid. Got to get that new belt on."

They bent over the engine again.

"I'll see what I can rustle up for supper. Will Angie be home in time to eat with us?"

Manuel peeked out from under the hood. "Almost forgot. She said to tell you not to bother cooking. She's bringing something home from Zoe's. She'll be here by six."

"Thanks." Betty backed away, her heart light at the scene of father and son working so well together, and the evidence that Carlos was taking the long view of his need for education.

oOo

A few days later, Betty arrived at the folk school early to help Patsy set up for the beaded moccasin class. As she walked through the door, her first glimpse of Patsy took her breath away. She was wearing a striking, beaded buckskin dress. Her blue-black hair formed one long braid that draped over her shoulder, and about her forehead was a beaded head band. On her feet, she wore beaded moccasins like those she would teach her class to make.

"Patsy, you look beautiful!"

She offered a shy smile. "Thank you."

Betty joined her at the table where she was setting out supplies, and she handed her the roster listing the registered students. "I've been looking forward to this class ever since you volunteered to teach. I'm really eager to make myself a new pair of cozy moccasins to wear when cold weather sets in."

Patsy studied the class roster. "I'm really glad you'll be in the class. I don't recognize the names of any of the other students." She set the paper aside and arranged pieces of deer skin, artificial sinew, and leather needles on the table.

Betty laid out squares of polar fleece for the lining and tightly woven woolen fabric for the vamps.

A truck roared to a stop in front of the building. Couldn't be Thad or Janna. The muffler was way too loud. Betty peered out the window. An older blue pickup truck was parked in front. The driver's door opened and Arthur, from the Ojibway community, got out. His shiny black hair was slicked back into a ponytail that was tied with a leather thong, and his black T-shirt bore the logo of the Ojibway casino.

No sooner had he slammed the door of his truck than Steve pulled up alongside. His motor stuttered to a stop and he emerged, camera in hand.

Patsy gasped. "What are those two doing here?" Her dark brows narrowed and the color deepened in her olive cheeks.

A moment later, the two men entered the building.

Before Betty could utter a word of greeting, Arthur addressed Patsy.

"I've got to talk to you!"

"Not now, Arthur. I'm preparing to teach." She turned her back to him and fussed with the supplies on the table.

He grasped her shoulder and turned her around. "It's important, Patsy!"

Steve snapped a picture, his flash exploding in their faces.

Patsy blinked, pushed Arthur's hand away, and scowled at Steve. "Don't you have something better to do than waste your camera battery on a photo you'll have to delete?"

"But it's evidence of this guy harassing you!"

"*Harassing* me?" She shook her finger in his face. "*You're* the one who's harassing me."

Betty stepped forward. "You heard her, Steve. This is no time for photos. Why don't you wait until the students arrive and class is underway, and then keep Patsy out of your viewfinder."

He shrugged, wandered to the other side of the room, and took a seat at the empty work table.

Arthur spoke again. "Patsy, I mean it. I really need to talk to you."

Her gaze locked with his. "Not now. I'm preparing for class. The students will be here soon. I need to give them my full attention."

"*I'm* one of your students. Don't *I* deserve your attention?"

Her eyes widened. "I didn't see your name on the roster."

"I signed up under an assumed name. I've got a confirmation to prove it." He pulled a printout from his back pocket.

She read it and chuckled. "So *you're* 'Justin Thyme'. When I saw that name, I thought, 'Who would name their kid Justin Thyme?'" She handed the confirmation back to him. "Justin, your time is out until we take a mid-morning break. Go have a seat until class starts." She pointed to the table where Steve was sitting.

Arthur shuffled across the room and sat at the table opposite Steve.

Betty approached Patsy and spoke under her breath. "Are you okay? I can boot both those guys out if you want."

She shook her head. "Just stay close during break. Arthur and I have been through some really bad times in the past. That's why I moved to Mossy Point. I didn't want him to know where I was—didn't want to be in any pictures that would end up in the paper or online. Then Arthur improved and my folks said it was safe to bring him here when we did the fire cleanup. But I still don't trust him. As for Steve, I know he means well, showing up to take photos for the folk school website. I suppose I don't have a reason to avoid exposure anymore, but still . . . ." She chewed her lip.

Betty's heart melted. "Don't worry. I'll be with you every second."

Within minutes, students began to arrive. Betty checked them in while Patsy handed out name tags.

Patsy called the class to order and described the process of making beaded moccasins, then invited the students to visit the supply table and take what they needed back to the work table.

Arthur was the last to find what he needed and return to his seat. When the sewing began, he fumbled with his needle and artificial sinew. Was he hoping for extra attention from the teacher?

Steve took a few photos and said he was heading off to the golf course.

At half-past ten, Patsy announced a ten-minute break and encouraged students to wander outside, where the summer sun sparkled off brilliant blue waves.

Betty stood and stretched, longing to head out the door. But Arthur remained at the table, so she sat and added more stitches to her moccasin.

Patsy pulled out the chair beside Arthur, sat down, and eyed his unstitched moccasin. "Looks like you need some help."

Arthur lifted Patsy's chin until their gazes met. "You've already helped me . . . when you left the reservation. You saved my life when you did that . . . put me at rock bottom. That's when I decided to turn my life around. No more drugs. No more drinking." He took a deep breath. "That's why I signed up to take this class—to tell you that. I should have told you sooner but . . . I wanted to wait until I'd been clean for a year." He gazed down at the deer skin he'd been struggling with. "As for this class, I don't think you're ever going to be able to teach me how to make a pair of moccasins." He pushed his chair away from the table and stood.

Patsy sprang to her feet, her hand on his wrist. "Arthur, you just give me a chance, and we'll see what happens." She gestured toward his unfinished moccasin.

They sat down, heads together as Patsy demonstrated the whip stitch.

Warmth radiated through Betty. Perhaps the moccasins would mark a step in the right direction for Arthur and Patsy's relationship.

CHAPTER 21

Two weeks later, at the Independence Day fish boil, Karen ladled a chunk of whitefish, two new red potatoes, and three small onions onto Betty's plate. Doris drizzled butter over the top and added a lemon wedge. Betty picked up a knife and fork, bundled in a napkin, and a cup of lemonade from a nearby table. The buttery aroma wafted up on the gentle Lake Superior breeze and Betty inhaled deeply.

"Mmm. Thanks, ladies! Haven't tasted fish boil in . . . I don't remember when." She nodded toward the lake, its tiny waves shimmering beneath a brilliant blue sky and full sun. "At least we got good weather for our event."

Karen grinned. "I said a special prayer. 'God, ya gotta come through for the fish boil. No leaks, no drips, just clear skies. And one more thing,' I says. 'Can ya work it out so's my ticket wins the drawing? I'll cut ya in for ten percent, I promise.'"

Betty chuckled. "He heard you about the weather. We'll see about the winning ticket. Angie said her accountant will be here at two to audit the drawing and award the check to the winner."

Steve Taylor stepped up, camera aimed their way. "Smile, ladies; you're on Candid Camera." The camera clicked and he reviewed the shot. "Excellent! Except for one thing, Karen. I heard what you said about your deal with God for the five thousand dollars, and I just want you to know you're not winning the money. *I* am."

"Oh, yeah? Did ya get that straight from God, a voice from heaven? 'Steve Taylor, I've been watchin' you. You've been a good boy and I'm gonna reward ya with five thousand bucks at the fish boil drawing'?"

Steve grinned. "You must be a prophet. That's exactly what happened. Gotta go shoot some more pictures. Save some fish for me, Karen."

"Yeah, with five thousand on the side. *Not!*"

Betty chuckled and turned away to look for Lee among the dozens of folks who'd gathered for the fish boil. She spotted him supervising the kettle where Patsy was serving. As she drew near, Wayne approached her. His gaze darted in the direction of the campground and back to her. "Hate to be the bearer of bad news on this fine day, but Frank Schram is headed this way."

She glanced over her shoulder. Sure enough, Frank was pulling his four-wheeler off to the side of the road near the folk school. Her stomach clenched. "Thanks for the warning, I think."

Wayne nodded, adjusted his Packers cap, and took off.

As she approached Lee, she pasted on a smile. "Can you tear yourself away to eat with me?"

His eyes sparkled. "Sure thing."

Patsy fixed him a plate of fish, potatoes, and onions smothered in butter. He grabbed silverware and lemonade, and then he led Betty to one of the extra picnic tables Thad had hauled in for the event.

She bowed her head for a moment of silent prayer. When she opened her eyes, Steve snapped a picture of her and Lee and then moved on to capture a shot of the family at the next table.

Lee took a bite of fish, stared past her toward the campground, and scowled. "Frank Schram's here, the old coot. Probably hoping to cash in on five thousand dollars." He speared a potato and swirled it in butter.

She took a bite of her whitefish. Its flavor was tainted by the acid in her mouth. She swallowed some lemonade and tried the potato, but it was no use. Her appetite had gone AWOL.

Lee's gaze moved from his plate to hers. "What's the matter? Karen's kettle of fish spoiled? Should've taken some from Patsy's kettle. It's perfect." He tucked a sizeable portion of whitefish into his mouth and chewed. Then his face crumpled and he swallowed. "Frank's coming to join us."

The old man approached with the aid of a four-pronged cane and sat down next to Betty without invitation.

She turned to him. At least he'd shaved and put on clean clothes. She forced a smile. "Frank, why don't you join us for some fish boil?"

"You blind or just plain stupid? I already done that, didn't I? I'm sittin' right here next to ya and this here's a fish boil, ain't it?"

Lee stiffened. "What's your point, Frank? If you've come here to make trouble—"

"Dang right I come here to make trouble! I'm gonna sue the pants off you people. Got me a 'tingency lawyer and a bulletproof case." He angled toward Betty. "Good thing that daughter o' yours won herself a pot of money 'cause there ain't gonna be none left in *your* account when I'm done."

Betty laughed. "You're too late, Frank. I already spent my money on start-up costs for the folk school."

"Well, the state ain't broke."

Lee leaned forward. "Oh, yes it is. Why do you think we started this folk school, anyway? Because the state's in deep financial doo-doo and was going to close this park at the end of the season. Didn't you see the article in the paper back in April? Or haven't you learned to read yet?"

"You son-of-a—"

"Beautiful woman." Lee smirked. "Thanks for the compliment, Frank. I know you didn't mean it that way, but that's how I'm going to take it. Now, you'd better go and get some fish boil, and be sure to throw your ticket into the bowl for the five-thousand-dollar drawing, 'cause that's the only money you can hope to get from the folk school." He came around the table and lifted Frank by the elbow.

Frank turned to Betty. "This silly folk school won't last another season, no matter how many millions of dollars that gal o' yours won. Money can't buy a good reputation, and when word gets out you're bein' sued, folks won't have nothin' to do with your school." He reached for his cane. "First of November. That's the day my lawyer says I can file a suit for a personal injury accident. You'll be hearing from me. I'll get what's due me, just you wait and see."

Lee sighed. "I have no doubt you'll get your due, and it won't be a fortune from an ill-conceived lawsuit. It'll be a plate of fish boil if you've got a ticket."

"'Course I got a ticket."

As they headed toward the fish kettle, Betty drew a deep breath and let it out slowly, releasing the angst Frank had stirred up.

Steve slid onto the bench beside her, his brows furrowed. "Did I hear right? Is Frank serious about suing you because of that stupid fall he took?"

"Evidently."

Steve slammed his fist against the table. "Why that slimy, money-grubbing . . . aren't you going to do anything?"

"What can I do? If he wants to file a lawsuit, I can't stop him."

Steve's gaze held hers, a light flickering in his lentil brown eyes. "You're right. You can't stop him, and maybe I can't, either, but I can certainly try."

"What are you getting at?"

His focus shifted to his camera. "Can't say. You just have to trust me."

Her spine tingled. "Don't make matters worse than they already are with Frank."

Steve threw his head back and let out a high-pitched hoot. "The man's about to sue you. On November first, that is. There's no way I can make things any worse than that." He rested his hand on Betty's arm and locked his gaze on hers. "Listen, Frank is nothing but a snarly, law-breaking, stupid old man. You're the savior of Mossy Point. I'm going to do everything in my power to make sure your reputation never suffers from the filing of a frivolous lawsuit by Frank Schram." He squeezed her arm gently. Then he rose and strode off toward Karen's fish kettle, pausing halfway there to pull a comb from his back pocket and run it through his hair.

Steve Taylor, a white knight, coming to her defense? The thought boggled her mind. What could he possibly be planning? She prayed it wasn't something illegal or immoral.

Carlos and Janna approached her, smiles on their faces and full plates in their hands.

"Hey, Gram, you look like you could use some company."

"I sure could. Have a seat, kids."

Carlos sat across from her. Janna, wearing a park T-shirt and khakis, slid onto the bench beside her.

Betty turned to Janna. "I see from the way you're dressed, you must be working today."

Janna nodded. "Got to get back to work as soon as I finish eating. I'll come by at two to see who wins the drawing, though. Got to be present to win." She tucked a forkful of fish into her mouth.

Carlos glanced at Betty. "If she wins the drawing, she'll put it toward tuition and books."

Janna grinned. "Yeah. Unlike you, I've got to pay my own way. Work at the park, win a drawing, do whatever . . . ."

Betty smiled. "I've known you since you were a little girl and there's one thing I'm sure of. You're a determined young lady and you'll come out just fine whether you win this drawing or not."

"Thanks, Mrs. Hanson." Her focus returned to Carlos, and as they bantered, Betty's gaze shifted to the fish kettle. Lee was carrying a plate for Frank, leading him toward a table with a single occupant, a much younger fellow with blond hair. Where had she seen him before? Oh, yes, it was right here, a couple of months ago. He came to the park with Mr. Engstrom when she and the others were fixing up the building. Chip Landers.

Lee returned to sit across from her, stabbed at his whitefish, and tucked it into his mouth. "Mmm. Cold fish boil. Still good, though."

"I see you paired up Frank with Chip Landers for a dining partner."

Lee's brows narrowed. "Who?"

"That blond fellow across from Frank. He visited the folk school with Mr. Engstrom when we were getting it ready to open. Don't you remember?"

He nodded. "I'd forgotten about him until you reminded me."

Janna turned to Betty. "I've seen that blond fellow in the park quite a lot the last couple of days. Some other fellows were with him, and they were walking all over the place. I even joked with them, asked them if they were geocaching and needed help. They weren't. Then I said they at least should have brought a metal detector to make all that walking worth their time. They laughed. Said they were thinking of renting out several campsites for a group campout and wanted to pick out the best area."

Betty lifted her brow. "What kind of group?"

"Didn't say. When I asked Thad if he's had any inquiries about group reservations, he said, 'No'."

Lee speared an onion. "Probably some scout leaders looking for a new camping experience for their troop."

oOo

"Ladies and gentlemen, five minutes until we pick the five-thousand-dollar winner." Angie, megaphone to her mouth, spoke from atop a picnic table a few yards from Betty. Manuel gazed up at her from ground level, an unmistakable look of pride and admiration sparkling in his dark eyes. Beside him stood an accountant with the glass bowl that held the tickets. Off to the side, Ursula Carlyle aimed her TV camera at them.

Betty remained seated while the fish boil guests migrated toward Angie: Carlos and Janna, Frank, Karen, the Reeds, Chip, Steve, Patsy, Thad, and a few dozen people she didn't know. She rose and followed the crowd to stand on the fringe next to Lee.

Angie spoke again. "Drum roll, please, while my accountant draws the winning ticket."

Carlos rapped his palms on the wooden table as if playing a Congo drum.

Manuel held the bowl above the accountant's head. He reached inside, stirred the tickets thoroughly, withdrew a green slip of paper, and passed it to Angie.

"And the winner is . . . " She held the green slip at arm's length and squinted. "I should have brought my reading glasses, but I think I can make it out. The winner is Chip Landers."

"Whoohoo!" Chip's yell cut through the air.

A smattering of applause broke out.

"Come on over here, Chip, and claim your check."

Angie handed the winning ticket back to her accountant. With a broad-tip marker, he penned Chip's name onto a two-foot-by-three-foot mock check. The two of them climbed atop the table beside Angie to pose with her and the check.

Angie gazed into Ursula's camera lens. "And there you have it, folks, the winner of the fish boil drawing here at Mossy Point Folk School." She turned to Chip. "What do you plan to do with your money, Chip?"

He smiled, his teeth gleaming. "I'm going to buy myself a new set of golf clubs and try them out at St. Andrews in Scotland."

"Need a caddy?" Steve called out. "I'll do it for free."

Chuckles rippled through the crowd.

"I'm serious!" Steve claimed.

Angie skewered him with a sharp look.

He aimed his camera at her.

She turned to Chip with a smile wide as a putting green. "Best wishes. I hope you get a hole-in-one. Now, you come back again soon to Mossy Point Folk School, ya hear? And bring your friends."

"Will do."

As the three climbed down, a gravelly voice rang out.

"Fraud!"

Frank Schram.

Ursula aimed her camera at him.

The crowd around him backed away.

He looked straight into the lens, jabbing the air with his index finger. "It's rigged! The drawing's rigged!"

"Liar!" Lee countered.

Betty shook her head. "Let it go. Angie's accountant will deal with him."

"He's got no right!" Color rose in Lee's cheeks as he started toward Frank.

Betty put her palm out. "Let me handle this." She approached Frank, reaching him just ahead of Thad, Manuel, and the accountant.

"Frank, you're in for a lawsuit if you make one more claim like that. It's called slander, and you won't stand a chance against Angie's accountant and lawyer. Ursula's got you on camera."

"You're one to talk about a lawsuit. Wait till I file mine! It'll be the end of you and this park, or my name ain't Frank Schram!"

Thad took him by the elbow. "The fish boil's over. You go on home now."

Frank shot him a smoldering look. "You kickin' me outta this park?"

"You can leave, or you can go with me to the county jail. I'm the law inside the park, and those are your choices."

Frank grumbled and limped away.

oOo

A couple of weeks later, while Betty was at the kitchen desk going over her credit card statement, the phone rang. She grabbed the portable handset and checked caller I.D. Carlos's cell number displayed. He must have finished his final sitting for the GED test at Superior Bay Community College.

"Carlos, how did it go?"

"Great! I got way more points than I needed to pass."

"Congratulations! I'm so proud of you! Did you call your mother?"

"I tried. Her phone must be off. I left her a message."

"She's probably at the folk school helping Zoe set up for the Pizza and Italian Cuisine night tomorrow."

"Oh, yeah. Listen. I'm going to hang out here a while and fill out the admissions application. Did you know I have to take another test before they'll let me start classes? Some kind of placement test."

"It's just to see whether you need any help with math, reading, or English. Nothing to worry about. When will you be home?"

"Not sure. I need some new duds. Next week I'm treating Janna to dinner at the Allumette, payback for helping me study. They won't let me in without a shirt, tie, and jacket. Mom gave me her credit card and said to find something at Christopher Banks."

"Have fun. See you later." Betty clicked off. She drew a deep breath and blew it out, releasing the worry and tension that had built over the past couple of months regarding Carlos's education. "Thank you, Lord. Carlos is finally back on track. Now, if we can only keep him there."

CHAPTER 22

Two months later, Betty slid the folk school check into the zippered pocket of her purse, slung the pouch-shaped bag over her shoulder, and grabbed the plastic bag containing the XXXL T-shirt she'd had specially made for Mr. Engstrom. She could hardly wait to see his face when she showed him the check that would put Mossy Point State Park in the black for the very first time in its existence. A turtle would fly today, if only on the logo of the T-shirt.

Angie came down the hall from her bedroom, car keys in hand, and checked her watch. "We'd better get a move on if we're going to stop by Mr. Engstrom's office and still get to our meeting with Eva Underwood on time. Got the T-shirt and the check?"

Betty held up the plastic bag and her purse. "Right here. Let's go." She followed Angie out the garage door and got into the passenger seat of the Lexus SUV.

As Angie drove out of the village, she flicked a side glance at Betty. "I'm thinking I might need to make some changes regarding the incentives for students and teachers next year."

"You mean you won't be offering huge cash prizes?"

"I mean those prizes had some unintended consequences."

Betty chuckled. "Yeah, like people signing up for my writing retreat who couldn't complete a sentence."

"And folks showing up for the birdwatching hike who didn't know a sparrow from a robin, didn't care, and were rude to Doris and the students who *did* care."

Betty pondered the dilemma. "There must be a way to weed out applicants who are only there for the prize money and have no commitment to the learning process."

Angie nodded. "Let me know if you come up with a solution."

"That will take some planning. Main thing is, we have the money to put the park in the black and keep it open."

"Thank God for that." Angie tuned to love songs on the satellite radio.

Betty reclined the cushy leather seat back, closed her eyes, and relaxed to the quiet melodies of Burt Bacharach.

o0o

"Wake up, Sleeping Beauty. Time to go see Mr. Engstrom and Eva and save Mossy Point State Park."

Angie's voice woke Betty from light sleep. She yawned, grabbed her purse and the plastic bag with the T-shirt, and followed Angie to the front entrance of the state office building. In no time, security issued temporary I.D.s, and sent them on their way. If Lee had been here, he'd have been humming "We're in the Money" and maybe even doing a little jig. Too bad he was in Michigan at his daughter's.

Mr. Engstrom's secretary, an older woman about Betty's age, greeted them with a smile the moment they entered the General Land Office suite. A sign on her desk identified her as

Shirley Ovesen. "Good morning, ladies. What can I do for you today?"

Betty held up the plastic bag. "Shirley, I have a Mossy Point Folk School T-shirt for Mr. Engstrom. I thought I'd drop it off on our way to Eva Underwood's office. We're going to present her with a check to put Mossy Point State Park in the black for this year and keep the park from closing."

"Congratulations! Bill—my husband—would be royally pi . . . put off if Mossy Point State Park closed. He loves to hunt and fish there."

Betty chuckled. "Him and tens of thousands of others who come through the park gate each year."

"Mr. Engstrom is in his office. You can go on in."

Angie opened Mr. Engstrom's door. He was leaning back in his chair, feet on his desk, hands linked behind his neck. He swung his feet to the floor, placed his palms against his desktop, and grunted as he slowly pressed himself to a standing position.

"Mrs. Hanson, good to see you." His focus shifted abruptly to Angie. "And this must be your daughter. Saw you on TV. Pleased to meet you." His minimal smile and quick check of his watch said otherwise.

Angie extended her hand, receiving a fingertip handshake. "Nice to meet you, Mr. Engstrom. We'll be brief." She nodded to Betty.

Her gaze flitted to the bookcase. The turtle she'd seen last spring was still there, as inanimate as ever. She focused on Ray. "Back in April, I told you the turtle would fly." Pulling the XXXL T-shirt out of the bag, she added, "This is for you. Wear it in good health." She unfolded it for him to see.

He gazed at the shirt, the corners of his mouth creeping upward. "Very clever."

She folded it so the flying turtle still showed and set it on the papers strewn across his desk.

Mr. Engstrom stared down at the shirt. "You really shouldn't have, Mrs. Hanson. You didn't need to do this."

Betty drew a breath to tell him she really *did* need to do it, but Angie spoke first.

"We won't take any more of your time, Mr. Engstrom. Thanks for seeing us."

He nodded. "Thanks for stopping by, ladies. You have a nice day, eh?"

Betty grinned. "We're having a *great* day!" She followed Angie out the door and closed it behind them.

Shirley looked up from her computer screen. "Good-bye, ladies. Thanks for coming in."

Angie paused. "Our pleasure. Have a nice day!"

"'Bye, Shirley." Betty stepped into the hall.

Angie closed the suite door behind her. "On to Eva Underwood's office." Angie led the way, pausing at the door.

Eva was on the phone but quickly concluded her call. "Mrs. Martinez, Mrs. Hanson, come in."

As Betty approached Eva's desk, she pulled the check from her purse. "Here's the money to put Mossy Point State Park in the black for this fiscal year."

Eva took it from her and read it, her expression solemn. "Thank you for bringing it in."

Betty pulled a folded paper from her purse and opened it. "Here's a letter to go with the check. Since checks always have to be made out to the State of Superior, it specifies that the money is to go into the Mossy Point State Park account.

Now, you have no reason to close the park." She set it on Eva's desk.

Eva placed the check on top of the letter and darted a glance at her watch.

Angie stepped back. "We won't keep you. Thanks for giving us a moment of your time."

Eva's phone rang. She grabbed it with one hand and waved good-bye with the other.

As Betty followed Angie out of the suite, a thick gray cloud descended within. Why was Eva so complacent? A major milestone had been accomplished, and she'd responded with complete indifference.

In the hallway, Angie turned to her. "Where to now, Mom?"

"Is it too early to go to lunch?"

Angie checked her watch. "Two diamonds before noon. Cocktail hour. How about the Hotel Amour? They have a great dining room and a wonderful cocktail menu—even if you're a non-drinker. We'll toast to putting Mossy Point State Park in the black."

"As long as you're picking up the tab."

"You're on."

A few minutes later, the maître d' showed them to a table overlooking Lake Superior. He handed each of them a leather-bound menu. A waitress took their drink orders—mulled cider for Betty and a cider cocktail for Angie. Outside the picture window, a brisk northwest wind had whipped the waves into rollers with extensive whitecaps, and the cooling temperatures had darkened the azure of summer to a fall-like shade of cobalt. A line of heavy clouds near the horizon hinted at snow.

Fall wouldn't even start until tomorrow, and already the white stuff was a real possibility.

The waitress delivered the drinks. "Are you ready to order, or should I come back later?"

Angie smiled up at her. "What do you recommend?"

"The daily special is a good choice—tips of beef with asparagus and rice pilaf."

"Sounds good."

The waitress turned to Betty. "And for you, ma'am?"

"Chef's salad, no cheese, no croutons, no dressing, lemon juice on the side."

"I'll be back with your orders in a few minutes."

Angie removed a swizzle stick skewered with apple chunks from her cocktail glass and raised the goblet. "To us, and to Mossy Point Folk School. May we all live long and endeavor to make Mossy Point State Park an educational and recreational experience for all who visit."

Betty clinked her glass with Angie's and took a sip of her mulled cider. The hot, spicy liquid with a hint of orange warmed her, as did Angie's words.

Across the table from her, Angie took a sip of her drink and set it down to gaze out the window. A faraway look played on her features.

"You look lost in the clouds. Do you see snow in them?"

Silent moments lapsed and then Angie shifted her focus to Betty. "Sorry. Did you say something?"

"I said you look lost in the clouds. Do you see snow in them?"

Her gaze darted to the clouds and back to Betty. "Now that you mention it, I suppose so. I wasn't thinking about that at all. I was thinking about our meeting with Eva. I hope she puts that check into the Mossy Point State Park account and not some general fund where it could be spent on a marina without boats at the other end of the state."

Betty sighed. "Eva may not be a cheerleader, but we have no control over what she does, so why worry?"

"But what if—"

"—she puts the money into some other account? It's only a problem if a decision is made to close the park because they didn't cover their expenses. Then we'll go after Eva with a dart gun. Until then, put it from your mind and think about where we're going after lunch. Did you say Carlos needed new duds for winter?"

Angie grinned. "You're pandering to my shopping addiction."

"Works every time."

oOo

The next Saturday morning, Lee stopped by to take Betty to the folk school building for one final clean-up. She unlocked the door and Lee followed her inside, standing beside her as they gazed about the nearly empty classroom.

He reached for her hand, giving it a squeeze. "Seems like we were just at your house for the first meeting to get this folk school organized. Who knew things would turn out the way they did?"

Betty nodded. "Thanks to Angie, every class filled up and twenty people won thousands of dollars they wouldn't otherwise have."

He smiled. "I thought Steve was going to wet his pants when Angie drew his name as the winning teacher."

Betty laughed. "That possibility occurred to me when I saw him dancing around this room like a madman last weekend. I hope he decides to put his winnings toward a new vehicle, instead of the golfing trip he said he wants to take. Goodness knows he needs a reliable car a lot more than a trip around the country to chase a white ball across the grass."

Lee reached for her other hand and drew her closer. "Now that you've put the park in the black, have you given any thought to setting a wedding date?"

"November, end of the month. I'll know by then what's going to happen with that lawsuit Frank's been threatening to file. If I'm in a big legal mess, we'll postpone the wedding until it's settled." She tried to release her hands.

Lee tightened his grip. "Lawsuit or not, marry me at the end of November, Betty. I'm going to watch out for you no matter what. I'd prefer to do it as your husband."

His earnestness tore at her heart and brought moisture to her eyes. "I can't promise you that, for both our sakes. But I can promise you this—after we finish here, we can take our rings to a jeweler and get him to design two new ones. That way, they'll be ready and waiting, no matter what day we say 'I do'."

His lips met hers briefly. "It's a date. Now let's get cracking here so we can get to the fun stuff. I'll vacuum the floor, you decide what to store at your place for the winter, and set it by the door." He began whistling "I'm Getting Married in the Morning," and danced a jig all the way to the broom closet.

o0o

On the drive to Superior Bay, Lee hummed "Love is Here to Stay" and then shot a side glance at Betty. "Have you given any thought to the design of your new wedding ring?"

She shrugged. "No. have you?"

"I thought I'd have mine engraved with fish all the way around, mouth to tail fish in a chain. What do you think?"

Was he serious? "What kind of fish?"

"Bass. Or maybe perch. And for your ring, how about a flying turtle top and center with a tiny little diamond for his eye?"

"Fish? A flying turtle? How perfectly ugly! Not to mention that they symbolize our individuality rather than our connectedness." She sighed.

He grinned and reached for her hand. "I was just kidding. But now I'm going to be serious. I was thinking the other day about how you love trillium. Why don't we have your ring designed with a trillium blossom and mine engraved with trillium leaves running around the outside?"

She squeezed his hand. "Now *that* idea I really like."

oOo

On Monday afternoon, as Betty stood at the open refrigerator contemplating what to make for supper, Angie came into the kitchen carrying her computer. She set it on the counter and pointed to the screen. "Look at the headlines on the *Superior Bay Journal* site today."

Betty stepped in front of the screen and read. "'Five State Parks Up for Bids. Mossy Point for Sale.'" Her heart skipped a beat as her gaze met Angie's. "Can't be. We were in Eva's office a week ago Monday with the money to keep Mossy Point open."

"As of yesterday, our check hadn't cleared the account. I'll call the bank again and see if that's still the case." She punched in numbers on the portable phone, waited, punched in more numbers, shook her head, and set the phone in the charger. "The check is still out."

A rock plummeted to the pit of Betty's stomach. "How could Eva have let this happen?"

"I just knew something wasn't right." Angie paced. "Her whole attitude didn't seem right when we were in her office with the check. It was as if she was going through the motions but they didn't mean anything. You'd think she'd have been jumping up and down for joy knowing one of the state's perennially unprofitable parks finally ran in the black, but no. She barely gave us the time of day." Angie marched back to the phone. "Do you have Eva's number?"

The phone rang. Angie checked caller I.D. "It's a State of Superior number." She clicked the "Talk" button. "Betty Hanson's residence . . . . Yes she is. May I say who is calling? . . . " She offered the phone to Betty. "It's Eva Underwood."

Betty punched the speaker button. "Hello, Eva. I've got you on speaker so Angie can hear you, too. What's this about Mossy Point State Park closing? She showed me the *Journal* headline. We haven't had time to read the article yet."

"I was hoping to reach you before the news came out, but this has been a mighty hectic day. I'm sorry about Mossy Point State Park, Betty. The state has decided to sell the unprofitable, least visited parks in order to better manage the rest."

Warmth flooded Betty's cheeks. "Unprofitable? A week ago, I gave you the check to put Mossy Point State Park in the black. Why haven't you deposited it? Our park doesn't deserve to be on a list of closures!"

"I know, I know. The decision to sell was all but a done deal the day you were in my office. Blame it on the capitalists in the legislature. They're the ones who hatched this egg-smashing scheme. I tried to tell them they're pushing Humpty-Dumpty over the wall, but they wouldn't listen—said it was better to privatize. I've got your check right here. You can come get it or I'll mail it out to you."

Betty drew a breath to answer, but Angie put palm out and stepped closer to the phone. "Angie here. We'll come get our check, Ms. Underwood. We'll stop by tomorrow and pick it up."

"See you then. Got to run. My phone's lit up like a Christmas tree." She clicked off.

Betty's gut churned. "I can't believe this happened. The park, the folk school, closed. After all we did—all your contest giveaways."

Angie picked up the computer. "I'm going to read this and find out how to place a bid. We're not done yet, not this gal, anyway!"

Minutes later, Angie returned to the kitchen. "The *Journal* article says to download a bidding form from the General Land Office website, but it's not working. I'll try again tomorrow morning. If it's still not working, we'll see if we can pick up a form from the GLO office when we go to get your check."

"Good idea."

o0o

The following morning, Betty stepped into Eva Underwood's office, followed by Angie.

Eva rose. "Good morning, Mrs. Hanson, Mrs. Martinez. I have your check right here." She lifted an agate paperweight, picked up the check, and handed it to Betty.

Betty gazed down at it. "I really never expected to see this again."

Eva's phone rang and she grabbed the receiver. "Good morning, Ray . . . . Yes, I know about the meeting. I'll be there in a just a moment." She hung up and focused on Betty again. "I'm truly sorry the way this turned out. Your folk school was just what was needed at Mossy Point State Park. I hope you find a new location to continue your operation. It's a real asset to the State of Superior. Now, if you'll excuse me, some folks are waiting for me in the conference room." She grabbed a portfolio and pen from her desk and ushered Angie and Betty out of her office.

In the hallway, Angie gestured toward the General Land Office. "Let's see if we can get a bidding form from Mr. Engstrom's secretary."

Moments later, Betty followed Angie into the Land Office suite.

Shirley looked up from her computer screen and smiled. "Good morning, ladies. Mr. Engstrom isn't here. He's in a meeting until noon. Is there something I can do for you?"

Angie nodded. "I'd like to get a bidding form so I can place a bid on Mossy Point State Park, seeing as how the state is selling. But the form web page wasn't working when I tried it earlier this morning. Could you please print a copy?"

"The website wasn't working?" Shirley grabbed her mouse, clicked a few times, and scowled. "By golly, you're right. I'll print a copy of the form for you."

She clicked a few more times. Her printer spit out a page and she handed it to Angie. "There you go. Good luck! Honestly, I think the new state legislators have their heads . . . you know . . . where the sun don't shine. Selling off parks is no way to balance a budget. And all that stuff in the *Journal* last night about decreasing inventory so they can do a better job with the remaining properties is just bull poop in my opinion."

Angie nodded. "Since that's what they've decided to do, I want to make sure I put in the winning bid for Mossy Point State Park. Got any tips?"

Shirley shrugged. "Follow the instructions on the state land auction website and bid high. The rest is pretty much out of your control."

"Thanks!" Angie folded the form, slid it into her shoulder bag, and turned to Betty. "Come on, Mom; let's get home. Manuel and I have some work to do."

o0o

As Angie drove into Mossy Point, she pulled up to a gas pump at the Quick Shop.

Betty turned an inquiring gaze on her. "Why are you filling up here? Gas was a lot cheaper in Superior Bay."

Angie shrugged. "Forgot. Had my mind on putting in a bid and didn't realize how low the gas tank was until we were halfway home. No matter. I'd just as soon patronize local businesses. Need anything from the store?"

"Maybe I'd better pick up some tortillas and deli meats for lunch."

Inside, Betty headed straight for the meat counter, coming up behind Frank Schram. Nausea set in. She hadn't crossed paths with him since the fish boil. If she'd known he was here, she'd have stayed in the car and let Angie do the shopping. Maybe she should just leave.

He took his package of meat and turned around, his gaze meeting Betty's.

Lord, please don't let him make a scene here.

He quickly walked past her without a word.

Knees shaking, she stepped up to the counter.

CHAPTER 23

Early on the morning after an uneventful Halloween, Betty reached for the calendar on her kitchen wall and flipped the page to November. "All Saints' Day" November 1st read. But were the saints really in charge today?

The General Land Office would open Angie's bid. What if her generous offer lost out to another bidder?

And Frank Schram's lawsuit was supposedly being filed today. Would a process server show up on her doorstep this week entangling her in a legal battle she didn't deserve? Her jaw tightened.

Oh, Lord, I hope you and your saints are ruling where Angie's bid and Frank's lawsuit are concerned.

oOo

A couple of hours later, with Carlos off to school, Angie at the pizza shop helping Zoe, and Manuel out on a Habitat for Humanity construction job, she sat down with her Kindle and opened to Psalm 139 in her Bible. The reminder that God knew where she was, knew her every thought and word, and hedged her in behind and before brought a measure of peace . . . until the phone rang, nearly making her jump out of her skin. Was her trust in the Lord so tenuous that a phone call could make it vanish?

She hurried to the kitchen desk and grabbed the handset. Lee's number showed on the display. She slumped onto the desk chair.

"Good morning, Lee."

"Hey, Betty, I just heard from Magnuss Jewelers. Our rings are ready. Want to go pick them up and then go out to lunch, my treat?"

"Absolutely. Give me ten minutes."

"You're on!"

She returned the phone to the charger. This was just what she needed to divert her attention from the things she couldn't control and must leave to God. She grabbed the phone again and speed-dialed Mossy Point Pizza.

On the third ring, Zoe answered. "Hey, Betty, I bet you want to talk to Angie."

"If you don't mind."

"I'll put her on."

"Mom, what's up?"

"Lee just called. Our rings are ready at Magnuss Jewelers. We're going to pick them up, and then go out for lunch. Just wanted to let you know. I'll be home in time to make dinner."

"Have fun! Can't wait to see the rings you guys had made."

"Nor can I. See you later." She made a beeline to the bathroom to comb her hair and put on makeup.

By the time she returned to the kitchen, Lee was pulling into the driveway.

o0o

Half an hour later, Lee pulled into the mall parking lot, jumped out, and with a spring in his step, came around to open her door. A couple of minutes later, they strolled into Magnuss Jewelers.

The gentleman who had taken their order for the custom rings weeks earlier approached them with a smile. "Mr. Nylund, Mrs. Hanson, you're here for your rings. Follow me." He led them to the end of the showcase, stepped behind the counter, and pulled out two small, black velvet boxes.

Flipping the lids open so only he could see the contents, he paused, his smile widening. "You're going to love these, I'm sure. The goldsmith has done an incredible job." Slowly, he turned the ring boxes around.

Betty drew a sharp breath. Her pulse fluttered.

Lee's brow narrowed. "Do you like them?"

Betty nodded vigorously. "More than like. These are gorgeous."

"Whew. You had me worried. Let's try yours on, make sure it fits." He took her ring from the box, reached for her left hand, and slid it onto her finger, easing carefully past her knuckle.

Betty held her hand up, turning it this way and that. The diamond in the center trillium blossom sparkled brighter than it had in . . . she couldn't remember when.

Lee took her hand in his and focused on the ring. "Looks mighty fine to me, Mrs. Nylund-to-be."

Betty nodded. "Now, let's try yours on." She removed his ring from its box, admiring the intricate details of the leaf pattern that wrapped around the solid gold band. Taking ahold of his left hand, she threaded the ring onto his finger, pressing with gentle determination to move it past his enlarged knuckle. It settled in place, looking as if it had always been there.

Lee wiggled his fingers. "Not too tight, not too loose. Fits perfectly, I'd say."

"Wonderful!" The salesman beamed. "In my opinion, the rings look extremely attractive on each of you."

Lee chuckled. "Now comes the hard part."

Betty cocked a brow. "Taking them off?"

Lee shook his head. "Taking them off could be a challenge, but that wasn't what I had in mind. I was referring to paying for them." He reached for his wallet.

Betty pulled her credit card from her purse and focused on the salesman. "Do you have our bills prepared?"

The salesman twitched his brows and grinned. "There will be no charge to either of you for these rings."

Betty leaned forward. "No charge? How can that be?"

"Your daughter called. She asked me to tell you that she is picking up the tab for both rings as her wedding gift to the two of you."

Betty gasped and turned to Lee.

He slid his wallet back into his pocket, his blue eyes glistening. "That Angela is really something, but then, so is her mother."

o0o

A leisurely lunch and an unsuccessful attempt to find a wedding dress gobbled up the afternoon hours. When Lee pulled up in front of Betty's house, Manuel's truck was already parked in the driveway.

Betty turned to Lee. "You'll stay for supper, won't you? Angie wants to see our rings."

"And I want to thank her." He opened Betty's door, slipped his arm about her waist, and walked her to the house.

The moment they stepped into the kitchen, Angie rushed toward them, her smile wide. "Okay, you two. I've been dying to see the rings!"

Betty opened the bag containing the rings and handed the two velvet boxes to her.

Angie opened them and stared. "Ohhh. Very nice. Very, *very* nice. Are you two happy with them?"

Betty nodded. "Thank you, Angie. You didn't have to do it, though."

Lee echoed her words and then began singing "You Are My Special Angel."

Angie set the rings on the counter, rested her hand on Lee's shoulder, and began dancing with him.

Manuel and Carlos came in through the garage door.

"Hey, whose stealin' *mi angelita*?" Manuel asked, grinning wide as he cut in.

Lee continued singing, taking Betty as his partner.

Carlos placed his hands on his hips. "Hey, what about me?" He tapped his father's shoulder.

"*Al rato, vato!* Later, dude!" Manuel pulled Angie closer.

Lee placed Betty's hand in Carlos's, stepped back, and kept on singing.

Betty smiled up at her new partner. "Dance with your grandmother. It'll be good practice for the wedding— whenever that will be."

Carlos wrapped his arm about her waist. "I don't know what you're waiting for, Gram. Now that you've got the rings, you oughta just get hitched."

"If only it were that simple." She rested her head against his rock-hard shoulder.

Lee transitioned into "Put Your Head on My Shoulder" without missing a beat. Halfway through, he cut in and reclaimed Betty as his partner. When the song ended, he released her.

Manuel kept his arm loosely about Angie as he turned to Betty and Lee. "We want to talk to you two about housing. Where you gonna live after you're married? Here, at Lee's, or do you wanna build a new nest?"

Betty turned to Lee. "I just assumed we'd live at your place."

Lee nodded. "That's the way I figured it. I've got my workshop and fish shed there, and the storage building for my boat and trailer. Besides, you and Harry helped us build the place all those years ago. It's only fitting that we live there."

Her gaze shifted to Angie and Manuel. "I guess I'll put this place up for sale next spring, if Lee and I are married by then."

Angie grinned. "You will be. But you won't have to put your place up for sale. We'll buy it from you. After the first of the year, we're heading back to California. We're going to spend winters there, and the rest of the year here. When we come back, Manuel wants to make some additions to this place."

Betty's stomach tightened. "But I haven't even set a wedding date yet. And if I get married this fall and move to Lee's, Carlos will be living all alone here while he goes to school."

"No, I won't." Carlos grinned. "Mom's getting me an apartment in Superior Bay so I won't have to drive over there during bad weather. I'd hate to crack up Gramps's Stude truck, especially after all the work Dad and I have put into it."

"Good move." Lee slipped his arm about Betty's waist. "You and I can check on this place during winter, keep the driveway plowed out and lights on."

Betty's thoughts whirled. It seemed like plans were spinning out of control.

Manuel released Angie and turned to Carlos. "Hey, kid, while the ladies make supper, we've got just enough time to check your tire pressure and fluids." His gaze shifted to Lee. "Come help us."

Lee followed them out to the garage.

Betty picked up the rings, set them on the kitchen desk, and turned to Angie. "What if I get sued? I can't marry Lee and drag him into that mess."

Angie wrapped her arms about Betty. "Put it from your mind. Intuition tells me it's not going to be a problem."

If only Betty could be so sure.

oOo

The following afternoon, as Betty sat at the kitchen desk balancing her checkbook, Angie came into the kitchen from her bedroom, computer in hand, tears dampening her cheeks.

"Angie, what's wrong?"

She set the computer on the kitchen counter and pointed to the *Superior Bay Journal* site's headline.

Betty read out loud. "'ExlandGroup Buys Mossy Point State Park'." An ice ball landed in the pit of her stomach. "Angie, I'm so sorry."

Angie grabbed a tissue from the box on the counter and dabbed at her cheeks. "I was so sure . . . we bid high enough. I guess being a millionaire . . . isn't everything. Oh, Mom, I'm so sorry!" Her quiet sobs increased to a blubbering wail.

Betty pulled Angie into her embrace and cried with her.

Minutes later, sobs subsiding, Angie released her and picked up the computer. "I'd better read the story and find out what this ExlandGroup is planning for the property they just bought." She wandered off toward the couch.

"Want some tea?"

"Yes, please. Tea with a large dash of sympathy."

Betty filled the electric kettle and pressed the start switch. The pot hissed softly.

As she gathered mugs, teabags, and spoons on the counter, her memory churned. ExlandGroup. It sounded familiar. But why?

Angie screamed and charged into the kitchen, computer open. "Mom, listen to this. 'ExlandGroup is a private investment firm with real estate holdings in several states according to Chip Landers, its Vice-President in charge of Midwest acquisitions.' Chip Landers! The very same Chip Landers who won five thousand dollars of *my* money! The enemy was in the camp all the time, a wolf in sheep's clothing!"

Betty drew a sharp breath.

Angie continued. "According to this article, Chip's ExlandGroup is turning the land into a gated resort for high-end clients. You can forget the public ever setting foot on that property again." She shook her head from side to side. "This is a disaster. Rather than drawing outsiders in to spend their money, they'll do just the opposite; fence them out with a big 'Not Welcome' sign in the form of a gate that's locked to all but the residents."

A wave of nausea soured Betty's stomach. She reached for the kettle, poured hot water into the mugs, and dropped a chamomile teabag into hers. "This calls for some calming of the nerves and a new plan. Look on the bright side, Angie. You've still got the money you'd have spent on the park. Maybe there's another way to put it to work to benefit this community." She pulled out a stool and sat.

Angie sat beside her and dropped a peppermint teabag into her mug. "Maybe. Manuel will be so upset when he hears we lost our bid; he'll probably start spouting Spanish curses. But like you said, it could act as a catalyst for some other project. And if I know Manuel, he'll go a hundred and fifty percent to make it work." She smiled. "I can just hear him now. 'If we're going to be locked out of the park land, let's put up some nice low-income housing on the adjacent property. That'll show 'em.'"

"Do you think you could get approval for that from the zoning board?"

"I doubt it. ExlandGroup will fight it with all they've got and probably win. But it's a fun thought."

oOo

Nine long days later, made even longer by the annual setting of the clocks back to standard time, Betty rested in Harry's easy chair after breakfast and opened her Kindle to Psalms. As she read, she struggled to push aside the sickening disappointment of the park sale and ever-present worries about a possible lawsuit from Frank Schram. Yet the words of assurance, faith, and peace lay beyond her grasp.

The ringing of the phone jangled her nerves and set her in motion. She headed to the kitchen and grabbed the phone from the charger, expecting to find Lee's number on the caller I.D. But the display read "Ovesen, William." Probably a wrong number.

"Hello, this is Betty."

"Betty, this is Shirley Ovesen, Mr. Engstrom's secretary. Is your daughter in? It's really important that I speak with her."

"Is it something to do with her bid to buy the park? Her *losing* bid?"

"I'm sick about the way it went. I really need to talk to your daughter if she's available."

"Just a minute." She headed for Carlos's room, where Angie was sitting at the computer and offered the phone to her. "Shirley, Mr. Engstrom's secretary, wants to talk to you. She says it's important."

Angie's forehead wrinkled as she reached for the phone. "Angie here."

Betty forced her feet to carry her out of the bedroom. She closed the door and returned to the recliner, bowing her head and clasping her hands. "Lord, I don't know what Shirley's calling about, but You do. I just ask that You guide Angie in whatever it may be. Amen."

She reached for her Kindle and returned to Psalms, but she couldn't focus on the words. Setting it aside, she stared up at the buck mounted over the fireplace. "What's going on, Zeb? Why is Shirley calling now, more than a week after Angie lost her bid? And why haven't I heard about a lawsuit from Frank Schram?"

The kindness in his steady, brown-eyed gaze somehow calmed her. Movement outside the windows on either side of the fireplace caught her attention. Snow, the first of the season, was drifting through the air, driven sideways by a gusty northwest wind. A new season with new challenges was blowing in. Would one of them be a new marriage to Lee?

She pushed out of her chair. Time to get to work, clean the place up. There was not a thing she could do about the unknown except wait.

Several minutes later, Angie came down the hall, returned the portable phone to its charger, and waltzed into the great room. A smiled beamed from her face. "Mom, you're not going to believe what happened!"

"Tell me quick, or call the undertaker."

"Huh?"

Betty grinned. "I'm *dying* of curiosity!"

Angie chuckled. "Very funny! Now listen up, because what I have to say isn't so comical. According to Shirley, Exland-Group didn't submit the highest bid. *I* did. But Engstrom called his friend Chip to tell him to raise their bid, and then he called the newspaper to announce that ExlandGroup was the new owner."

"Does she have evidence? Otherwise, it's a he-said-she-said deal."

"She's got evidence. I'm meeting with her and a lawyer in an hour. Want to come?

"Wouldn't miss it!"

"Could you do me a favor and brew me a cup of coffee? I'll take it with me when we hit the road."

"Sure thing."

She set the one-cup coffeemaker to brewing, then poured the café con leche into a travel mug and capped it. Half an hour later, she and Angie hit the road.

o0o

The following morning, with Angie off to Superior Bay to help Zoe with a catering job and Manuel working at the Habitat construction site, Betty perched on a kitchen stool, head bowed, hands clasped. "Lord, thanks for watching over us yesterday in the meeting with Shirley and her lawyer. Please let justice and righteousness prevail in this situation with the park and the bidders and Mr. Engstrom. And keep Angie and Manuel safe on the roads today. Angie hasn't driven in snow in decades, and Manuel isn't used to these conditions. And help me to move ahead with my service to you, regardless of what happens with Frank Schram. Thank you, Lord. Amen."

She headed for the great room to sort through the stack of magazines piled up on the coffee table. About halfway through the job, the phone rang. This had to be Lee. But when she checked the display, it showed Steve Taylor's number. She hadn't seen or talked to him since he'd won the $10,000 prize in the teacher drawing over a month ago. She picked up the phone.

"Good morning, Steve."

"Hey, Betty, how's it going?"

"I'll know better after you tell me why you called. I hope it's not bad news."

"Nah. Just checking to find out whether Frank Schram ever made good on his threat to sue you. He kept saying he'd file the first of this month. If he did, seems to me you'd have heard by now."

"My thoughts exactly. I keep expecting someone to knock on my door and shove an envelope at me as soon as I open it, but so far, nothing."

"Since that's the case—oops, poor choice of words. Since that's the situation, I think you can lay to rest any worry of a lawsuit."

"Why? What do you know that I don't know?"

"Will you be there for a few minutes?"

"I'll be here."

"I'm coming over."

CHAPTER 24

By the time Betty had tidied up the great room, tossed old newspapers and magazines into the recycle bin in the utility room, and set the kitchen counter in order, the doorbell rang. She opened it to Steve and a gust of frigid wind. In the driveway stood an SUV she didn't recognize.

"Come in out of the cold, Steve."

He grinned as he stepped inside onto the doormat. "Very appropriate. I *am* the spy who came in from the cold."

Betty narrowed her brows. "How so?"

"You'll see." He removed his fur hat and ran a comb through his hair. Then he pulled an envelope from his jacket pocket and held it up. "I want you to see what Frank saw the day after the fish boil when he made those threats to sue you." He kicked off his boots and padded to the kitchen counter where he laid out several photographs.

Betty studied the images. Every picture showed Frank. In some, he was dragging a dead deer through the woods. Some showed him landing fish he'd caught in the river below the falls. Still others showed him cutting down tall plants.

Betty looked up at Steve. "What does all this mean?"

He pointed to red numbers on the corner of a photo. "Did you see the dates on these shots?"

She looked closer. "I hadn't noticed, but I see them now."

"Every picture of the deer and the fish shows Frank poaching, taking fish and game out of season. The agricultural shot—"

"Is that marijuana?"

Steve nodded. "Grown on state land before it was legal as medicine. The picture was taken in late August of last year when he harvested the crop."

"How did you happen to get these shots? Were you really spying on him?"

Steve shook his head vigorously. "Not at all. I was out there on public land to shoot wildlife. I'd wait in places where I knew deer came to drink at the river. Little did I know Frank Schram was going to show up."

"So you took these pictures of him without him ever knowing it?"

Steve nodded. "I never really planned to do anything with them. Everybody knows poaching is common and so was pot-growing. And everybody knows the state prosecutes vigorously for poaching and for illegal pot-growing."

Pieces of the puzzle fell into place. "So the day after the fish boil, you paid Frank a visit and showed him these pictures."

A mischievous smile curved his mouth. "Here's how it went. When I got to Frank's house, I warmed him up with some friendly chit-chat. Then I asked him if he was really planning to sue you. He was adamant. Of course, he was going to sue. His daughter insisted. You were at fault. The park was at fault. He'd wrench as much cash out of you and Angie as he could. He didn't really need the money, but Vickie's consignment shop in Appleton was going broke so he'd send most of the settlement her way."

Betty's cheeks burned. "Why that money-grubbing little viper!"

Steve nodded. "He went on about that for a while, and then I eased the subject around to hunting and fishing and asked him if he planned to get back to his two favorite pastimes. Wrong question. He didn't think his hip would ever be good enough for hunting—another reason to sue for damages. His lawyer was all ready to go on the case. They were just waiting for the first of November to file."

Betty raised a brow. "Is that when you pulled out your photos?"

He grinned. "I laid a set of them out on his coffee table. You should have heard the cursing! Then he started tearing them up. I reminded him that they're digital and I can make as many copies as I want. He sputtered and told me to get out. On my way to the door, I said, 'Frank, are you still planning to sue Betty and the park?'"

"What did he say?"

"I won't repeat the names he called me. Then he stammered and stuttered until I made it crystal clear I'd turn my evidence over to the authorities if he didn't promise to drop his lawsuit plan. We went back and forth about it for a few minutes. By the time I left, he looked like a defeated man. But I couldn't be sure he'd dropped the suit idea until this month rolled around and nothing came of it."

"Weren't you afraid he'd accuse you of extortion, or something?"

He shook his head. "I wasn't trying to get anything for myself. And even if he *were* to accuse me, it was worth the risk. I mean, what's right is right, and I had to take a stand for justice."

A burden lifted from her heart. She rose up on tiptoe and kissed Steve on the cheek. "Thanks, buddy. You saved my skin and the park's."

A wry smile curved his lips. "Glad on your account; not so glad the park's been sold to a developer. What a rotten kettle of fish after all you and your daughter have done to put that place in the black and keep it open."

"It's not over till it's over. I can't divulge details, but yesterday morning Angie learned about some irregularities with the ExlandGroup bid. A lawyer is on the case."

Steve turned thumbs up. "I hope Angie comes out the owner. Everybody in town does." He grew thoughtful. "Say, on a different subject, not to pry or anything, but are you and Lee planning to tie the knot? I heard you're getting married November 30th."

"I've been waiting to hear about a lawsuit against me. Maybe I can lay that one to rest and move forward with the wedding plans."

"Need a photographer? I'll work cheap. Free, even. Call it payback for the $10,000 your daughter forked over to me when I won the teacher drawing."

"You're hired!"

Steve laughed. "I hope Lee won't mind. He's not exactly my biggest fan."

"I'll take care of Lee. You take care of photography."

"Got it!" He scooped the photos into a stack, tucked them into the envelope, and handed it to Betty. "You keep these as insurance."

"Thanks, Steve. For everything."

He nodded and pulled on his hat and boots. "Let me know the when and where for the wedding."

"Will do!" She opened the door and nodded toward the vehicle in the driveway. "Did you decide to get a new SUV with your winnings?"

"I got it on lease, thanks to Angie."

"I'm pleased for you. Take care, now, on the roads."

With a nod, he stepped out into the snowy weather.

As she watched him get into his car and drive away, she prayed. "Thanks, Lord, for Steve's help. It's a huge burden off my shoulders. I think. Frank wouldn't sue me, would he? I mean, I haven't heard it straight from the horse's mouth, but it seems like a safe assumption. Should I go ahead with wedding plans?"

An inner voice spoke. *Go ahead. Forget about Frank.*

She set the photos on the kitchen counter, headed for the phone, and punched the preset for Lee's number. He answered on the first ring.

"Betty, what's up?"

"Let's go ahead with a November 30th wedding."

"What happened to finally make you commit to a date?"

"I'll come over and explain it all, and we'll make plans, if that's okay?"

"*Mi casa es su casa.*"

Betty chuckled. "Now you're starting to sound like Manuel."

"Just getting in practice."

"I'll be there in a few."

"I'll put the water on. Tea or coffee?"

"Better make it herbal tea. I'm so excited, if I drink any caffeine, I'll be up all night."

Betty pulled on her down jacket, grabbed her purse and the envelope of photos, and headed over to Lee's at a cautious pace. Snow swirled on the road and rose in clouds, obscuring visibility at times. But when she turned into Lee's driveway, protected by cedars on both sides, the white flakes drifted lazily onto the evergreen branches, painting a romantic winter scene undisturbed by whirling wind.

As she parked in front of Lee's log home, his door opened and he stepped onto the porch.

She hurried up the steps and into the kitchen, opened the envelope, and spread the photos out on the granite countertop. "Steve Taylor came by my place just before I called you and brought me these. Take a look. Frank Schram poaching fish, poaching deer, and growing pot."

Lee bent over the photos, picking up one after another and laying them down again. Then he let out a low whistle. "Looks like Steve really has the goods on Frank."

"Exactly. We assume it was enough to convince him to drop his lawsuit against me and the park since I haven't heard about any filing and it's way past the first of November."

Lee picked her up and whirled her around, setting her gently on her feet again. Then he bent over, groaning, and placed his hand against his lower back.

Betty's pulse raced. "Lee, are you all right? You shouldn't have lifted me up like that. I'm not exactly a lightweight . . . not yet, anyway."

He quickly straightened and flashed a smile. "Just kidding! The water's hot. What kind of tea do you want?"

oOo

When the teacups were empty, Lee made a call to their pastor to see about a November 30th wedding at the church. Pastor Tom confirmed the date, and then Betty helped Lee prepare his place for her to move in. At the end of the afternoon, with four inches of new snow covering Lee's long driveway, Betty got into her truck and slowly headed for the main road. "Lord, I haven't had to drive in snowy conditions in a long time. Please protect me—and Angie, Carlos, and Manuel too. They aren't used to this white stuff on the roads. And thanks, Lord, for working everything out so Lee and I can go ahead with our wedding plans. Amen."

Minutes later, as Betty pulled into her driveway, she clicked the garage door opener. Angie's Lexus was already there. Betty parked her truck beside it, headed out to the mailbox to collect the mail, and sorted through it on her way back. One envelope, addressed to her and the folk school, showed an IRS return address. She eagerly ripped it open and read.

We are pleased to inform you that upon review of your application for tax-exempt status we have determined that you are exempt from Federal income tax under section 501 (c) (3) of the Internal Revenue Code.

Her heart soared. Lee would be pleased. But would they even have a folk school to open, come spring? She grabbed Steve's photos from the truck and carried them, along with the mail, into the kitchen.

Angie was sitting on a stool at the counter, mug in hand, laptop computer in front of her. She gazed up, a quizzical look on her brow. "Where have you been? I was starting to worry, with all the snow that's coming down."

Betty smiled. "I was at Lee's. How did your catering go?"

"Great! I love helping Zoe. So what were you and Lee up to? Or shouldn't I ask?" She cocked her brow.

"First things first. Look at what just came in the mail." She handed Angie the IRS letter of declaration.

Angie read it and handed it back. "Congratulations, Mom! File it someplace safe. We'll need it once this park land matter is resolved. Now, tell me what you were doing at Lee's."

"Do you remember the lawsuit Frank Schram threatened to file against me and the park?"

Angie nodded.

"I think we can lay that worry to rest. Take a look at these." Betty laid out the photos from Steve on the countertop, repeating the explanation she'd given Lee earlier. "So unless we hear about a lawsuit in the next few days, we're planning to get married on November 30th. Pastor Tom says we can use the church and he'll do the ceremony. Once we got that nailed down, Lee and I spent the rest of the afternoon doing some much-needed cleaning and rearranging at his place."

"But Mom, November 30th is less than three weeks away." She started typing on the computer keyboard.

"I know. It doesn't have to be fancy, just our family and friends, and some church folks. A cake afterward would be nice. Steve offered to do the photography for free. We're going to announce the wedding in church this Sunday and invite the congregation. No need to mail out invitations."

Angie made a few clicks with her mouse and pointed to the screen. "Look at these fall wedding decorations, Mom. Apple pie jars, a pumpkin carved with the names of the bride and groom, cider served in scooped out apples, spiced deviled eggs that look like pumpkins. And how's this for a wedding cake?" She pointed to a photo of a cake served on what appeared to be a tree slab.

Betty studied the image. A tree slab? Really? "That's all very nice, Angie, but there's no need to fuss."

Angie looked up, her blue eyes aglow. "I'll take care of everything—be your wedding planner—and the wedding and reception won't cost you a penny. I'll ask Zoe to do the catering. All you and Lee have to do is show up. What do you say?"

"Well . . . all right. But only if you promise *not* to put my wedding cake on a tree slab."

"Promise!"

CHAPTER 25

Betty woke from a nightmare on Sunday morning. What if she were wrong? What if Frank Schram really *was* going to sue her, and she just didn't know it yet? The more she progressed with wedding plans, the more she dreaded that possibility.

She drew a deep breath and exhaled slowly in hopes of expelling her fears. Then she headed for her closet to find something to wear to church.

A cold, brisk wind and glowering skies did nothing to improve her outlook when she stepped out of the Lexus in the church parking lot. Once inside, Carlos headed for a pew on the right where Janna was sitting with her folks, while Manuel and Angie followed her to the left where Lee was sitting. From his bright smile and cheerful greeting, it appeared he was suffering no ill effects from the gloomy weather, or the possibility that a lawsuit might materialize.

She offered a tentative smile as she sat beside him. He gently leaned against her and spoke quietly in her ear. "This is a great day, don't you think? I finally get to announce our wedding."

She nodded. No point in sharing her unfounded concern.

The organ prelude came to an end, and as Pastor Tom made his way to the podium, the sanctuary door opened. Betty craned her neck to see who the latecomer could be, and nearly choked. Frank Schram removed his fedora and slipped into the last pew beside Steve.

Betty's heart raced. Frank hadn't darkened the door of the church since his wife's funeral twenty years ago. What was he doing here now? And why would he sit beside Steve, of all people?

She nudged Lee, who was focused on the bulletin he held, and whispered in his ear. "Frank Schram just came in and sat beside Steve. Do you believe it?"

He cast a quick glance over his shoulder and shrugged.

Pastor Tom spoke into the microphone. "Good morning, everyone, and welcome! This is the day that the Lord hath made. Let us rejoice and be glad in it! If you'll take up your bulletins, I'd like to draw your attention to a few announcements." He mentioned the men's breakfast, youth group, and women's fellowship meeting. "Does anyone else have an announcement to make?"

Lee raised his hand.

"Yes, Lee."

He rose, his gaze sweeping across the congregation. "I'd like to announce that Betty and I are getting married here on November 30th, 2 p.m., and you're all invited!"

"Congratulations," rippled through the congregation as Lee sat down, and a new concern sent chills down Betty's spine. What if Frank Schram showed up at the wedding and caused trouble?

Pastor Tom grinned. "I'm looking forward to that wedding, a very special one indeed. Any other announcements?" His gaze settled on someone at the back of the sanctuary. "Yes, Frank?"

Betty whipped her head around.

Frank Schram was on his feet, fussing with the brim of his hat. "It's been a lot of years since I was here. You're probably wondering why I came today. Well, I'll tell ya. I done a lot of thinking since I broke my hip last spring. I was real angry about it, put the blame on others for that, and a lot of other things over the years. Then I saw the light, so to speak." His gaze shifted from Steve, to Betty, to Pastor Tom. "I came here today to honor the memory of my wife, Erna. If she'd a lived, we'd a been married fifty years today." He looked down at his hat, and then up at Pastor Tom again. "Seems like the day she died, I stopped livin' the way I should. I see now I wasted these last twenty years. But I'm turnin' things around." He sat, eyes lowered.

Pastor Tom spoke again. "Glad to hear it, Frank. Thanks for sharing with us. And remember, we're here to give you the support you need on that turnaround you mentioned. Anyone else with an announcement?" When no one else raised a hand, he shuffled the papers on the podium. "Now, let's have a few moments of silence to prepare our hearts for worship."

Betty bowed her head. What did it all mean? Was Frank really a changed man? Or was he still going to spring a lawsuit on her? *Lord, if Frank is really sincere about turning his life around, please give him all the support he needs. Amen.*

Pastor Tom delivered another thought-provoking sermon in his month-long series on gratitude, dismissed the congregation with a benediction, and headed to the door to shake hands as the parishioners left the service.

As Betty and Lee made their way down the aisle toward the door, Karen, Doris, Wayne, Janna, and others offered their congratulations and made promises to attend the wedding. Betty shook Pastor Tom's hand, thanked him for the sermon, and stepped outside. A sliver of sunshine peeked out through an opening in the heavy clouds, lifting her spirits . . . until Frank Schram started toward her. Where was Lee? She glanced over her shoulder. He stepped beside her and slipped his arm about her waist.

"Hello Betty, Lee." Frank's gaze settled on Betty. "I just want you to know I ain't filing any lawsuit . . . and one more thing." His eyes grew moist. "Congratulations on your weddin'. After Erna died, I wish I coulda found someone . . . ." He bit his lip, turned, and wandered off.

A lump clogged Betty's throat. She gazed up at Lee and shrugged.

He squeezed her waist. "I guess we can lay that problem to rest."

o0o

Five months later.

Betty rose early, quietly slipped out of the bedroom so as not to wake Lee, and headed for her recliner. Zorro, the senior black lab mix they'd adopted from the shelter last Christmas, followed and settled nearby.

In a couple of hours, volunteers would meet at Mossy Point Folk School to prepare for its second season. Hard to believe an entire year had passed since the first work session. So much had happened. The park had been deeded over to Angie and Manuel, and Mr. Engstrom had gone to prison. Lee was about as perfect as a husband could be, and Zorro—bless his heart—

had helped both of them lose weight by demanding walks through the woods each morning and evening. She and Lee had even had to learn how to snowshoe just to keep up with him.

With a full heart, Betty bowed her head and whispered. "Thank You, Lord, that Mossy Point Folk School and the park have a really bright future now that Angie and Manuel are the owners. Help us to have a good work session today. Thank You, too, for a wonderful husband, and for Zorro. I couldn't have asked for two nicer gentlemen in my life. Amen."

She turned on the reading lamp, reached for her Kindle, and opened her Bible to Psalm 105. *O give thanks unto the Lord; call upon his name: make known his deeds among the people . . . .*

o0o

From the passenger's side of Lee's truck as he approached the folk school, Betty counted half-a-dozen vehicles already parked in front—Angie and Manuel's Lexus, Carlos's Stude truck, Steve's SUV, Wayne and Doris's truck, the Ojibway tribal van, and Karen's rusty old Ford.

A lump forming in her throat, she reached for Lee's hand and gave it a squeeze. "The old gang is all here."

He turned to her with a smile and squeezed back. "Now we have some work to do." His gaze drifted to some point beyond her and his brows furrowed.

"What?" At the sound of a four-wheeler approaching, she shifted her focus. A rock plummeted in her gut. "Frank Schram. He shouldn't even be allowed on this property."

"Now, Betty. Give the man a chance. After all, he's turned his life around. You were there when he stood up and announced it to the whole congregation last fall. Do you doubt his sincerity?"

"Talk is cheap. I haven't seen him in church since."

Frank's gaze and his smile were fixed on her as he drew near her window.

Zorro, standing in the storage area behind the seats, let out a low growl.

Lee grasped his collar. "It's okay, Zorro."

Betty rolled her window down. "Good morning, Frank."

"'Mornin', Betty. You got a holds-harmless agreement for me to sign? I heard we all gotta sign one before we can start."

"Angie's got them inside. She's the new boss here. I'm sure she'll be glad to fix you up." *Not.*

Frank gave a nod and headed for the open front door.

Betty sighed. "If I were Angie, I'd absolutely ban that man from my property. He's an accident waiting to happen. I wonder who told him about the work session?"

Lee lowered his gaze. "He overheard me talking to Wayne and Doris the other day at the Quick Shop and said he'd help us."

Betty sighed and bowed her head. "Lord, keep us accident-free today, especially Frank."

"Amen." Lee kissed her cheek and got out. Zorro leaped out and trotted into the folk school as Lee came around to hold her door.

Betty stepped down and drew in a deep breath. Spring was in the air, the time for rebirth, new beginnings. Maybe Frank really *did* have a change of heart. Who was she to question? After all, Mossy Point had been saved, and turtles could fly.

ABOUT DONNA WINTERS

Donna adopted Michigan as her home state in 1971 when she moved from a small town outside of Rochester, New York. She began penning novels in 1982 while working full time for an electronics firm in Grand Rapids.

She resigned from her job in 1984 following a contract offer for her first book. Since then, Thomas Nelson Publishers, Zondervan Publishing House, Guideposts, and Bigwater Publishing have published her novels.

Her husband, Fred, a former American History teacher, shares her enthusiasm for history. Together, they visit historical sites, restored villages, museums, and lake ports purchasing books and reference materials for use in Donna's research.

Donna has lived all of her life in states bordering on the Great Lakes. Her familiarity and fascination with these remarkable inland waters and her residence in the heart of Great Lakes Country make her the perfect candidate for writing *Great Lakes Romances®*.

When *Mackinac* and the *Great Lakes Romances®* series first launched in May 1989, the author and her husband and two dozen friends and relatives from Michigan, New York State, and Illinois visited Grand Hotel to celebrate, enjoying the Victorian ambiance and superb cuisine.

GREAT LAKES ROMANCES®

Visit
GreatLakesRomances.com
for excerpts and pricing
on all of the following titles.

Mackinac, *First in the series of Great Lakes Romances®* (Set at Grand Hotel, Mackinac Island, 1895.) Victoria Whitmore is no shy, retiring miss. When her father runs into money trouble, she heads to Mackinac Island to collect payment due from Grand Hotel for the furniture he's made. But dealing with Rand Bartlett, the hotel's manager, poses an unexpected challenge. Can Victoria succeed in finances without losing her heart?

The Captain and the Widow, Second in the series of Great Lakes Romances® (Set in South Haven, Michigan, 1897.) Lily Atwood Haynes is beautiful, intelligent, and alone at the helm of a shipping company at the tender age of twenty. Then Captain Hoyt Curtiss offers to help her navigate the choppy waters of widowhood. Together, can they keep a new shipping line—and romance—afloat?

Sweethearts of Sleeping Bear Bay, Third in the series of Great Lakes Romances® (Set in the Sleeping Bear Dune region of northern Michigan, 1898.) Mary Ellen Jenkins has successfully mastered the ever-changing shoals and swift currents of the Mississippi, but Lake Michigan poses a new set of challenges. Can she round the ever-dangerous Sleeping Bear Point in safety, or will the steamer—and her heart—run aground under the influence of Thad Grant?

Charlotte of South Manitou Island, Fourth in the series of Great Lakes Romances ® (Set on South Manitou Island, Michigan, 1891-1898.) Charlotte Richards, fatherless at age eleven, thought she'd never smile again. But Seth Trevelyn, son of South Manitou Island's lightkeeper, makes it his mission to show her that life goes on, and so does true friendship. Together, they explore the World's Columbian Exposition in far-away Chicago where he saves her from a near-fatal fire. When he leaves the island to create a life of his own in Detroit, he realizes Charlotte is his one true love. Will his feelings be returned when she grows to womanhood?

Aurora of North Manitou Island, Fifth in the series of Great Lakes Romances® (Set on North Manitou Island, Michigan, 1898-1899.) With her new husband, Harrison, lying helpless after an accident on stormy Lake Michigan, Aurora finds marriage far from the glorious romantic adventure she had anticipated. And when Serilda Anders appears out of his past to tend the light and nurse him to health, Aurora is certain her marriage is doomed. Maybe Cad Blackburn, with the ready wit and silver tongue, is the answer. But it isn't right to accept the safe harbor he's offering. Where is the light that will guide her through troubled waters?

Bridget of Cat's Head Point, Sixth in the series of Great Lakes Romances® (Set in Traverse City and the Leelanau Peninsula of Michigan, 1899-1900.) When Bridget Richards leaves South Manitou Island to take up residence on Michigan's mainland, she suffers no lack of ardent suitors. Nat Trevelyn wants desperately to make her his bride and the mother of his two-year-old son. Attorney Kenton McCune showers her with gifts and rapt attention. And Erik Olson shows her the incomparable beauty and romance of a Leelanau summer. Who will finally win her heart?

Rosalie of Grand Traverse Bay, Seventh in the series of Great Lakes Romances® (Set in Traverse City, Michigan, and Winston-Salem, North Carolina, 1900.) Soon after Rosalie Foxe arrives in Traverse City for the summer of 1900, she stands at the center of controversy. Her aunt and uncle are about to lose their confectionery shop, and Rosalie is being blamed. Can Kenton McCune, a handsome, Harvard-trained lawyer, prove her innocence and win her heart?

Isabelle's Inning, Encore Edition #1 in the series of Great Lakes Romances® (Set in the heart of Great Lakes Country, 1903.) Born and raised in the heart of the Great Lakes, Isabelle Dorlon pays little attention to the baseball players patronizing her mother's rooming house—until Jack Weatherby moves in. He's determined to earn a position with the Erskine College

Purple Stockings, and a place in her heart as well, but will his affections fade once he learns the truth about her humiliating flaw?

Jenny of L'Anse Bay, Special Edition in the series of Great Lakes Romances® (Set in the Keweenaw Peninsula of Upper Michigan in 1867.) Eager to escape the fiery disaster that leaves her home in ashes, Jennifer Crawford sets out on an adventure to an Ojibway Mission on L'Anse Bay. In the wilderness, her affections grow for a native people very different from herself—especially for the chief's son, Hawk. Together, can they overcome the differences of their diverse cultures, and the harsh, deadly weather of the North Country?

Elizabeth of Saginaw Bay, Pioneer Edition in the series of Great Lakes Romances® (Set in the Saginaw Valley of Michigan, 1837.) The taste of wedding cake is still sweet in Elizabeth Morgan's mouth when she sets out with her bridegroom, Jacob, from York State for the new State of Michigan. But she isn't prepared for the untamed forest, crude lodgings, and dangerous diseases that await her there. Desperately, she seeks her way out of the forest that holds her captive, but God seems to have another plan for her future.

Unlikely Duet—Caledonia Chronicles—Part 1 in the series of Great Lakes Romances® (Set in Caledonia, Michigan, 1905.) Caroline Chappell practiced long and hard for her recital on the piano and organ in Caledonia's Methodist Episcopal Church. She even took up the trumpet and composed a duet to perform with Joshua Bolden, an ace trumpet player whom she'd long admired. Now, two days before the performance, it looks as if her recital plans, and her relationship with Joshua are hitting sour notes. Will she be able to restore harmony in time to save her musical reputation?

Butterfly Come Home—Caledonia Chronicles—Part 2 in the series of Great Lakes Romances® (Set in Caledonia and Calumet, Michigan, 1905-06.) Deborah Dapprich's flighty ways had earned her the nickname, "Butterfly," in childhood. Now, as a young woman of eighteen in the year 1905, her impetuous wanderings brought unanticipated trouble. A marriage of convenience to her childhood friend seemed the only way out. Tommy Rockwell knew that life with his Butterfly would never be dull, but he wasn't prepared for the challenges of his new bride. From Caledonia to Calumet he pursued her, only to discover that he was running second to her first love, the theater. Would she ever light long enough for his love, and the will of God, to work their way into her heart?

Fayette—A Time to Love, Eighth in the series of Great Lakes Romances® (Set in Fayette, Michigan, 1868.) The new iron-smelting town of Fayette, Michigan held no promise for sixteen-year-old Lavinia McAdams. The moment she arrived, she took an instant disliking to its muddy streets, acrid smoke, and dirty furnace men. The sooner she could return to her hometown in Canada, the better. Then Huck Harrigan came along to challenge her thinking and soften her iron will. Could she really find happiness in this raw, new town with a "pig iron" Irishman from across the bay?

Fayette—A Time to Laugh, Ninth in the series of Great Lakes Romances® (Set in Fayette, Michigan in 1879.) The greatest love of Flora McAdams' life had always been her love of animals. From girlhood she had made it her mission to care for orphaned wild creatures and hurting family pets in the pig iron town of Fayette. Now, at age eighteen, she has no lack of four-footed patients needing her skill, and no time or thought of romance, until a quiet Norwegian machinist comes to town. Sven Jorgensen hoped his first encounter with the feisty Flora McAdams would be his last. Whether at the village vegetable garden or the town racetrack, he can't seem to avoid her. But time works miracles. And after witnessing her transformation of hurting, homeless canines into healthy, loving pets, his own heart is transformed as well. Can he somehow convince her that he has much more than friendship in mind for their future?

Fayette—A Time to Leave, Tenth in the series of Great Lakes Romances® (Set in Fayette, Michigan, 1885-1891.) At age fourteen, Violet Harrigan encounters dual tragedies: the death of her father, and the resulting need to move several miles north to Fayette. The situation is more than she can bear. But a true friend sticks closer than a brother. Guy Legard visits Violet faithfully. Months turn into years, and the seed of friendship blossoms into love. Then Guy disappears into the woods for several long months and Violet turns her attention to a suave and debonair newcomer, Reggie Vanderveen. Will he steal her away to a new life of excitement in Boston, or can Guy rekindle the flame of enduring love?

Bluebird of Brockport, A Novel of the Erie Canal (Set in western New York State and on the Erie Canal, 1830.) Dreams of floating on the Erie Canal have flowed through Lucina

Willcox's mind since childhood. Yet once her family has purchased their boat and begins their journey, they meet with one challenge after another. An encounter with a towpath rattlesnake threatens her brother's life. A thief attempts to break in and steal precious cargo. Heavy rain causes a breach and drains the canal of water. Lucina comforts herself with thoughts of Ezra Lockwood, her handsome childhood friend, and discovers a longing to be with him that she just can't ignore. Can she have a future with Ezra and still hold onto her canalling dream? Ezra Lockwood's one goal in life is to build and captain his own canal boat, but two years into the construction of his freight hauler, funds run short. With his goal temporarily stalled, and Lucina Willcox back in his life, his priorities begin to change. Can he have both his dreams—his own boat, and Lucina as his bride?

For the Love of Roses (Set in western New York State, 1984.) Reeling from the loss of her parents in a tragic auto accident, Carey McIlwain resigns her teaching job to take up the reins of the family florist business, unaware of the challenges that await her. Gavin Jack, the darkly handsome rose supplier threatens to cut off deliveries due to lack of payment. Alex Hensley, the college botanist, wants more than friendship from their casual dates. Her younger brother Todd, who is supposed to step into the business after graduating with his Master's degree, develops a disabling addiction that threatens both his and Carey's future. Can she somehow weather the storms to find security, satisfaction, and that special someone who will steal her heart?

MORE DONNA WINTERS TITLES

Picturing Fayette Fayette Historic Townsite in the Upper Peninsula of Michigan offers visitors a step back in time to a nineteenth century company town. Here, nestled beneath a towering limestone bluff on Lake Michigan, the Jackson Iron Company operated two iron smelting furnaces. From December 25, 1867 to December 1, 1890, hot iron poured forth into casting houses, was cooled and separated into "pigs," and shipped to Ohio aboard schooners. Today, several original structures give testimony to Michigan's industrial past—from the laborers' log cabin, to the managers' salt box homes, to the "Big White House" on the bluff that was occupied by the superintendent. In the center of all these stands the working core of the once-thriving village—the furnace stacks, casting houses, company store, warehouse, town hall, company office, machine shop, and hotel. Through the pages of this book, tour this fascinating open air museum that offers million-dollar views of the harbor, bay, and quaint remnants from nearly 150 years ago. Quotes from newspapers of that era serve as captions, bringing the town to life. Fayette Historic Townsite is without a doubt one of the best-preserved company towns in America and a gem of Michigan history that is unlike any other.

Adventures with Vinnie Handsome. Affectionate. In need of a forever home. And we were in need of another rescue dog. Thus began our Adventures with Vinnie.

From his first day to his last, the only predictable thing about Vinnie was his unpredictability. Loving and loyal, an escape artist to rival Houdini, and a genuinely comical fellow, his antics will make you laugh, give you a fright (but only for a moment), and melt your heart.

So join us, won't you? With Vinnie, there's never a dull moment!

o0o

Having retired to the Upper Peninsula of Michigan, we decided to choose older shelter dogs for our family pets—dogs not easily placed because of their age. When an opportunity arose in March of 2012 to add a Lab/Dobie mix to our family, we didn't hesitate. Nearly forty years of dog parenting had given us confidence that we could provide a safe, loving home for this senior pet fallen on hard times.

We hadn't anticipated the likes of Vinnie.

Learn how that loving shelter dog with bright, longing eyes, led to adventures never expected the day we welcomed him into our lives!

This book contains twelve full-color photographs of Vinnie and his family.

GreatLakesRomances.com